# PRAISE FOR ADINA SENFT

### *Herb of Grace*

"Senft is a talented author and her research on various herbs is a welcome surprise to readers. The story incorporates facts about herbs, what each of them can be used for and what will happen if used incorrectly. This sweet romance has a believable storyline with a lot of heart."

—*RT Book Reviews*

"[A] genuine must read for those who love Amish fiction. Readers will not be able to put this book down until finished, it is just that great and filled with rich characterization....HERB OF GRACE is a five star recommended book."

—AmishReader.blogspot.com

### *The Wounded Heart*

"This relatable story, which launches Senft's Amish Quilt series, shows that while waiting to see God's plan can be difficult, remembering to put Jesus first, others next and yourself last ('JOY') is necessary."

—*RT Book Reviews*

"With this quai͏ series is off to a good start for Jerry S. Eicher readers

*Library Journal*

"Senft perfectly captures the Amish setting of the novel. Amelia is an endearing character, and there were a few laugh-out-loud moments for me that I wasn't even expecting. Although this is the first book I have read by the author, she has been added to my 'must read' list. If you are a fan of Amish fiction, then plan on reading *The Wounded Heart* soon!"

—Christian Fiction Addiction

### The Hidden Life

"I absolutely loved *The Hidden Life*! Nothing is as enjoyable as feeling the same way the characters do throughout the story and believing that you are mixed into the same world... *The Hidden Life* is full of conflict, romance, and drama! Overall I felt Adina captured the Amish way of life with fine detail. Be prepared to become an even bigger fan of Adina's after you read this book and you will be eagerly anticipating the next installment, *The Tempted Soul*, just like me!"

—Destination Amish

### The Tempted Soul

"I do declare that Adina has saved the best story for last. I loved this book! Saying that it is a heartfelt story just doesn't seem like it does the book justice."

—Destination Amish

ALSO BY ADINA SENFT

The Healing Grace Series

*Herb of Grace*

The Amish Quilt Series

*The Wounded Heart*
*The Hidden Life*
*The Tempted Soul*

**Available from FaithWords wherever books are sold.**

# KEYS *of* HEAVEN

## A HEALING GRACE NOVEL

## ADINA SENFT

New York  Boston  Nashville

Copyright © 2015 by Shelley Bates

Excerpt from *Balm of Gilead* © 2015 by Shelley Bates

FaithWords
Hachette Book Group
1290 Avenue of the Americas
New York, NY 10104

www.faithwords.com

Printed in the United States of America

RRD-C

First Edition: February 2015
10 9 8 7 6 5 4 3 2 1

FaithWords is a division of Hachette Book Group, Inc.
The FaithWords name and logo are trademarks of Hachette Book Group, Inc.

The Hachette Speakers Bureau provides a wide range of authors for speaking events. To find out more, go to www.hachettespeakersbureau.com or call (866) 376-6591.

The publisher is not responsible for websites (or their content) that are not owned by the publisher.

Library of Congress Cataloging-in-Publication Data
Senft, Adina.
  Keys of heaven : a healing grace novel / Adina Senft.
    pages cm
  ISBN 978-1-4555-4866-8 (trade pbk.) -- ISBN 978-1-4555-4864-4 (ebook)
  I. Title.
PS3602.A875K49 2015
813'.6--dc23
                          2014013998

*For my plain friends, near and far*

# ACKNOWLEDGMENTS

My thanks to potter Anne Lewis, who brings me back to earth with kindness and humor, and to herbalists Paula Grainger and Darren Huckle, who always have the answer. Thanks to my editor, Christina Boys, and my agent, Jennifer Jackson, for their support of this series. And thanks always to my husband, Jeff, who thinks nothing of driving across country or mucking out a cow barn in support of my fiction.

*Red valerian, sometimes called "keys of heaven" or "Jupiter's beard," often grows in rocky places where other plants don't flourish, such as in stone walls or against fences. But adverse conditions can produce a beautiful plant, brightening hard places with its sprays of red flowers.*

*There are people like this, too. They grow in hard places where others wouldn't flourish—staying where God has put them, even if they might not have chosen to grow there. But they stay because they're needed, because their spirit transforms the hard place and makes it beautiful...*

# KEYS *of*
# HEAVEN

For the Lord shall comfort Zion: he will comfort all her waste places; and he will make her wilderness like Eden, and her desert like the garden of the Lord; joy and gladness shall be found therein, thanksgiving, and the voice of melody.

—Isaiah 51:3, KJV

# CHAPTER 1

The young Amish mother in the mint-green dress, black bib apron, and crisp organdy *Kapp* looked at Sarah Yoder a little doubtfully. "Chickweed?"

The June sun shone through the sparkling windows of the guest room on the first floor of the farmhouse, which Sarah had begun to use as her dispensary. Gripping his mother's hand and trying manfully not to cry was her little patient—a boy of four so sunburned that his skin had already begun to peel.

Briskly, Sarah took the big bunch of chickweed that she'd pulled from the bank near her garden, and demonstrated as she talked. "It's a humble little plant, but it's *wunderbaar*, truly. You scrunch it up and rub it between your hands, like this, *ja?*" The plants began to break down, their juicy stems and leaves forming a wet mass (*mucilaginous*, her herb book said, when *goopy* would have done as well). When it was good and ready, Sarah gently applied it to the little boy's arms and shoulders. "Were you working in the field with your Dat, Aaron?"

He gulped and shook his head, flinching in spite of himself. "We went swimming in the pond. *Mei Bruder* and the boys from the next farm."

"Ah, I see. And when you're swimming, you don't feel

the sun working on you, do you? Does this feel better?" She dabbed the juicy mass on his cheeks and forehead, and he nodded.

"It feels cool."

She stepped back and smiled at him. "You look like a duck who just came up out of the pond, all covered in weed. What does a duck say?"

Instead of saying "quack-quack," the boy gave a perfect imitation of a mallard's call.

"I see a hunter in the making." She brushed his fine blond hair from his eyes and tried to ignore the pang in her heart.

*Simon. Caleb.* No longer little boys who she could cuddle and sing to. And now, Simon was gone.

He and his best friend Joe Byler had done a bait-and-switch a few weeks ago, making them all think they were going to an Amish community in Colorado for a working vacation, and all the time they'd secured jobs at a dude ranch, wrangling horses. They were working among worldly people and all the temptations to a young man that living outside the circle of their people would bring.

*Oh Lord, be with him and keep him safe.*

"How long should I leave the chickweed on him?" Aaron's mother asked.

"Not long," Sarah assured her, coming back to herself. This was work she could do, a difference she could make right here with another woman's child. Worrying about Simon profited her nothing. The Lord had him cupped in His hand, didn't He? There was no reason to worry. "Rinse it off when you get home, and if you can, squish up some more and put it on when he goes to bed. He might need to sleep on a towel, to save the sheets."

"*Denki*, Sarah. I'm so glad you knew what to do. Sunscreen

is no good after the damage is done, and vinegar didn't seem to help him."

Sarah accepted a payment that still seemed to her to be too much for such a simple solution, but the young mother seemed happy with both the treatment and the new knowledge she'd gained. When they clopped away down the drive in the gray-sided buggy the churches used here in Lancaster County, Sarah could already hear Aaron begging to take the reins, just the way Caleb, her youngest, always had when he was that age.

Boys and ponds. Boys and horses. Boys and dirt. You could count on the magnetic attraction between them the way you counted on the turn of the seasons.

She turned and walked across the lawn to her garden—or as her sister-in-law Amanda was fond of saying, "that crazy quilt patch you planted." The patterns she had seen in her mind's eye back in the muddy days of spring had come to full fruition, the way a complicated star-and-flying-geese pattern materialized out of fabric when Sarah's mother-in-law, Corinne, made Yoder a quilt.

First there was nothing, and then there was something, patterns emerging to create beauty where there had been none before. Was this how women reflected God as they went about the act of creation in small ways and large?

Sarah knelt to inspect the progress of the peas climbing up their teepees of string. Was she being prideful even to think such things? Because baking, gardening, and sewing were all small acts of creation, when you got right down to it. Leaving out the miracle of conception itself, what about bringing up children? There was no creation as beautiful as a child who worshipped God and learned to love Him at an early age.

"Hallo, Sarah!"

And speaking of...

She stood and shaded her eyes against the sun. "Hallo, Priscilla. *Wie geht's?*"

"I'm well, *denki*." She waved an envelope and Sarah felt a leap in her heart. "I have a letter from Joe. I thought you might like to read it."

From Joe. Not Simon.

As the pretty blond sixteen-year-old crossed the grass, Sarah took a deep breath to settle herself and made her way between the squares of culinary and medicinal herbs to join her under the maple trees. "You're lucky. Joe is a much better letter-writer than Simon, as it turns out. My boy has never been away from home this long—never had to write me letters. The things we find out, even when we think we know someone so well."

"That's why I thought you might want to share it with me."

"Come back to the house. Do you have time for a root beer? I made some on Saturday."

"I do. It's my day off from the Inn—Ginny doesn't have anyone come in on Sundays, and her other helper is working today. I can't stay long, though. Mamm is doing the washing."

Nearly all the women in their district did on Mondays. Sarah had just finished taking in hers before the sunburn patient had arrived.

When they were settled with cold root beer fizzing in tall glasses, Sarah opened Priscilla's letter from Joe.

Dear Pris,

    I hope you are well. I'm writing this from the porch of the bunkhouse, where all us hands sleep. Yesterday was officially the longest I've ever been gone from home, including that time we went to Holmes County when my two cousins married twin sisters and there was a tornado during the wedding. Hard to believe.

Simon sends his regards.

We been real busy. Like I told you in my last letter, this ain't no fly-by-night outfit. The ranch house alone must have cost a couple million to build, even if it is just a real big, fancy log cabin, and don't even get me started on the barns and bunkhouses. Everything is first class. Guess that's why they hired us, ha ha.

We just got back from a week-long trail ride. Me and Simon went along to tend to the horses, because a herd of Japanese businessmen don't know much about 'em except which end to put the bridle on.

They treated us real good, and I have to say, I never seen such pretty country as I have here. You really see what God was about when He made the earth. We saw two bears and a mountain lion and a bald eagle. I took a picture of the she-bear with my phone because I didn't think any of the boys would believe I really saw one.

We worked with the guests to teach them about their horses, and by the time we got back, all but one of the Japanese men could saddle and curry his own horse. The one who I guess is the boss of them was real happy with what he called the "team building exercise"—he gave us a nice tip. A hundred dollars is pretty nice, I'd say! I sent it home to Dat.

I've had a letter from Mamm. I think Dat is still pretty mad at me, but he'll come around.

Okay, it's time for supper.

Yours,
Joe

Sarah folded up the letter and handed it back. "Do you think it's true about Paul?"

Priscilla shrugged one shoulder under her deep rose dress and matching cape, and pushed up her glasses with one finger. "I don't know. I think he'd have been less mad if the boys had been more honest. It wasn't the ranch he objected to, so much as the lie."

Sarah could well imagine Paul's feelings of betrayal. She'd struggled with the same. On top of it, she didn't have a big farm to run with one less pair of hands.

After a moment, Priscilla said, "Do you think they're coming back?"

"It's only for the summer." Sarah wanted to encourage her, but it was hard when she wondered the same thing. "Whinburg Township is home. I'm sure they'll be back when the snow flies and they're laid off, even if they're not in time to help with harvest."

Priscilla nodded, and as though this had reminded her of something, she changed the subject. "Is Caleb over at Henry's?"

"*Ja.* Henry needed help no matter how he fought against it—did you hear that he got an order from some big kitchen store in New York to make jugs and batter bowls?"

"I did, and I know why, too. One of the men who works for the company in New York spent the weekend at the Inn with his girlfriend. He got Henry's name from Ginny and spent the whole Saturday in the barn with him. His girlfriend didn't mind, though. You should see the quilts she bought— one of them was Evie Troyer's 'Rondelay'—her most expensive one. Mamm worked on it last winter. She said Evie was delighted—and so was her husband the bishop."

Good for Henry, to find such a good commission so soon

after moving here. Sarah wished him well—and as for any other feelings…

After Henry had tried to help her stop Simon from leaving, things had been…different between them. Oh, they were cordial and neighborly and Sarah still sent over a plate of baking with Caleb when she could, but under it all was the faint sound of an alarm bell ringing.

An Amish woman could be neighborly with an *Englisch* man. The Amish were friendly to everyone. But Henry was more than *Englisch*. He had grown up Amish and chosen to leave rather than join the church. He and Sarah might share a fence line, but between them there was a great gulf fixed…and any feelings that might have gone beyond friendship could never cross that gulf.

After Priscilla went home, Sarah spent the afternoon weeding the herb beds next to the house, where she grew the plants closest to her heart. The fragrance of lemon balm, rosemary, thyme, and lavender rose up around her the way prayer must rise to God. The Bible called it a "sweet-smelling savor." Maybe it smelled something like this to the Lord, too.

Her chickens, interested in the disturbed soil, came to investigate, yanking out worms and chasing butterflies. The way they threw themselves wholeheartedly into whatever they did made her smile. People thought chickens were stupid, but she was beginning to learn that wasn't so. She and Carrie Miller over in Whinburg had got to talking when they'd run into each other at the discount barn, both of them looking for shoes for their *Kinner*. When Carrie explained that the birds could learn their own names and understand phrases, Sarah hadn't believed her—until she'd tried it herself.

One of the Red Stars was nipping at the leaves of the sage. "Here, you," she said. "Not for chickens. You go eat the grass." The hen ignored her, so she said it again, and gently moved the bird toward the lawn. The hen made one final attempt, and when Sarah repeated, "Not for chickens," at last she turned away and pulled up a few blades of grass instead.

Sometimes it took a few reminders to do the right thing. Content with her garden and her flock, Sarah found herself giving thanks for her blessings.

She didn't need to look over that fence where forbidden things grew.

On Friday evenings, Sarah and Caleb usually crossed the creek and walked up the hill to the home of Jacob and Corinne Yoder, her late husband's parents. But since they were expecting a visit by their extended family and the van was to arrive on Friday, the immediate family supper had been moved up to Wednesday.

Amanda met them at the door. At nearly twenty-one, she was the baby of the family, unmarried and still living at home, and she and Sarah had become such good friends that Sarah had dispensed with "sister-in-law" and simply called her "sister."

Her own three sisters were far away in Mifflin County, busy with husbands and children, and while they exchanged letters every week, and saw each other at least once a year, it wasn't the same as the everyday companionship she'd been used to, growing up. Amanda and her other sister-in-law Miriam, who owned the local fabric store, had stepped into the gap, and Sarah thanked God for them daily.

While Caleb galloped out to the barn to find Jacob, his Daadi, Sarah followed Amanda into the kitchen to be hugged and absorbed into the busyness of getting a family meal on the table.

She found a moment to pull Amanda aside, and took a small package out of the pocket of her dress. "I made you some things for your skin," she said. "Chickweed and cleaver tea—I wrote out a recipe that tastes *gut*—like breathing a meadow. It will clear your glands if you drink a cup every morning. And here is a jar of rose cream. Use it everywhere, not just your face."

Amanda touched her jaw, where a couple of blemishes had appeared, her gaze falling self-consciously. "Is it that bad?"

Sarah gave her a squeeze. "Of course not. But there is nothing wrong with using the plants God gave us to make things better."

"But to care about how I look is vanity," Amanda objected in her gentle way.

"Our bodies are God's temple," Sarah reminded her. "And there is nothing vain about providing a healthy place for God's spirit to dwell."

Amanda laughed and accepted the packet. "All right. There is no arguing with a *Dokterfraa*."

"I don't like people calling me that," Sarah said, following her upstairs to her bedroom, where Amanda put the packet on the dresser. "Mostly I'm just muddling through the books Ruth lent me, experimenting on poor Caleb, and hoping I don't hurt anyone."

"That's not what I hear." Amanda's loyalty touched Sarah's heart, but before she could respond, Corinne called them down to help put the food on the table.

Later, after a dessert of lemon meringue pie and homemade ice cream, while the four women were doing the dishes and the menfolk were relaxing with full bellies in the living room and girding their loins to take on Caleb at Scrabble, Amanda brought it up again.

"I hope you don't mind that I mentioned you to Linda Peachey on Sunday. I know you have your regular patients, but it can't hurt to expand, can it?"

"Linda Peachey?" Corinne's hands stilled in the hot dishwater. "Isn't she well? Not that I wouldn't believe it, living on that tumbledown farm with all those wild children. I don't understand why Crist doesn't move out of his brother's place and give her a home of her own."

"I doubt he can afford it, Mamm," Miriam said, wiping plates dry with speed and precision. "They live off the land as it is—both theirs and their neighbors'."

Sarah remembered the first time she'd gone for church at the Peachey farm, back when the old folks had it. It had sparkled with fresh paint and you could swear the lawn had been trimmed with nail scissors, so beautifully was it kept. But Crist Peachey and his brother Arlon didn't seem to have the gift either for farming or for keeping the yard and barn in good condition. The old place seemed shabbier and more run-down every year they hosted church. Their wives did their best to grow food, but it seemed that the only things that grew without effort were Arlon and Ella's children.

Crist and Linda, married five years, had not yet begun a family.

"What is Linda's trouble?" Sarah asked.

Amanda looked a little embarrassed. "You know."

There were only a few subjects on which Amanda didn't have the confidence to speak—subjects where you had to have experience before you could have an opinion.

"Oh," Sarah said. "I don't think anything I can do will help her conceive. That's in the Lord's hands."

"At least talk to her," Amanda pleaded. "She's such a nice little thing and she hardly gets a chance to open her mouth with that tribe rampaging all over the place."

"They shouldn't be rampaging." Corinne dropped a pot into the sink with a clang. "If those boys spent half the energy on helping Arlon in the fields that they waste on climbing trees and running wild in the woods, that farm would be a different place."

"They're still in school, aren't they?" Sarah said.

"The two younger are, if you can pin them down long enough to go," Amanda said. "One of the elder two just got back from a month with Arlon's relatives in Lebanon County and the other is putting the *i* in *Rumspringe*."

"But why don't they help?" she wanted to know. "It's their place to honor God and their father by helping him now that they're old enough. With four boys, that farm should be fixed up and producing enough to keep them by now."

"I don't know what the problem is," Corinne said. "They're a cheerful lot, and all smiles in their dirty faces, but a firm hand should have been applied years ago, if you ask me. I don't know what Arlon and Ella are thinking."

Arlon and Ella were not Sarah's business. But Amanda seemed to think that Linda was. "If you see Linda, let her know I'm happy to talk with her," she said at last. "I don't know how I can help, but at least I can give her a nice big slice of pie and some fresh milk. Everything else is up to the Lord."

Amanda's smile broke out, making her quiet face with its broad forehead and small chin beautiful. "I'll tell her."

"Speaking of things being up to the Lord, I hope you're coming Friday," Corinne said. "Did you have anything else planned?"

Sarah shook her head. "Only writing letters. My sister is

expecting again, so we're all excited as can be. She had a miscarriage this past winter, you know."

Corinne nodded. "I've been praying for her—I'm so glad! Well, that's *gut*, then. Our company will be here in time for dinner—you remember my cousins Zeke and Fannie King? One of Fannie's relatives who is farming east of there is coming, too. We hardly ever get to see Zeke and Fannie except in the winter. This is a treat."

"I'd love to. What can I bring?"

"One of those funny salads with the flowers in it," Amanda said promptly. "I love those."

Sarah laughed and said, "A salad it will be. Maybe I'll put nasturtiums in it, just for you."

She reached up to put the dry drinking glasses in the cupboard, and missed the conspiratorial look and raised eyebrows that Amanda exchanged with her mother. When she turned back again, they had wiped it from their faces and the conversational river flowed on as if that silent exchange of secrets had never been.

# CHAPTER 2

Henry Byler hadn't been around kids much after he'd left home. When he'd climbed down from that bus in Missouri after leaving his parents' Holmes County farm in the middle of the night, he'd felt as aged as his own Daadi, and at the same time, as young and inexperienced in the ways of the *Englisch* world as any toddler on his mother's lap in church.

He'd lucked into a job in the back of a garden store that sold clay urns and decorative pottery, and met the potters who supplied them. From there, he did rather like Caleb was doing now—hanging out and absorbing as much knowledge as he could before someone noticed and chased him away.

Busy with survival and then later, making a living, then getting his GED and going to college...there hadn't been a lot of time for getting to know any kids.

He was paying his dues now.

"Slam it down harder, Caleb," he instructed the gangly fourteen-year-old who had somehow morphed into his unofficial apprentice. "You're not going to hurt the clay, and the bubbles have to be flattened out of it completely."

"Oomph!" The boy hefted a big lump of clay like a bag of chicken feed and slammed it on the wedging table.

"Try cutting it in half," Henry suggested, then returned his attention to the batter bowl he had on the wheel.

"I can manage," Caleb panted. "Do you think I'll have muscles like yours by the end of the summer?"

"I think you'll have a slipped disc and carpal tunnel syndrome. Don't try to save time by wedging a big piece and then cutting it. Cut one or two pounds at a time, enough for a single mug or bowl. I tacked up a chart for you, see? You'll be better able to pound the bubbles out of a smaller lump."

"This is an important commission and we can't mess it up. *Ja*, I know." He took the words out of Henry's mouth, which made him realize just how often he must have said them in the last couple of weeks.

"Point taken," Henry told him. "Now you take mine. And yes, you'll have some definition by the end of this job, if that's what you're after. Working clay is hard physical labor."

"Daadi doesn't believe me. He thinks I ought to be helping him and Uncle Josh in the fields." Caleb took the cutting wire and sliced the lump into three as easily as Henry himself might have. The boy was a quick study in some things, he'd give him that.

"Maybe you ought to obey your grandfather."

"But I want to do this." *Slam! Slam!* "Anybody can follow a horse up and down. But not everybody knows how to work clay. Can I make the handles?"

"I need someone to wedge more than I need someone to make handles. Those only take a minute. That's probably enough on that lump, Caleb. If you overdo it, then it won't do what I ask it to on the wheel."

"How do you ask it?" The boy wrapped the damp clay in plastic and set it with the row of others that would be today's batch.

"With my hands."

Was that what had happened to him when his fiancée, Allison, had died in that car accident? Too many slaps—too much slamming against the brick walls of life, rendering him unable to do what God asked him to do?

Maybe.

But things were better now. He didn't know why. Coming to the home his aunt had left him, to the community of Amish relatives he'd visited in his youth, should have made things worse. He'd been running from his upbringing for most of his life, so it was strange that running back to it had brought him a measure of peace and allowed him to get his hands back into clay again.

Not that he was coming all the way back to it, mind you. That was never going to happen. But he was getting used to living in the quiet, nonelectrified farmhouse that had once rung with the voices and shouts of someone else's family. Of living on a farm that other men tilled and cared for. Of making friends with other people's children.

Like Caleb, and a few of the teenagers like Priscilla Mast, whose dad's farm abutted his and Sarah Yoder's on one corner. After a hoedown party had ended in a grass fire a couple of months ago, the local teens had evidently decided he was on their side when he didn't press charges or hand anyone over to the local sheriff. He overlooked the fact that nonretaliation was the Amish way, and told himself it was because they hadn't really done much harm to that old fallow field. The *Youngie* would greet him on the road when they were driving by in their courting buggies, and now and again he'd find a plate of cookies or a pie on his doorstep when he came in from the studio he'd created in the barn.

Sarah Yoder sent the odd plate over, too, but not with this kind of frequency.

It felt a little strange to be accepted by a bunch of local kids. A nice kind of strange. As Caleb had pointed out in a rare moment of sense in all his chatter, Henry and the local teenagers were on the same side of the baptismal fence. They hadn't joined church yet, and neither had he.

Except in his case, there was no *yet*.

Through the open doors, he heard the crunch of tires on gravel, rolling slowly past the house and coming to a stop on the wide piece of ground he'd paid Caleb to clear for a parking lot between house and barn. Not buggy wheels, but tires, which meant an *Englisch* car. It was either a curious tourist, drawn in by the small placard bearing a pot and the word AR-TISAN that he'd ordered off the Internet, or it was—

"Hello in there!"

Ginny.

Caleb grinned over his shoulder as Henry brought the wheel to a stop. "Hello," he called as her curvy form appeared silhouetted against the light between the open barn doors. "Give me a second—I'm just pulling this bowl off and I can't leave it."

"Take your time," she said cheerfully. "Hey, Caleb. 'Sup?"

Caleb, whose mouth ran a mile a minute, got inexplicably tongue-tied in Ginny's presence. Henry could never decide if it was because she was an *Englisch* woman, or an African-American one, or simply because she was Ginny, and she tended to silence people while they adjusted to her brilliance, the way eyes had to adjust when they came out of a dark room into the sunlight.

He lifted the bowl, still on the bat—the flat surface in the middle of the wheel—and took it over to the workbench, where he used his thumb and two fingers on its soft rim to pull a spout into shape that was wide enough to accommodate the thicker flow of cake batter. Then he cut it from the bat with his cutting wire and set it on the drying shelf.

"There. Done." The water in the deep sink was cold, fresh out of the ground, with a tendency to be hard, but it felt good as he washed his hands.

When he was dry and presentable, he turned to Ginny with a smile, and she, as irrepressible in her way as Caleb normally was, gave him a hug instead of a handshake. "I hope that old thing isn't interfering with my mugs."

Today she was wearing yellow jeans and a lime-green T-shirt with a quilt square and the words SISTERS' DAY EVERY DAY written on it in curly script. Her earrings were tiny yellow birds.

On any other woman, the effect would have made him flinch. But on Ginny, they made you feel like all the sunflowers in the field had turned their beaming faces toward you and all was right with the world.

"Not a bit. I did five this morning, before I got started on the D.W. Frith order." He smiled into her amber eyes. "I haven't forgotten who my number one customer is."

"You'd best not." She gave him a poke in the ribs and said, "But I'm not here on business. I actually have an afternoon off and I'm here to tempt you into two hours of dissipation and frivolity." He took a breath, and before he could say a word, she went on, "I know those are foreign concepts to you, but for once in your life, just go with it and come with me, okay?"

He hadn't had a day off in two weeks—since starting the Frith order, in fact. Temptation flooded in, warring with the thought of the bowls and jugs that needed to be completed, glazed, fired, and shipped to arrive by the fifteenth of August.

Ginny appealed to Caleb. "Help me convince him. A man can't work twelve hours a day, seven days a week without losing it."

"Go on, Henry," said Caleb, the traitor. "I'll finish wedging this block of clay and clean up. It'll all be ready for you tomorrow."

Henry wavered, but it was the pleading in Ginny's eyes that did him in. The novelty of someone actually asking for his company was still too fresh, too unusual. He was powerless against it.

Which was how he found himself on a sunlit hillside an hour later, looking out over the valley from under a big chestnut that had probably been there since the original Amish settlers had come to the township in the seventeen hundreds.

"There, now," Ginny said happily, setting out sandwiches, a basket of berries, and bottles of cold limeade she'd probably made herself to match her T-shirt. "Isn't this nice?"

"You have a gift for making an event out of the simplest things." He bit into a fresh, flaky roll to discover it contained a fat slice of Brie cheese, a layer of cranberry sauce, and some leafy greens he couldn't identify. He finished it in about two seconds and reached for another.

"Not a gift," she said, making herself comfortable on the quilt she'd fished out of the trunk of her car. "I just pay attention to details. And one detail I noticed was that you hadn't been out in a long time. So I came to rescue you from the tyranny of the pots, marching around your studio like the brooms in that Disney cartoon."

He laughed at the image—and at the unconscious assumption that he would get the reference. "You forget I didn't have a childhood that contained cartoons. But I did go to Disneyland once, and I know what you mean. *The Sorcerer's Apprentice*, right?"

She nodded. "That scared me silly when I was a little kid. Inanimate objects behaving with minds of their own—don't like 'em. I don't like dolls that talk and move their eyes, either, or clowns. Creepy."

"Not a fan of the circus, then?"

She shook her head so that her spiral curls, tied back in a yellow scarf wrapped around her head like a headband, danced. "You couldn't get me to go on a bet. The one and only time my parents took me and my sisters, a clown came leaping into the stands to give out candy or something, and I had a total meltdown. They had to carry me out before I burst a blood vessel from screaming. Or so Mama said. After that first sight of the darn clown coming at me up the stairs, I don't remember very much."

"The most traumatic thing that ever happened to me was falling through the hay hole when I was seven. That doesn't really compare."

"It would if there was nothing underneath. Did you get hurt?"

"No, luckily my dad had just filled the stall, so it was a soft landing. Still, I treated the loft with a lot more respect after that."

"Do you miss it, Henry?"

"What? The hayloft?" The words came out defensively, instinctively.

"No, silly. Being Amish."

*Deflect—deflect.* "Did your husband?"

She took his question at face value. "I don't think so. He

was happy in the Mennonite church, and so was I, for a time. But after our divorce, I didn't find the satisfaction in it that I used to, so I left."

"I can say the same."

"Our situations are different, though. I still have my family, all happy Gospelpalians, in Philadelphia."

"Gospelpalians?" That was a new one.

"Episcopal Gospel Church of Douglastown, but that's a mouthful. Mama couldn't get her tongue around it when she was small, so her family started using her word for it. Gospelpalians. It's a family tradition now, even when she got married and Daddy took over the pulpit."

"I still have my family."

"But you told me yourself, you can't go home again."

"I can, technically. I'm not under *die Meinding*. But I don't want to. I'm happy living here, and my relatives are civil and don't have their fingers in my life, and it all works out." He finished up the last roll as if that were the end of it.

Ginny gazed at him, then out at the pretty view, and back to him again.

"What?"

"I'm trying to decide if you really mean it."

He met that gaze, as sober now as it had been twinkling and full of laughter before. "What brought on this serious conversation anyway? I'm supposed to be having an afternoon off."

"You can still use your mind, even if your hands aren't busy," she pointed out. "Where do you see our friendship going, Henry?"

"I see it blooming like the daylilies down there by the road."

"Aren't you the poet. I'm serious."

"So am I. I don't ask more of a flower than that it simply exists, and in return, it makes me happy."

"But people aren't flowers. We do more than just exist."

"Sure. But isn't it enough that our friendship exists, and that it makes us happy?"

She sighed, a short, choppy sound of frustration. "Never mind."

He knew he should answer her question in the spirit in which she'd asked it. But he couldn't. Not yet.

Not until he knew the answer himself.

# CHAPTER 3

Except for cleaning toilets, which she didn't like doing at home, either, Priscilla enjoyed her job at the Rose Arbor Inn. Ginny was not only nice to work for, but also fair about extra wages for extra work, and flexible about things like time off. Pris could see now that, had she gone to work on the retail floor at the Hex Barn in order to be close to Simon, she would have gone crazy in the first week. The disappointment of incurring her father's wrath in order to be near him, only to have him leave within a few days, would have been bad enough, but to add the tourists and the strangeness of having to tell people that the made-in-China things they bought were Amish-made would have made it worse.

There were plenty of tourists at the Inn, but at least she could say with perfect truth that *ja*, the quilt on their bed had been made by a local Amish or Mennonite woman. In fact, the Kentucky Storm in the Peace Room had been made by Evie Troyer, and Priscilla herself had helped with the quilting before it went to the auction last September.

She'd spent the morning stripping beds and scrubbing bathrooms. The other *Maud*, Kate Schrock, a Mennonite girl from the church Ginny used to go to, worked Tuesdays, Thursdays, and Saturdays while Priscilla worked Mondays,

Wednesdays, and Fridays. Kate wore a lace doily on her coiled-up hair, held on by a couple of bobby pins, which were discouraged by the *Ordnung* for any Amish woman. Kate was older than Priscilla, and getting married the following year.

"Anytime you want to take a few days off, you just let me know," she'd told Priscilla not long ago. "I want to get in as many hours as I can and save as much as possible so we can put a down payment on a house."

Ginny wanted all the guest rooms made up, the dishes done, and the public rooms tidied and dusted by two o'clock each day so that when guests checked in at three, there were no buckets lurking in the upstairs hall or glasses left over from the night before sitting on the coffee table.

Kate usually vanished the moment her chores were completed, to go and do bride-to-be things, but Priscilla liked to linger a little. When she brought in a bouquet of flowers for the entry hall where the registration book lay open, Ginny had been delighted and the job of doing a few things "just for pretty" had become hers.

Ginny wasn't back yet from wherever she'd gone all dolled up in yellow pants with birds in her ears, and when the doorbell rang at two forty-five, Priscilla jumped and put down the bowl of snowball flowers on the dining room table so abruptly it was a good thing the water didn't slosh out onto the gleaming wood.

What should she do? She wasn't supposed to be seen—she was the *Maud*. Ginny was the public face of the Rose Arbor Inn. If Dat found out she was putting herself on public view, he'd be upset, since he had pretty strong feelings about a woman's place.

The doorbell rang again.

She couldn't very well leave them standing on the step with their luggage, now, could she? What kind of a welcome would that be at a bed-and-breakfast with a reputation for hospitality?

Priscilla touched the three straight pins in her *Kapp*, smoothed down her apron, and opened the door. "Hello," she said. "Welcome to the Rose Arbor Inn."

The man in the business suit smiled and his wife dragged her gaze off the riot of climbing roses over her head. "There really is a rose arbor," she said, following her husband in.

"It'd be false advertising if there wasn't, Mom."

Priscilla turned at the sound of a younger voice and looked straight into the greenest, liveliest eyes she'd ever seen.

"Hey," the young man said. "Wow, are you for real?"

She couldn't have replied if her life depended on it. She'd never seen anyone so handsome—better looking than Simon, even, and that was saying something. His hair was the color of dark chocolate, and was shaggy, like it hadn't seen scissors in a few months. It hung in those eyes and emphasized the clean angle of his jaw.

"Don't be rude, Justin," his mother told him, then said to Priscilla, "We're the Parkers from Connecticut. I booked the Peace and the Sonya Rooms for two weeks. No cell phones, no computers, no video games. We're going to have an unplugged family vacation—right, boys?"

Silence greeted what Priscilla thought was a perfectly reasonable plan.

"J-Just let me make sure," she finally whispered, when it was clear no one was going to speak, and slipped past Justin to look at the reservation. Sure enough, there they were, booked almost to the end of June. "*Ja*—I mean, yes, it's right. Let me show you upstairs."

She'd heard Ginny say this often enough. But she still felt awkward as she preceded them up the steep staircase, as though at any second, someone—like Justin—would discover she had no business taking over and would demand to speak to the real innkeeper. "Mind your heads," she said as they passed under the lintel to the second floor. "It's low here because people were shorter in 1813."

"Fascinating," Mrs. Parker said. "I've been looking forward to this for weeks. Where's the nearest farm that sells quilts, miss?"

"My name is Priscilla," she said shyly. "And I believe Ginny—that is, Mrs. Hochstetler—has a booklet on the table downstairs that shows all the places in the district where you can buy quilts. We get a lot of quilters here."

"Do you make them, too?"

Priscilla opened the door of the Peace Room and showed her in. "I worked on that one." She nodded at the bed and the woman made a beeline for it. "But our bishop's wife, Evie, she pieced it."

"Kentucky Storm?"

"*Ja.*" Priscilla smiled at her. "You know the pattern?"

"I sure do. And I know how complex it is, especially when—"

"Whoa, Isabel, easy does it," her husband said, coming through the door sideways with both rolling suitcases. "Let us get our bags in the room, at least, before you head off down the road like a racehorse, okay?"

Priscilla hovered in the doorway, unsure how extensive a tour of the room should be—or if she should even give one.

"Don't forget about us."

She whirled to see Justin lounging against the banister. "Oh, I'm sorry, I haven't—"

"Let's go to our room." He raised an eyebrow and grinned at her.

"Justin, stop teasing," his mother called from inside the en suite bathroom. "You're in the Sonya. Where's Eric?"

"Here." A younger boy wearing a hoodie and a sulky expression stepped out of the shadows behind his brother. Priscilla wondered how she'd managed to miss him when the registration book had plainly said there were four people in the Parker party.

Justin caught her eye. "Well?"

Blushing, and annoyed at herself for doing it, Priscilla pushed open the door to the Sonya Room. It held a pair of twin beds on either side of a three-light window that had a nice view of the old covered bridge. "This is yours."

"Nice. Too bad it's pink."

There was nothing pink about it. Wedgewood blue walls with cream drapes and pillows and—oh, the quilts. "That isn't pink. It's peach, like the Sonya rose. There's not very much of it, but it matches that picture, and it's why she calls this room the—"

"Sonya. I get it. What did you say your name was?"

"Priscilla."

"Is there a Priscilla rose?"

She mustn't look at him. She could count on one hand the number of *Englisch* boys she'd ever spoken to, and none of them strung as many lines as this one. She definitely preferred the younger boy, who simply wheeled in his suitcase and occupied one of the beds without saying a word. "If there is, I've never seen one. Enjoy your stay."

"Will I see you around?"

What did he mean? Why would he care? "Maybe. I work here."

There was that wicked grin again. "So I will, then."

"The guests don't usually see us. They're here to see the sights."

"You're a sight. I'd like to see more of you."

His brother sighed. "Justin, give it a rest."

She had to get out of here. What did the *Englisch* say? "Have a nice day."

And before any more outrageous things came out of his mouth, she fled down the stairs. Fortunately, Ginny had an open-door policy, and never minded guests coming and going or even being on their own in the house. Priscilla grabbed her handbag out of the hall closet, left the house, and emerged from under the rose-covered arch to the parking lot to see Ginny getting out of her car.

"Hi, Priscilla," she said. "Is this the Parkers' car?"

"*Ja*, they just arrived. I got them settled in the Peace and the Sonya, like it said in the book."

"Did you offer them tea?"

Priscilla clapped a hand to her mouth. "I forgot."

"Never mind, not your job. Thanks for stepping in for me." She came around the front of the car, her picnic basket in one hand. "I kidnapped Henry Byler and made him take an hour for lunch...and it turned into two." She checked her watch. "Oops. Almost three."

Aha. So that was the reason for the bright outfit. "Did you have fun?"

Ginny's warm eyes seemed to darken. "*I* did. But I don't know if that man knows how to have fun. At least he can hold up his end of a conversation, so that's a plus. Do you know him very well?"

Pris shook her head. "He seems nice." If Ginny didn't know about the hoedown fire, she wasn't about to tell her.

The fewer adults besides Henry and the sheriff and her father who knew about that, the better.

Ginny gazed at the roses, nodding in the warm June breeze. "I don't know what it is about him," she said, almost to herself. "Maybe I have a rescue complex." Then, as Priscilla stared at her, wondering what on earth she was talking about, she gave herself a little shake. "Never mind. Are you off? Want a ride home?"

"No, thanks. Mrs. Parker probably needs that cup of tea more. Besides, it's not far to walk."

"See you next time, then. It'll be busy this weekend—we have a full house, thank the good Lord."

The shortest way home was by the path along Willow Creek, a path worn into the bank by the feet of many *Youngie* who didn't have access to their own buggies, hikers, and the occasional fisherman looking to pull a brook trout out of the riffles for his supper. The creek cut across lots, avoiding the busy corner where the highway intersected with the county road, which Priscilla would just as soon not have to negotiate, especially as tourist season was beginning to swell the traffic into a flood.

She'd barely gone fifty feet when someone behind her called her name.

A male someone. She turned to see Justin Parker coming along the path, and when he saw he had her attention, he lifted a negligent hand in a wave.

Oh, good grief. Just what she didn't need any more of.

Priscilla whirled and headed off down the uneven path at a healthy clip. If she could get around the first bend, she could dodge through the hanging branches of the big weeping willow and climb up to the road without him seeing where she'd gone. She'd take the traffic on the highway any day over more of his jokes and insinuations that she only half understood.

But she underestimated both his surefootedness on the creek bank, and what was clearly his determination to escape day one of the "unplugged" family holiday his mother had planned.

"Priscilla! Wait up!"

She wasn't going to make it, so with a sigh, she turned to see what he wanted.

"What's the hurry?" He wasn't even breathing hard. He jammed his hands in the pockets of his jeans and grinned, as if he'd caught her hanging around on purpose hoping to catch a glimpse of him. "Aren't you done for the day?"

"No." She began to walk again. Maybe if she kept her replies short and her pace fast, he'd get the hint.

Unfortunately, his stride was longer than hers, and even though the path narrowed and widened depending on rocks and bends in the creek's course, he still kept up. "Do you have another job to go to?"

"*Ja.*"

"Where's that?"

"At home."

"Your family have some kind of business there?"

Were all *Englisch* boys this nosy? "*I* have business there. I have chores to do."

"What kind of chores?"

What a question! "The same kind your mother has, I suppose."

"Oh, like picking up the dry cleaning and ordering takeout and telling the cleaner which rooms to do?"

That put a hitch in her thinking, but only for a second.

"No, like sewing and mending and washing the clothes, and cooking the dinner, and cleaning the rooms myself."

"Yourself? You do all that by yourself?"

"No, my two sisters help. And Mamm. She does the most of all of us."

They passed under the willow, and bars of sunlight flickered over his face. He stopped and looked up, into the golden heart of the tree, and for a moment, thank goodness, stopped asking questions. The chuckling and endless whisper of the creek flooded in to fill the silence, and over in one of the Byler boys' fields, a three-note call sounded.

"What was that?"

"What, the bird? That was a bobwhite. He's probably calling for a mate."

"Smart guy. So no takeout or dry cleaning, huh?"

She was finally goaded to look him in the eye. "How much do you know about our ways? Are you really asking me this because you want to learn, or are you just trying to get a rise out of me?"

He blinked at her for a moment before the smiling veneer flowed over his face again. That shield of "I've got this under control" that he seemed to wear as comfortably as he wore his gray T-shirt and black jeans. But just for a moment, she'd made it crack with her honesty. Maybe he wasn't used to being called out on all the silly things he said.

"Oh, I want to learn," he replied. He touched the sleeve of her work dress, pleated, not gathered, into the arm hole, as the *Ordnung* said. "Especially about you."

"There is nothing to learn." She took off again. At this rate, she'd be home in ten minutes. She had to get rid of him before anyone saw them. Dat would have a fit if he got wind of it. "I'm not special."

"I bet you are."

"I hope not." She didn't slow her pace, or waste breath trying to think of ways to soften her words. "If I thought I was, that would be prideful, and pride is a sin."

"There's no such thing as sin."

She choked on her own breath for a second, before she got it back enough to set him straight. "You're wrong. How do you explain all the bad things in the world?"

But he only shrugged. "People do bad things."

"And that's called sin."

"Semantics. So what do you do for fun around here?"

She'd better look up what *semantics* were in the dictionary when she got home. There was nothing more irritating than for a know-it-all to actually know something.

"You could go to the water park. Or the mini-golf. There's a quilt museum in town your mother would probably like. And—"

"I meant you, Priscilla Rose. What do you do for fun? Do you have a boyfriend?"

Well, this was the limit! She had made a mistake even to talk to this boy. They were nearly to the bridge on County Road 26. She had to lose him, and quick.

"That's none of your business."

"So you don't."

"I do, too!"

"Where is he? Is he going to take a buggy whip to me for talking to his girl?"

"He would not do that. We do not believe in violence."

"So he won't mind me talking to you?"

Here they were at the bridge, and she had reached the end of her patience. "*I* mind you talking to me. I'm sure your parents are wondering where you are."

"I'm sure they're not."

"Go away and stop bothering me," she said in rapid *Deitsch*, and scrambled up the bank like a rabbit. When she crossed the bridge, she did not look down, but she had the distinct feeling he was watching her.

# CHAPTER 4

Sarah practically floated over to Jacob and Corinne's on Friday night. A letter had come from Simon—only his second since he'd been in Colorado. But what made her happy was not so much the news it contained, which was much like Joe's to Priscilla, but the simple fact that he was safe and well and able to do prosaic things like write letters. A letter meant a measure of normalcy in his life—paper, a pen, a quiet place. She could be grateful for that, even if the rest of his days were taken up with horses and chores and dealing with people he was never likely to meet here on the farm in Willow Creek. For one thing, around here, horses were meant to work—pulling buggies or plows or harrows—not to ride.

"When he gets back, he'll be itching to ride Dulcie," Caleb said as they climbed the steps to his grandparents' kitchen door. "I wonder if they learn rope tricks out there?"

"The only thing he'll be roping around here will be you." Sarah grinned at her youngest, who was always in motion and often had to be roped in, and pushed open the door so that he could precede her.

He carried the big deep bowl of fresh-picked garden salad, with cucumbers, lettuce, raw peas, shredded carrot, sliced strawberries, and for a little surprise, even a few Johnnyjump-ups she'd found in the rockery. But what delighted her most was the cheerful, unexpected orange of the nasturtiums and calendula petals.

"You did it." Amanda hung over the bowl for a moment, as if she could smell the flowers, before she took it from Caleb and set it in the middle of the dining table, which was set for sixteen.

"Ask and ye shall receive," Sarah said with a smile. She knew all but one of the women in the kitchen from family gatherings, and the busy time before dishing up went quickly with introductions, catching up on family news, and hearing about the trip down, for which they'd hired a big van and a driver.

When Corinne began to mash the potatoes, she glanced around the room until she caught Sarah's eye. "*Liewi*, would you go call the men in? It'll take them longer to wash up than it will to get all this food on the table."

Belatedly, Sarah realized that Caleb had handed over the salad and vanished in the direction of the barn, so they didn't have him to send. "I'll be right back."

Her father-in-law was a prosperous and careful steward of the land—so much so that Joshua and Miriam had been able to build a home on the property, and Sarah's late husband, Michael, had been given five acres of his own when he had returned to the district after the death of his first wife and had courted and married Sarah. Since Michael hadn't intended to farm, he was quite happy for his father and older brother to continue doing so for a third and fourth generation, and left his machine shop to pitch in and help during planting and harvest. That is, until the cancer had sent him home to God.

In the dark hours of the night, sometimes Sarah had to light a lamp, open her Bible, and remember that his spirit had been delivered to a better place, where there was no pain and no tears. The garden reminded her daily of God's mercy, but during the first years, the Bible had been the authority she'd turned to, and found comfort there.

Sarah passed her mother-in-law's enormous garden, which was becoming more Miriam and Amanda's as Corinne got older. The barns and sheds were neatly painted white, the trim a decorous black, as were most of the homes and buildings in this district.

Just where the drive widened out so the buggies could turn around, and before the paddock where the horses grazed and the gate opened into the orchard, the men had drawn up chairs in a circle to visit and joke and make plans for their fields. Jacob waved as he saw her coming along the gravel drive.

She waved back, and called, "Dinner is ready—time to wash up."

Jacob slapped his knees and got up, tossing a joke over his shoulder to the other men as they folded up the old wooden chairs that were too rickety to use in church, and took them into the barn. They straggled up to the house—her father-in-law, his oldest son Joshua and Joshua's two boys, Caleb, Corinne's cousin Ezekiel King, and a man she didn't know. Was this the relative she'd mentioned before? The husband of one of the women in the kitchen?

But no, he had no beard. She looked away as Ezekiel caught up to her. "Sarah, it's good to see you. Caleb tells me Simon is working in Colorado. How is he?"

She shook his hand. Zeke, according to Corinne, was the family jokester, so you never knew what he was up to. Every time Michael had talked about him, it had been with a reminiscent smile. "He's well, Zeke. I just had a letter from him today, in fact—all about a trail ride with some Japanese businessmen."

For once, she had been the one to surprise Zeke King, and not the other way around. "Caleb said he was working on a dude ranch, but I couldn't believe it was true."

"It's true. He and his buddy Joe are looking after the horses, from what I understand—and, I hope, keeping themselves as separate from bad influences as they can."

"It's big country out there," said the stranger. "More country than people, I think. He'll be all right." He held out his hand. "My name is Silas Lapp."

Zeke finally remembered his manners. "And this is Sarah Yoder, my cousin Corinne's daughter-in-law. She was married to Corinne's second boy, Michael, before the Lord took him."

Sarah shook his hand. "Have you been to Colorado, Silas?"

"I have."

Anxious to get everyone to the table, Sarah turned and chivvied them toward the house. They'd be the last ones seated at this rate. But at the same time, she was vitally interested in finding out even the smallest things about the state, which might as well be a foreign country, it was so unlikely she'd ever get the chance to visit.

"I hope you'll tell me a little about it. I want to picture my boy somehow, and the only way I've been able to do it so far is to check books out of the library."

"We'll have to talk it over at dinner, then."

And he was as good as his word—especially since the only two chairs left at the table when they finally got inside were right next to each other at the opposite end from where Sarah and Caleb usually sat on Friday nights.

After a silent grace, when plates and cups began to clatter,

Silas passed the big bowl of potatoes to Sarah and said, "Where is the ranch your boy works on?"

"The postmark is Buena Vista, so that must be the nearest town with a post office, but he mentioned once that the ranch is in a place called Cottonwood Springs."

Silas smiled, a look in his eyes as though he was appreciating a memory. "The closest Amish settlement would be in Monte Vista, then."

"Is that close enough that a boy in Cottonwood Springs might have an opportunity to go to church?"

If so, she would write to Simon that very night and suggest it—even if they had to ride one of their trail horses to get there.

"No, I don't think so. It's a hundred miles or more—but there is a bus service."

So far? Imagine living a hundred miles from church. Her mind could hardly take in a country so vast. "I could write and suggest that for his next weekend off. *Denki.*" And she smiled at him, determined to join him in looking on the bright side. Even if the boys were too far away to ride in one day, just knowing there were some of their own people only a couple of hours away on the bus was a gift. The knot of worry that had been plaguing her despite her confidence that God held Simon in His hand loosened just a little. The evil one took every opportunity he could to sow doubt, and now this good man had allowed himself to be used by God to sweep it away.

"Where have your travels taken you?" Amanda asked shyly, handing him the bowl of salad.

He picked up the tongs and was about to take a scoop of it as he answered her, when he stopped. "Is that a flower?" He laid it on his plate.

"It's a nasturtium. I like them in the salad, so Sarah puts in a few for color."

Sarah added, "There are tiny pansies and some marigold petals, too."

"It has color, all right. Are you sure they're safe to eat?"

"Oh, *ja*," Sarah assured him. "And good for you."

"Sarah is an herbalist." Amanda took back the salad bowl to steal the last nasturtium and crown her little pile of greens with it.

"Herbalist-in-training, you mean," Sarah said. "Jacob's sister Ruth is the real *Dokterfraa* in this area."

"Ruth Lehman in Whinburg?" Zeke asked. "Fannie, wife, we should go up there and pay them a visit while we're here."

"I can take you on Tuesday, if you like," Sarah said. "I go for lessons with her every week."

"That would save us hiring a driver." Fannie helped herself to chicken and dumplings. "*Denki*, Sarah. Silas, why don't you come with us? You're always interested in new things. Maybe you could learn a thing or two."

"I'm glad he takes an interest in what's around him," Sarah said with a smile. "He's been telling me about Colorado, where my boy is working."

"Better you should tell these girls about your farm, Si, and your plans for it," Zeke said. "Did you know, Sarah, that the phone company wants to put up a repeater tower on his land? They'll pay him a fortune and he doesn't have to do one thing to earn it, just let them build it."

What on earth was a repeater tower? "What do those do?"

"Pay money," Zeke chortled.

"They pass on a signal to cell phones," Silas said quietly. "And it's not for sure. They came around many of the farms to ask permission from our men."

"They wanted the same thing from Deacon Moses Yoder in Whinburg," Jacob said. "I think he was wise to turn them down. What does it say of a man when he can work and doesn't? Sitting back and watching a metal structure sending its signals doesn't glorify God."

"And it puts one whole field out of commission," Silas agreed.

"I'd say you could plant beans or corn for six generations and not get the money for them that a tower could bring in six months," Joshua put in.

"And there's no sin in being clear of debt. 'Owe no man anything, but to love one another,'" Zeke quoted.

"Maybe it does contribute to the use of cell phones," Corinne said, "but at the same time, a fruitful field is a fruitful field, and if the phone company is willing to pay fairly for it, I don't see any sin in it."

"I have had this discussion with myself many times," Silas told them. "And come to no better conclusion than we have right here."

"What does your bishop say?" Sarah asked him. "You would be guided by his thoughts in any case."

Silas nodded. "He is in favor of it."

Jacob shook his head. "You're lucky you don't have a bishop like Daniel Lapp in Whinburg, then. He told Moses no, flat out. Of course, Deacon Moses had to be an example."

"I am not a deacon," Silas agreed. "But the Lord's will could change at any time."

Every man in an Amish community had to be prepared for that. When the lot fell upon you, there was no declining it, or putting it off, or asking someone else to take your place. A man simply submitted himself to God's will and entered upon a life of service to church and community that would not end until his death.

The conversation turned to other things, and Sarah urged another helping of dumplings on Silas. "Tell me something else about Colorado. Since we have you here, I find myself thirsty for information like a hart for water brooks, knowing I may not get this chance again."

"I'll be here for a few days," he said. "Perhaps we might go for a drive and I can tell you more."

Sarah swallowed her surprise at his forwardness; he hadn't seemed like that kind of man. But she could not react too strongly or Corinne would see it, and a little idea might grow in her mind that should not be there.

"You can tell me more now," she said, with a smile to let him know she wasn't offended. "Did you see the Rocky Mountains? What are they like?"

Again, his eyes took on the distant gaze of a good memory. "I did. Picture the earth flinging itself toward heaven and then being frozen there in the sky, thousands of feet high."

"I can't picture it—or I can, but only because of the photographs in the books I borrowed."

"I had not been so smart before I left, so I was stunned by the mountains. You can see them for a hundred miles off, and they stay in the distance—until between one moment and the next, there you are in the midst of them, looking up and up until you get a crick in your neck."

"That I can well believe."

"But up until that point, you go through what they call the foothills. They aren't like the hills here in Lancaster County." He nodded in the direction of the window, which faced north toward a view of Battle Ridge. "They're much higher and wider—almost mountains in themselves. I believe the ranch your boy works on must be in the foothills, if he is near the Cottonwood Valley."

"If there are ranches, there must be water for the animals, too."

"*Ja*, the rivers are precious, because the land is what they call high desert, covered with golden grass in the summer. But the rivers aren't like the ones here. Instead of running deep and quiet, they fling themselves through granite canyons and off hundred-foot precipices. Even in the shallower grade of the foothills, they still roar among the rocks, as cold as the glaciers they spring from."

She gazed at him, seeing the picture he painted in her mind's eye as well as she could the sharp angles of his jaw and forehead. "You are a good storyteller. I can almost see the land."

Beside her, Caleb was transfixed, too, and Sarah noticed out of the corner of her eye that Amanda was listening so intently that her supper was only half eaten, her fork lying limply in her fingers.

"I am not, not really," Silas said with becoming modesty. "I am just describing the wonderful things God has made."

"Do you think you'll go back?" Amanda finally managed to ask. "You said there was a church established near there?"

"There are a few, but I don't know what God has planned for me," he said. "At the moment, I have a farm and enough work to keep two men busy, so another trip west is probably not going to happen for a few years yet."

Caleb leaned over to see him better past Sarah's shoulder. "When you get married and have a family, you could take them there on a holiday."

Silas laughed. "I could, when God reveals the woman He has planned for me."

For some reason, Amanda blushed, but since everyone was looking at Silas, Sarah was pretty sure no one noticed.

And then her boy put his foot in it for sure. "You could marry Mamm and then we could all go."

"Caleb Yoder!" Sarah exclaimed, and dropped her fork. Creamy gravy spattered down the front of her cape.

While everyone got a good laugh out of it, Sarah dabbed at the fabric, thankful that it was a good, sturdy polyester crepe that repelled liquids and wiped off easily. She wished his words could be wiped away as easily. Honestly, the things he got into his head!

By the time she got her clothes looked after and was mopping up the last of her supper with a piece of Corinne's homemade bread, the conversation had moved on to the likelihood of a thunderstorm and some rain to give the knee-high corn a boost.

When Sarah glanced at her mother-in-law to see if she wanted to begin clearing, there was a look on Corinne's face that she had never seen before. She was gazing at Silas Lapp as though that new idea had occurred to her in the last minute or so.

Sarah did not want to know anything about it.

She stood and began to clear the dishes herself.

# CHAPTER 5

I n its niche next to the barn door, the telephone rang. Not for the first time, Henry was glad he spent most of his day in the barn, where he wouldn't miss the calls that came more often now. Eventually he'd get around to letting the phone company know he wanted a jack in the house, but until then, it was working out not too badly, having the only phone on the place this close to where he worked.

"Henry, this is Dave Petersen at D.W. Frith. Is now a good time for a conversation?"

He wiped the grit off one hand on his jeans and switched the phone to the other ear. Petersen was the vice president of procurement, which sounded like too grand a title for a guy who spent his days scouting for things that people might like to buy. It must be important if he was calling at the tail end of the week instead of getting on the train to commute back to his home in Connecticut.

"Hi, Dave. Sure. I was just putting some green ware out to dry. That makes six batter bowls so far, out of the twenty-five you ordered for the initial launch."

"Glad to hear it. Say, I just got out of a meeting and the marketing guys had some questions."

Platters and batter bowls were pretty straightforward in

Henry's mind, but considering what they'd offered him for this commission, whatever the East Coast luxury housewares chain wanted, he'd provide. He made himself comfortable, leaning on the barn door. "Go ahead."

"Well, it's this whole Amish thing. The catalog girl figures she can get you a two-page spread in the fall book that goes to a million DM subscribers, and that automatically means a slide on the home page of our site."

"That's great news." More than he'd ever expected, in fact. "What's DM?" Definitely money?

"Direct mail. Glad to hear you're pleased. They just need a short paragraph about you—not a bio exactly, but more like a two-liner on who you are. So I was working on it and thought I'd run it by you."

"Better you than me. Marketing gives me hives. Shoot."

"How's this: 'Amish potter Henry Byler creates his pieces in the barn that his ancestors built a hundred years ago, finding his inspiration in the flowers and fields his family has cultivated for generations.' Huh? Sound good?"

Henry hesitated. "It sounds like marketing copy, all right. I like the flowers and fields part." For some reason, that reminded him of Sarah Yoder.

"Great! That was easy. So we'll run with it."

How to put this in a way that a guy from New York City could understand? For once, Henry was glad to have had the experience with the reviewers in Denver, which had taught him all too well the power of the written word.

"Are you going for accuracy or for atmosphere?" he asked, hoping Petersen wasn't about to hang up.

"Both," Dave said promptly. "Did I get something wrong? Is it the farm? You told me when I was there that it had been in the family since the turn of the last century."

"Well, it has—the extended family. My own family is out in Ohio."

"Oh, well, family's family. That all?"

"No. About the Amish part, Dave..."

"What about it? It's an Amish farm, right? You grew up Amish?"

"Well, yes, but—"

"Then we're good to go."

"But I'm not Amish now. You can't say 'Amish potter Henry Byler' when I'm not. Not since I was nineteen."

A heavy sigh came down the line. "You're splitting hairs here. It's one word in one sentence in one catalog. Are you going to hold up production over that?"

"I don't like misleading people."

"Who's misleading? You were once Amish. That's good enough for me—and good enough for the customers who will be buying your bowls."

"Just take out that one word. Maybe 'Pennsylvania potter,' or 'Longtime potter,' or—"

"But Amish sells. That's the marketing hook, my modest friend. We're trying to differentiate ourselves from the noise out there. I can tell you this, Pottery Barn and Pier One don't have real Amish potters making their pieces."

"Neither do you."

"What's that supposed to mean? Don't tell me you're going to do something drastic, like pull out of the deal over an adjective?"

Henry's stomach plunged, and he steadied himself with his back against the sturdy door. He could feel the warmth of the sun coming through the wood from the other side. "No, of course not. Not when I've already signed and sent back the contract and begun the order."

"Good. That's good. Because I've got this check ready to send out and I'd hate to think you'd changed your mind."

Was Petersen *threatening* him? Who said anything about changing his mind? He needed that money to eat and buy clay.

"So we're good to go on this copy, then? Amish and all? Because I need to get this in before close today if you're going to get the spread. Those spots in the catalog book up months in advance, and I'd hate to see you lose it because we gummed up the works over wordsmithing."

*You say wordsmithing, I say truth.*

But what did it matter whether it was the truth or not? How much advertising was actually truth? It was a fact that the reviews of his own work back in Denver hadn't held any truth, and that hadn't stopped them from being published—or people from believing what they said.

"Fine," he said, pushing a hand through his hair and gazing at the green ware, which needed to be attended to. "Run with it, if you think it will do the job."

"That's the spirit, Henry. That's all it is, right? Copy doing a job. My job is to sell your pieces so you have a job making them. And what's it going to hurt? You were once Amish, and you live on an Amish farm. Close enough for government work, eh?"

"Sure," he said.

"Great. I'll get this check in the mail today. Nice talking to you. You take care now." And Dave hung up before Henry could even say good-bye in return.

He pictured the other man in his suit and expensive tie, dashing off to take the check down to the mailroom himself, and then shook his head at the image. Pushing a shoulder off the door, he walked over to the drying boards and picked up where he'd left off, setting out today's work so that the air could circulate around the pieces and dry them out.

There was probably as much truth in the existence of that check as there was in his currently being Amish. Maybe Dave had just been blowing smoke, holding payment over his head so he'd agree with whatever the marketing guys wanted.

Well, it wasn't his catalog, and no one was going to drive out here to see if he was really Amish before they bought a batter bowl. Half those catalogs would probably go straight into the recycling bin anyhow.

Meanwhile, he still had some work to do on the final glaze design, which he kept playing with, dissatisfied. He didn't really have six bowls ready to ship. They were still at the green ware stage, waiting for the first of their two firings, while sketches lay all over his kitchen table, and a few attempts at molding organic forms sat here on the workbench in various stages of completion.

After pulling plastic over the wedged clay waiting to go on the wheel, he washed his hands and forearms at the deep, two-bay porcelain sink and dried them on an old towel. Then he set off in the direction of Willow Creek along the path that Caleb had worn into the hill between the Yoder place and this one.

He needed some inspiration from the flowers and fields on this warm summer evening—in that way, at least, he could put some truth into the marketing copy.

There was something beguiling about moving water. Henry climbed down the slope into the creek bottom, where a path meandered along a grassy bank. Alders, maples, and willows leaned over the water, which chattered and bubbled along in its course, turning rocks over and cutting the channel infinitesimally deeper every day. Clusters of purple flowers grew among hillocks of wide-bladed grass, and hummingbirds and sparrows flitted among them. Two swallows dove and swooped after mosquitoes, no doubt with the aim of taking them back to a barn somewhere to feed hungry young before night fell.

The water had scoured the soil from a couple of wide, flat stones, and as Henry sat and leaned back on his hands, he felt the warmth of the afternoon sun stored in the granite permeate his skin.

With a shock of recognition, he looked up into a maple above his head and saw a rotted old piece of rope tied around a branch. This was where he'd gone into the creek that December day, egged on by Michael Yoder and his brothers. The rope had broken and dropped him into the swimming hole right over there, and it had been a good thing they were having a green Christmas, or he might not have survived the experience.

Or so he'd thought at the time. Somehow it didn't look quite as deep and scary as it had when he was a boy.

The breeze and the whispering rush of the water calmed him the way the voice of a trusted friend might—a friend you could count on to be there no matter what the season or circumstance. The creek eddied and swirled, always in motion, always changing—yet still the same, all these years later.

Motion. Liquid motion.

Henry sat up and pulled his sketchbook out of the breast pocket of his shirt, along with a number eight Micro pen. He sketched in the outline of a batter bowl. Liquid poured from the spout, but if he treated the handle as the source and the motion went from here to here…

No, that wasn't right. Too obvious. Like giving the baker instructions on how to use his tools.

He tried again, the swirl and eddy of the creek in his mind—the stillness of the rocks—the sound of wind and the way it moved through trees—

Five bowls appeared on the page now, none of them quite right. Six.

Birds. The swoop and dive of the birds against the light as they sought to feed their families—the way a baker wanted to feed his or her family—sky, water, bird, light, all in motion—

That was it.

The seventh bowl came into being under his pen, a line at a time, a shadow here, a curve there, a swirl and a dive, light as air and brilliant as water. He could use one of the delicate shades of blue he'd already developed in his glaze recipe book, but there was more to it—the luminescence of water, a pearly, swirly effect—he had the ground minerals on hand to produce that, he was sure of it, somewhere in the boxes he hadn't yet unpacked.

It was unusual. It suggested light and movement, whether at rest or in use.

Down the margin of the page, he made notes. Oh, this was going to be good.

He had to get back to the barn right away.

Over the rush of the creek, he heard voices around the bend, and scrambled to his feet. But before he could get across the path and up the slope, three people came around the curve. He recognized Priscilla Mast's blond hair and glasses right away. But who were the two city kids with her?

"Hallo, Henry," she called, relief in her voice.

"Hi, Priscilla." Teenagers wouldn't expect him to stand there and visit. He'd be polite and then they could all be on their way.

"What are you doing down here?"

"Taking a walk. How are you?"

"I'm well, thanks." Her gaze pleaded with him to do something.

And then he put one and two together. "You okay, Pris? These kids bugging you?"

"Hey," the taller one said. "Way to make assumptions."

He was a good-looking kid, maybe seventeen, with a cocky step and an "I own you" gaze. The younger one had the same hair color, but if they were related, the resemblance ended there. If he could have pulled his black hoodie over his head and rolled up like a hedgehog, Henry would bet he would have.

"Not much of an assumption," he said calmly. "Two *Englisch* boys tailing an Amish girl—that never turns out well. Take some friendly advice and leave her alone."

The kid took a deep breath, as if he was trying to keep his temper. "Who are you? She's got no problem with us. We're staying at the place where she works. You want her to lose her job?"

"I don't think Ginny will give you that much power."

The kid deflated a little and Henry wondered when the last time was that someone had spiked his guns.

"Come on, Justin," the younger one mumbled. "Knock it off."

"Priscilla Rose?" Justin appealed to her.

"I'm going home now," she said, and crossed to the track that led over the hill past Sarah Yoder's garden—the one that Henry himself had been about to take. "Nice to see you, Henry."

Justin looked as though he might follow her, and probably would have, but the younger one's gaze reluctantly locked on Henry's sketchbook, which was sticking out of his pocket.

"Are you an artist?" Justin turned as if a rock had spoken, and while he was distracted, Priscilla disappeared over the top of the rise.

"I suppose you could say so. I'm a potter." He held out a hand. "Henry Byler."

The kid shook the hair out of his eyes and took Henry's hand as if he wasn't quite sure he was doing it right. "Eric," he said reluctantly.

Henry gave it a firm shake, and the kid's fingers toughened up their grip, mimicking him. Had he never shaken a man's hand before?

"What are you doing out here?"

It was the same question Priscilla had asked, but with a different meaning. The kid had recognized a Moleskine sketchbook when he saw it. Maybe he was interested in art.

"Don't talk to strangers, Eric," Justin said.

His brother—for they had to be brothers—ignored this hypocrisy as he waited for an answer.

"I'm making batter bowls, but I got stuck on a design for the glaze." To his own amazement, he pulled the sketchbook out of his pocket. He never shared his process. But there was something in this kid's eyes—a hunger that he would never put into words for fear of being mocked—that Henry recognized with the accuracy of shared experience. "So I came down here for some inspiration."

Eric took the book with something close to reverence, opened it to the pages Henry had been working on—and Justin tapped it in the middle so the book folded shut and fell through his brother's fingers.

As neatly as a basketball player stealing the ball, Justin caught it before it hit the ground. "What's this?" He flipped it open, riffling through the sketches of mugs, bowls, and even an art piece or two that were in the first few pages.

Henry was both taller and faster—and knew a thing or two about basketball. In less than a second, the book was snapped shut and back in his pocket.

"None of your business."

"But it's Eric's business?"

"If I choose to make it so, yes."

Justin's brows drew down over his eyes. "What is *up* with you, dude?"

"Not a thing. But something's up with you. You might consider sharing the spotlight with someone else once in a while. Selfishness is a total bore, dude."

"What the— Where do you get off?"

"Right here. Have a nice afternoon, boys."

He made it halfway up Yoders' hill before he turned around.

And saw Eric—alone—standing knee high in the corn at the top of the creek bank. He had followed Henry up the slope and stood watching him go, like a small child in the ocean who had no clue how to swim.

# CHAPTER 6

The Saturday afternoon sun was beginning its descent, the light catching in the branches of the trees, when Sarah finished picking the peas. Her bowl was full, and with them she planned to make a chicken potpie for supper, with new potatoes and the baby carrots she'd thinned from the feathery square that made up one element of the Ohio Star design in her garden.

A buggy turned into the driveway and rolled up to the house, so Sarah took the bowl and made her way across the lawn to greet her visitor.

Linda Peachey looped the reins over the rail in front of the rock garden with hands that shook. She turned, a hesitant smile flickering on her lips and the inside of one wrist pressed protectively to her stomach. "Hallo, Sarah. *Wie geht's?*"

"It's *gut* to see you, Linda." No matter how close it might be to dinnertime, Sarah couldn't look at a woman this thin without wanting to feed her. Not only that, she felt a little guilty for not having gone to see her long before this. "*Kommscht du.* I'm hungry for some blackberry pie, and if you keep me company, I won't feel guilty about having a piece."

"*Neh*, I don't want to trouble you."

"No trouble at all. I like people to indulge my bad habits."

Linda smiled and followed her into the kitchen, where Sarah didn't waste an instant cutting the pie, pouring cream over it, and setting it down in front of her guest. A pot of what she had taken to calling *meadow tea* followed, which filled the kitchen with the scent she loved, and would do this young woman's body some good even as it lifted her spirits.

"You have such a way of making food seem like a gift," Linda said on a sigh of contentment as she scraped up the last of the pastry.

Sarah cut another piece and slid it onto her plate. "Food *is* a gift—from God."

"And I'm thankful for every bite." She hesitated, concentrating on her pie so that, Sarah suspected, she could put off telling her what she'd come for.

"My sister-in-law Amanda was telling me the other day that you might stop by." Sarah took a sip of tea. "I'm glad you came."

"Amanda is a *gut Freind*. Did she say what I was looking for?" Any other woman might have taken offense at being talked about, but Linda seemed to find it a relief that a way to start the conversation had already been opened.

"Not really. She seemed a little shy about it. About *die Bobblin*, I mean."

"It's not easy." Two slices of pie seemed to have taken the edge off, and Linda picked up her mug of tea and breathed in the scent. The tremor in her hands made the china clink against her teeth as she sipped. "Crist doesn't want to talk about it anymore, so I'm left to bend my friends' ears." Her blue gaze met Sarah's. "At least with you, there's a hope of being able to do something besides talk."

"I'm no expert, Linda. I'm still learning."

"Then we can learn together. If you think you can do

something for me, then I'm willing to do as you say. I can't pay you very much, but in the fall, the boys will go hunting and I can see that you get some meat for the winter."

"I'd never turn down that offer." She gathered her words together. "So if we are successful, have you thought a little about the situation you would bring a little *Boppli* into? Is there a chance that you and Crist will have a home of your own?"

Linda's gaze fell once more to her mug. "I don't think so. We can't afford to buy in this county, and if we moved away, we'd be leaving both his family and mine. Neither of us are willing to do that—and we don't think it's God's will that we do, either. But it's all we can do to pay a little rent to Arlon and help with the farm."

"Shouldn't his boys be helping, too?" The question shot out of Sarah's mouth before she could stop it. "I'm sorry. It's none of my business how he and Ella bring up their family."

"I can see why you would say so. The boys are high-spirited, but they have good hearts."

"But Linda, if they helped their father and uncle, they wouldn't have the energy for such high spirits, and the farm would be more profitable—would be able to support you better. And make an environment that you could bring a baby into. A calmer environment."

Linda took another sip of tea—something a woman did when she disagreed with you, but didn't want to argue. Then she said, "I am in the place that God has put me, and I'm content there. If it's not His will to bless us with children, then I must be willing for that. But if there is something I can do, I want to do it."

Sarah reined in her human nature, which wanted to tell this trembling reed of a young woman that living hand to mouth on a tumbledown farm with no peace was not conducive to bringing life into the world, and her body was telling her so. How could God want her there when she could not do His will for a woman and a wife?

Sarah didn't have the answer, but she could do a little to help.

"There are some things you can do," she said gently. "You have plants growing in your yard and in the woods behind your place that can nourish you. We'll start with this meadow tea. I'll give you the recipe and I want you to drink four cups a day—one with each meal, and one in the evening before bed."

Linda nodded. "That will be no burden at all. I love the smell of it—like a fresh-cut field in summer. What does it do?"

"Besides cleaning out the lymph system, which promotes healthy breasts, it's a nerve tonic. It reduces stress."

"I'm not stressed," Linda protested.

"When you came in, you were shaking."

The other woman waved a hand. "I was just hungry. I was so busy today I forgot to eat lunch."

Sarah knew when to knock on a door, and when to go around the side and open a window. "The body needs calm and a good sleep at night, so this will help you there as well."

"And you said that some of the ingredients grow around us, so I won't need to buy them?"

Sarah made up her mind between one word and the next. "I'm not going to charge you for the things I give you. We're experimenting." Linda tried to protest, but with a smile, Sarah kept right on going. "There's also a plant called lady's mantle. Ever heard of it?"

Her patient shook her head.

"I'm just learning about this one, but Ruth Lehman says it's excellent for fertility. She says that when you look at the plant, you can picture a lady—a mother—covering you with her cape to protect you and the baby. That's how the herb works."

"I'll take her word for it."

"I know, a little fanciful, but no more than smelling a fresh-cut field in our tea, *neh?* I'll give the lady's mantle mixture to you as a tincture. Just put a couple of drops in a glass of water and drink it. You'll be running to the bathroom every five minutes if I ask you to drink two kinds of tea."

"I'll be running to the bathroom anyway. Between tea and this lady's mantle, that's a lot of water every day. More than I drink in a week, I think."

Sarah made a mental note to write this down in her patients' journal. Poor Linda was probably dehydrated as well as being under stress and suffering from clogged-up plumbing. "We all need water, and lots of it. You may not think so, because I can see you're retaining water, but the more you drink, the less you'll retain. There's a reason the Bible tells us the water of life flows from the throne of God. We can't live without lots of it—or Him."

At last Linda smiled, and Sarah could see that her resistance was crumbling. That was *gut*. A patient who was motivated to do the right thing wouldn't stop after a day or two and then wonder why she wasn't getting well.

"*Kumme mit*, and I'll show you what plants to pick and how to prepare them."

When Linda went away an hour later with a cardboard box containing a bottle of tincture, some packets of dried herbs, and several handfuls of cleavers and chickweed, Sarah waved farewell.

"See you in church tomorrow," she called, and Linda waved through the buggy's open door in acknowledgment.

*Let these things help her, Lord. Even if it isn't Your will that she be blessed with a baby, I pray that You would bless her with a return to health. You have given us these humble plants that contain so much that is good for us. You have given us water, as necessary to us as Your love. Help her to use them wisely, so that she can serve You with joy.*

Because that, Sarah suddenly realized, was what had been missing in Linda's eyes.

Joy.

There was resignation, and she had said she was content. But in someone who loved God and was loved in return, a person should be able to see more than those pale substitutes.

*Give her back her joy, Lord.*
*And as You do, I'll find mine.*

# CHAPTER 7

Priscilla had never been so thankful for a Sunday as she was today. Church was held that week at Bishop Dan Troyer's home, on the other side of Willow Creek and down the county highway about four miles...so far away that the likelihood of running into Justin Parker was zero.

She was looking forward to a whole day where she'd be guaranteed a little peace.

Though why he should disturb her peace so much was not quite clear yet. He made her nervous. He wanted too much of her time. And yet there was something about him that was causing a little root of compassion to grow in her heart— though he would be the first to tell her that he felt sorry for her and not the other way around.

She and Katie and Saranne had breakfast on the table by the time Mamm and Dat got in from the milking, and once they'd cleaned up and changed into clean *Kapps*, their blue Sunday dresses with the white organdy capes and aprons, and their good black oxford shoes, Dat had led out the horse and harnessed him up to the family buggy.

The sun had barely lifted its face above the trees when they were on their way. Church began at eight thirty and lasted until eleven thirty—which was about the length of time it took for Priscilla's behind to begin going numb from the hard wooden bench.

The sermon was on faith, from Hebrews 11 and 12, and Priscilla listened to the preacher tell the stories of those in the Old Testament who had been faithful no matter what their circumstances. Who had believed that faith was the substance of things hoped for, the evidence of things they couldn't see.

Some people might think that was a contradiction in terms—you had to be able to see evidence, didn't you?—but to Priscilla there was no contradiction. Her faith in God, in her church, in the rightness of it, was a faith in something that was real and had form. Like the breeze in the trees outside, you might not be able to see it, but you could see what it did.

Nobody could argue that the wind didn't exist.

God had allowed Justin to come here, the way He allowed mosquitoes and the burrs that formed in the forget-me-nots when they went to seed. Annoying and persistent though they were, they had their season, and their season always passed.

The Parkers would be gone on Wednesday, and she could stop looking over her shoulder. She wasn't afraid of him—not at all. He was more like a newborn puppy or a baby, all noise and need, unable to look after itself without someone nearby to pay attention to it. Frankly, since he was neither puppy nor baby, she didn't have the patience. Or the time. And maybe that was what made him so persistent.

Dat's edict from the spring was still in effect, with no sign of relenting. To keep her out of trouble and from thinking about frivolous things like band hops and dates, none of her chores had been given to her sisters despite the fact that she worked three days a week at the Rose Arbor Inn. So Sundays were a relief in more ways than one. She could rest without the list of things to do ticking itself off in her mind.

After a tasty lunch of cheese, pickles, peanut butter spread in a thick layer on Evie's homemade bread, jam, and two kinds of pie, everyone trickled outside to enjoy the warm sunshine and visit for a while before the ride home.

Pris's buddy bunch had already congregated in a circle at the far end of the garden, exchanging news and taking sidelong glances at the sixteen- and seventeen-year-old boys hanging out by the barn door.

Rosanne Kanagy, her sidekick, as a girl's best friend was known in their district, bumped shoulders with her as Pris merged seamlessly into the group and the girl on the other side made room for her. "I haven't seen you in days. I miss you."

"I miss you, too. But until Dat sees that I've learned my lesson after that field caught on fire, I may as well be working two jobs."

"You didn't start that fire—you put it out. But we've plowed that ground before. Any news from Joe?"

"He writes every week. They've just been on a trail ride with some Japanese businessmen, and Joe says it went well."

Rosanne looked as if she couldn't believe it. "What are Japanese businessmen doing at a dude ranch riding horses?"

Priscilla shrugged. "Joe says it was a team-building exercise. I don't even know what that means, or why they needed to come all the way from Japan to do it, but the end result was that he and Simon both got a hundred-dollar tip."

By now everyone was listening, and Pris pushed her glasses up her nose self-consciously.

"Do you like being a *Maud* at the Rose Arbor?" one of the other girls asked. "I've never been in there—I've heard it's nice."

"It is nice," Pris said, glad to share something she enjoyed. "Each bedroom is named after a different kind of rose, and

Henry Byler made mugs for Ginny Hochstetler, with the roses painted on the side."

"I hear he's sweet on her," Rosanne said. "Isn't she Mennonite?"

"Her husband was. Very liberal—they're divorced. I don't know what church she goes to now."

Rosanne nodded. "I saw them driving together in the car, her and Henry. She was laughing."

"She laughs a lot," Pris told them with a smile. "Ginny can see the funny side of just about anything. Even the Parkers. They're staying there right now. She made eggs on stuffed French toast and the husband asked her to do his eggs over. They weren't cooked right."

"How can you cook an egg wrong?" someone wanted to know. "You put it in the pan, cook it until it's not runny, and eat it."

"He wanted his just so, runny but not transparent, and finally he went into the kitchen with her and did it himself," Priscilla said. "I was in there folding napkins and couldn't believe anyone would be so ungrateful for the meal served to him that he would criticize it. But she just laughed and said she'd learned something."

"He'd be making his own breakfast every day if it was me," Rosanne said. "But I guess for two hundred dollars a night, he can afford to pay for two breakfasts."

"I can see why his kids are the way they are," Priscilla confided, and the little circle leaned in to listen. "The older boy flirts all the time and follows me around while I make the beds. He's supposed to be on vacation, but he has nothing to do so he's bored silly. I finally asked him if he'd like to help and he went away, only to follow me down to the creek and try to walk with me."

"Is he good-looking?" the girl on her left said with a laugh.

"He's so exhausting I've stopped paying attention to his looks," Priscilla said with some asperity. "Lucky thing Henry Byler was there and distracted him long enough for me to get up to the field and home. I don't want him knowing where I live or he'll be whining at the door like a lost puppy."

"Cheer up—it's not forever," Rosanne said. "They have to go back to wherever they're from sooner or later, *neh?*"

"Wednesday. So really, it's only Monday that I'll have to deal with him." She stopped, and looked past the shoulders of the girls on the other side of their circle. "Don't look now, but the Peachey boys are trying to sneak up on us."

"The Peachey boys don't sneak," Rosanne said in a low tone. "They just stampede in and laugh at you when you tell them how rude they are. Come on, let's take a walk."

And before Pris could agree or disagree, Rosanne had looped her arm through hers and that of another girl, and the three of them broke the circle on their side just as Benny and Leon Peachey intruded on the other, teasing the nearest girls and laughing as they scattered.

"Any other boy would wait until a girl was alone or at least ask politely if she wanted to take a walk," Rosanne grumbled. "Who else would bust in like that where they weren't wanted?"

"Maybe they think they are wanted," Barbie Kaufman said, looking over her shoulder at the brave girls who were actually talking to them.

But Benny spotted that glance, and before the three of them could join a group of grown-ups or do something sensible like go in the house and wash dishes, he had loped over to take Priscilla's other arm, mincing a little as if he were mimicking their steps.

"Hi, girls," he said. "Want to go for a walk?"

"Not with you," Rosanne told him, as severe as a spinster chasing little boys out of her apple trees. "Let go of her and go away."

"Why? I was talking to Priscilla. Say, Pris, does Joe know you're keeping company with *Englisch* boys?"

Priscilla shook him off, but he kept walking up the driveway with them. Just wait. If he was still at her elbow when they got to the ditch, he was going to get a surprise.

"I don't keep company with them," she told him stiffly.

"That's not what I saw Friday, down in the creek bottom."

"Where were you? I didn't see anyone."

"Me and Leon were up in one of the maple trees. We were going to do cannonballs into the creek, but when you walked by underneath, we thought we'd better give you two some privacy."

"I wish you *had* done a cannonball," she told him, the words tumbling rashly out of her. "Next time, give me a hand getting rid of him instead of hiding up in the trees like a pair of scared birds."

"Scared!"

Good. Maybe she'd offended him.

"Wasn't us who was scared, I bet."

Or not.

"Not scared exactly, but I sure was glad to see Henry Byler. But still, it would have been nice if you'd showed your faces and let him know I wasn't all alone down there."

For once in his harum-scarum life, Benny Peachey didn't laugh. In fact, the merriment faded from his blue eyes as he searched her face, looking for the truth. "You serious, Priscilla Mast? This *Englisch* boy bothering you?"

"He's a nuisance." She wished now she'd never said anything. Now they would all think she saw bogeymen in the bushes. "He's staying at the Inn and I don't want to be rude in case it reflects badly on Ginny and hurts her business."

Benny looked thoughtful for all of five seconds before the grin broke out on his face again. "A little thing like you couldn't hurt anything. Say, can I take you home from the singing tonight? It's here, so everyone is staying on for supper."

Rosanne and Barbie both gaped at the effrontery of him, asking such a thing right out in front of a person's girlfriends.

"Benny, for goodness' sake," Pris said in exasperation. "You know I'm writing to Joe!"

"But he ain't here, and I am. What do you say?"

"She says no, she's coming home with Malinda and me," Rosanne told him with perfect timing. See, this was why they were best friends. They looked out for each other. "We live way closer to her place than you do."

Priscilla nodded, never letting on for a moment that this was the first she'd heard of it. "Sorry, Benny."

But if she thought he was going to break his heart over being turned down, she learned differently when not ten minutes later, she saw him walking under the trees with one of Malinda Kanagy's friends, who was at least a year older than he was.

Boys. Honestly.

The more she knew of them, the more she wished Joe Byler would come home sooner rather than later.

# CHAPTER 8

It was far too soon to expect results, but Linda Peachey still gave Sarah an update, pausing as she crossed the lawn. "I drank two cups of meadow tea and a glass of tincture water yesterday," she said with a glint of humor. "I thought you'd want to know."

Sarah laughed and said, "I'm glad you did. Just keep it up for a month and see how you feel."

"I'm going to ask the boys to look for some of the ingredients when they're rambling around in the woods. Benny has sharp eyes."

As Linda returned to her family, Sarah wondered again at Arlon's allowing two grown boys to run so wild. Did they have chores at all? Because looking at that farm, you'd sure believe they didn't. Well, they'd all see it in two weeks, because Arlon and Ella's house was next in the rotation.

Now that the lunch was over, the men had begun loading the benches into the bench wagon, while the women boxed up the plates, cups, and silverware and put them in their cubbyholes. Everything had its place, and the wagon went from home to home so that no one family bore the burden of keeping seating and eating utensils for use only once a year or so by the two dozen families in the *Gmee*.

In minutes, the job was done, and the cupboards and doors closed up.

Sarah was hovering around Evie's big garden when she felt an arm slip around her waist. "Covet not thy neighbor's flowers," Amanda teased. "I see what you're looking at."

Sarah squeezed back. "I don't think that's in the Scriptures."

"Maybe not specifically, but I'm sure the spirit of it is there. What's caught your eye?"

"I was thinking of making a skin preparation for you and I to try, and the recipe calls for four cups of rose petals. I wonder if Evie would let me have a paper bag full?"

"You wouldn't. Evie loves them so much. Nobody can grow roses like she can, and these have just hit their peak. Surely you don't want to spoil them by tearing all their petals off?"

"I wouldn't tear them off... here. But you can see that they could use a little thinning. It would be good for the plants."

"I'm sure Evie will see it that way."

Sarah had to laugh. "All right. I'll wait a couple of days until they're just past their best, and offer to help her thin them in exchange for some of this facial splash."

Amanda's gaze turned curious. "So you're coming to enjoy it, then, being a *Dokterfraa?*"

"I'm not one, I told you. I'm just learning. But it's interesting. I think my mother was an herbalist—not like Ruth, preparing things as a business, but because it came naturally to her. She might even have learned it from her mother." She drew in a long breath, scented with roses and marigolds. "I wish I'd known back then. I could have learned from her instead of starting from scratch."

"Maybe when you get more experience, you could—"

Amanda stopped, gazing past Sarah's shoulder, and Sarah turned to see Silas Lapp strolling up, hands in his pockets, smiling as though he was enjoying the picture they made.

That Amanda made.

"Hallo, Silas," Sarah said in a sisterly tone. "It didn't take long for you boys to get the benches put away."

"It never does when so many hands share the work. What are you looking at?"

"Evie's roses," Amanda said shyly. "God has given her a gift with them, but we're the ones who enjoy the benefit of it."

"God has given our bishop's wife many gifts," Sarah said. "She's an accomplished quilter, and I hear there's another baby on the way, too."

"I'm sure His hand was just as generous with you," Silas said. "I came to ask if you girls had a ride home."

Why was he talking to them both but looking at her? "*Ja*, Caleb and I came in our buggy." She craned to look around him for Zeke or her father-in-law, Jacob. "Did you get left behind?"

"If I try hard enough, I will," he joked. "Then I could ride home with you."

She laughed as if he'd made a joke. Of course he had.

Then he said, "You're coming for dinner at Jacob's, *ja?*"

"*Ja*, I am." She turned to Amanda. "Do you want to come home with Caleb and me, or are you staying for the singing?"

Amanda had joined church the year before, but until she was married, she could join the *Youngie* for singing and volleyball and games. Some people might think a twenty-year-old woman was too old for that, but how else was she to find a husband if she didn't go places with the singles?

"It's a fine afternoon," Silas said. "You might have the chance of a drive."

Amanda blushed, and to draw attention away from her, Sarah said, "If you had a buggy here, you could take her for one yourself." Then she had a bright idea. "In fact, why don't you do that? I want a chance to visit with Zeke and Fannie, so you take Dulcie and Caleb and I will go with them."

And before either of them had a chance to demur or make themselves scarce, she bustled off to arrange it with Zeke, who thought it a fine joke.

"I see what you're up to," he said, wagging a finger at her. "You're matchmaking."

"I am not, and don't you say a word. Silas suggested it, but Amanda needs a little help. Now, let me go find Caleb."

By dinnertime, when they arrived at Jacob and Corinne's, she was bursting with curiosity about how the ride had gone. It must have gone well, because she couldn't see her buggy in the yard...and there were plenty of quiet lanes to drive on that might delay a couple's arrival.

Oh, how she hoped Amanda might hit it off with Silas. Her young sister-in-law was so shy that she could barely bring herself to speak to a young man, never mind be so forward as to suggest a ride home. She had her father's slimness and Corinne's blond coloring, and her own gentle spirit shone in her face. If she'd use the skin wash that Sarah planned to make to brighten up her complexion, any man would take a second look at her and like what he saw.

Not that a good husband would count a woman's looks to be of as much value as her faithful service to God, or her skill with *Kich* and *Kinner*, but you couldn't deny that getting his attention was a place to start.

Preparations for dinner were fairly leisurely, since Jacob planned to barbecue steak on the grill outside, and that meant that potatoes and vegetables didn't take long to prepare. Even still, Jacob's barbecue fork was in his hand and he was ready to begin when they finally heard the crunch of wheels in the lane.

Silas tied Dulcie to the rail while Amanda hurried into the kitchen, already unpinning her cape. Sarah followed her up to her room, where she found her changing into a soft green dress.

"Did you have a nice drive?"

Amanda turned eyes filled with pleading on her. "Oh, don't tease me. Cousin Zeke is going to make hay with this and I don't think I can bear it."

"What does it matter, *Liewi?* As long as you enjoyed Silas's company, it doesn't make a bit of difference what anybody says. What did you talk about?"

Amanda pulled a bib apron off a peg, shrugged into it, and slowly tied it behind her. "Everything. Nothing. He told me a little about Colorado—different from what he said the other night—and he asked about Simon. About you, and your learning to make cures. About our Michael, and what a shock it was when he was diagnosed."

"You took an awfully long time getting home."

"He's not a fast driver. And we were talking."

"That's *gut*. I'm glad to hear it."

"Do you think he likes me, Sarah?"

Sarah pushed her shoulder off the door frame and crossed the room to give her a hug. "It would be impossible not to."

"You're just saying that because you love me."

"I'm saying it because it's the truth."

"But you practically tricked him into driving me home."

"If a man didn't want to in the first place, he couldn't be 'tricked' into doing anything. I just gave him an opportunity, and he took it. What else did you talk about?"

At last Amanda calmed her agitation enough to smile. "Silly things. He doesn't believe that chickweed can be good for anything but feeding to chickens. I told him some of the things you do with it, but he still wasn't convinced."

"You should sneak some into the salad tonight and see if he notices."

Sarah smiled inside at Amanda's laughter. This was the girl she knew, not the anxious, tense person who was so unsure of herself that she could hardly enjoy a ride without worrying about being teased about it.

"I certainly will. That will teach him."

They went down to supper then, and Amanda was as good as her word. And when she told Silas what she'd done, his laughter made everyone around the table smile and exchange interested glances.

Even Zeke didn't spoil the mood by making a joke or teasing Amanda to distraction.

It wasn't until later that night, after Sarah and Caleb had said their prayers together and she'd gone to bed, that she opened her eyes wide in the summer dark as a thought struck her.

Amanda and Silas had talked all the way home.

Was it her imagination that every subject seemed to have something to do with her?

Sarah shook her head at herself. That couldn't be. And she had better do some serious praying on the subject of pride.

# CHAPTER 9

On Monday, after she and her sisters made breakfast, and then she helped Mamm do the week's laundry, Priscilla arrived at the Rose Arbor Inn a few minutes after eight thirty. Thank goodness one of the Byler uncles had been going into town and had offered her a ride; otherwise, she'd have been nearly half an hour late. She was going to have to fetch her old scooter out of the barn, if Dat didn't relent soon, so she'd have a way to speed up the trip.

"Good morning, Ginny." With a glance into the dining room, which was empty but set for breakfast, she knelt by the storage cupboard to get out the basket of cleaning supplies. "Has everyone gone for the day?"

"Oh, no," Ginny said. "The Parkers aren't even down to breakfast yet. The weekenders I had in the other four rooms left yesterday afternoon, so you might as well get started in the Wild Rose Room."

That was what Ginny called the attic, which had been opened up as a family suite and had a queen-sized bed as well as two bunk beds and a twin.

"But first, have a sticky bun. I just took them out of the oven."

"I've already had breakfast, but thank you." She didn't

want to be here when Justin came down. If she was up on the third floor, and had any luck, he would have finished breakfast and gone out for the day before she was finished in the Wild Rose Room.

"A sticky bun isn't breakfast. Come on. I know you love them."

Priscilla wavered. Ginny made the best sticky buns in the county, rich with cinnamon and pecans and melting sugar. And the floors weren't creaking with footsteps going back and forth upstairs. Maybe just this once. "Ohhh...all right."

Which meant that the minute she sank her teeth into the luscious bun, sneakers padded down the stairs and Justin walked into the dining room. In the next second, he spotted her sitting at the prep table in the kitchen.

She should have gone up to the third floor as soon as Ginny had mentioned it. This was her punishment for indulging the lusts of the flesh. At least the kitchen was gated off. He could talk to her, but he couldn't come through and invade her space.

"Good morning, Justin," Ginny said. "Can I get you some orange juice?"

"Sure, thanks. Hi, Priscilla Rose."

Ginny gave her a puzzled look, but said nothing as she poured a glass of juice and handed it to him. "If you like, I'll put some mugs of coffee on a tray and you can take them up to your folks."

Now it was his turn to look puzzled at the outlandish thought of doing something considerate for someone. "They'll be down in a few minutes. Dad's just getting out of the shower."

"All right." Clearly, Ginny knew better than to say what Priscilla was thinking. "Sticky bun?"

"Is that what that is?" he asked Pris, and she nodded, though she would rather have ignored him. "Okay. Cool."

"What have you got planned for today?" Ginny asked him.

"I don't know. I guess my parents want to go to the Strasburg Rail Road and ride a train or something."

"You'll enjoy that. I always do."

"I doubt it. I stopped playing with trains when I was three. I figured maybe I'd hang out with Priscilla."

"Priscilla has work to do. I don't pay her by the hour to provide entertainment for my guests."

Thank goodness for Ginny. At this rate, Pris wouldn't have to talk to him at all.

"She doesn't have to entertain me. She can work and talk at the same time, can't you?" He appealed to Priscilla, who swallowed the last bite of bun as Ginny handed him his on a napkin.

She got up and washed her hands at the double sink. "I'd rather work than talk."

"I think you've got it backward." And he chuckled, as though that was a joke.

"She's Amish," Ginny pointed out. "And like some of us, they don't mind working. In fact, the Amish think work is good for the soul."

Justin shook his hair back as if he were squaring up to a challenge. "Want me to give you a hand making the beds and stuff, Priscilla?"

"No, thank you."

She picked up the cleaning supplies and headed for the stairs.

"Why not? You'd get it done in half the time, and have the rest of the day off."

"I would just go home and have more time to take the laundry in and do the ironing."

"Who irons anymore?" He took a big bite of his bun as he followed her down the corridor. "Mm, this is good."

"Justin, please leave Priscilla to her work," Ginny called from the kitchen.

"Oh, she doesn't mind. Hey, I didn't know the Amish could wear flip-flops."

"I mind." Ginny came out of the kitchen with a look in her eye that Priscilla had never seen before. She took the opportunity to scamper up the flight to the landing. Once around the turn in the stairs, she could hear, but no one down there could see her—or her bare feet in their flip-flops.

"Dude, chill," Justin protested. "Hey, give me back my bun."

"One, my name is Ginny, not *dude*, and two, in this house we eat our food at the table—especially things as sticky as this. Right here, Justin, where I've set your juice."

"I'm not a little kid."

"You're behaving like one, and getting in my business. Now, sit."

"I don't think I want the juice or the bun, thanks. I'm going back to my room."

But by that time, Priscilla was on the third floor with the door to the Wild Rose Room closed.

And locked.

She had never been so glad to clean the big room, which took up most of the top floor. Every bed had been slept in, every bar of soap and towel used, and both bathrooms had been left in disarray, with trash all around the wastebasket. It took two hours to restore it to its usual welcoming order, with fresh soaps in their paper wrappings set out for the next guests, and fluffy towels hanging on the racks. The quilts on all the beds lay smoothly, clean sheets under them ready for tired bodies.

And the Parkers were gone off to the railroad.

It was hard to miss their departure, what with Justin arguing every step of the way. She didn't hear Eric's voice, but that wasn't surprising. The poor kid hardly had a chance to get a word in edgewise even when he did come out of his shell long enough to speak.

What a strange family. They seemed so disconnected, so out of tune with one another and the people around them. She knew that not all *Englisch* people were like that, so it couldn't just be the effect of the city. It had to start with Mr. and Mrs. Parker, who were amassing quite a cache of souvenirs in their room—even a bookcase they'd bought at the Amish Market that Pris had to clean around every morning—while their sons were going stir-crazy from boredom.

Their big SUV accelerated out of the parking lot and onto the road with hardly a pause to look for anything coming. With a sigh of relief, Priscilla picked up the basket of supplies, unlocked the door, and—

—practically fell over the body sitting on the top step of the staircase outside.

"Eric! What are you doing here? I thought you went with your family to the train."

He put away his phone, on which he had been playing a game, and scrambled to his feet. Priscilla maneuvered past him and descended to the staircase landing, where the light was better and she could see his face.

He looked so abjectly miserable that her heart softened. An unhappy kid who was out of his element, and hardly older than Saranne. But Saranne had the advantage of a place in a family that loved her and showed it by giving her tasks that were hers alone, to support the rest of the family and help out.

What did this boy have to do but go to school and play games on his phone?

"Is everything all right?"

He shrugged, and followed her down to the second floor, where she opened the door to the room his parents were staying in and put the basket on the floor.

"Why didn't you go to Strasburg? I think you would have liked the train. I always like it when I get a chance to stop and watch it go by, all puffing with steam and people waving out the windows."

He shrugged.

"Justin seems to have gone, though he didn't want to."

"They had tickets for eleven o'clock and had to leave. They looked for me, but not upstairs where you were."

She stopped in the act of pulling the quilt off the bed. "You hid from them on purpose?"

Another shrug.

"Eric, what is going on? Why would you stay here in a house that's practically empty instead of doing something fun with your family on your holiday?"

He didn't answer. Instead, he watched her pull the sheets taut, tuck the corners in, and fold the top one back over the blanket, each layer precisely aligned with the one below. "Why do you make the beds when everyone is just going to mess them up again tonight?"

"Because that's my job." She went around to the other side to do the same. "Besides, who wants to sleep in wrinkly old sheets? We don't change them every day, and it's much nicer to climb into a bed that's been made. Much nicer for people to look at a made-up bed during the day, too."

"I keep my bedroom door closed."

"If you made your bed, maybe you wouldn't have to."

"I don't know how."

She paused in the act of fluffing the pillows and aligning them. "You don't know how to make a bed? Didn't your mother teach you?"

"She doesn't make them. The house cleaner does, but we're never home when she comes."

She indicated the quilt. "Toss that over, would you?"

He did, and she caught it, shaking it out over the bed. "Fold back the top and I'll put the pillows on it."

He caught on quickly, and even helped her smooth the quilt down and tuck it in at the footboard.

"Come on and I'll show you how to do yours."

Without waiting to see if he would follow her, she crossed the landing to the linen closet next to the bathroom and got fresh sheets, even though technically for a longer-term stay, they were only to change them every other morning.

"My sister and I can make a bed in less than a minute, top to bottom," she said, stripping his sheets. "It goes way faster when there are two doing it. So. Fitted sheet first." Snap. Pull. Tuck. "Top sheet." Snap. "Hospital corners so it won't travel while you're sleeping." She demonstrated. Pull up. Tuck under. "Blanket—just tuck it under the end of the mattress. Then fold the sheet on top of it. Good. Now the quilt and the pillows."

She pretended to check the clock on the mantel. "Five minutes. Not bad for a beginner. Let's do the next one."

They made Justin's bed in three minutes, but only because Eric told her not to bother with fresh sheets. Hiding a smile, she had him take the old ones off anyway and start from the beginning. "Otherwise we'll be cheating on the clock."

By the time they had the beds made in the other three rooms, Priscilla was far enough ahead of schedule that she could go downstairs and fetch a couple of sticky buns as a treat.

"You do good work," she said. "You could be a professional."

For the first time, a smile flickered across his face. "There's more to it than I thought."

"There is if you want a bed to look nice and be comfortable. Ginny wants everything to welcome her guests—and beds are important."

"Guess I never thought about that before. What else do you have to do?"

"Tidy up, sweep the floors, clean the bathrooms, empty the wastebaskets. But I won't ask you to help me do that. Otherwise I'd be taking money that belongs to you for doing the work."

"When do you get off?"

"When I'm done—usually around two. Ginny likes us to be finished then, because the guests begin checking in at three. Oh, and I have to dust and tidy up downstairs, too, but the bedrooms come first. And sometimes, if I have time, I cut flowers for the dining room and the entry hall."

He shifted on the sofa in the reading niche, where they were enjoying their buns without a word from Ginny about sitting at the table. "What?" she asked.

"Are you going home along the creek?"

What an odd question. "I don't know." *It depends on whether your brother is back by then.* "Maybe."

"Do you think that guy will be there?"

"What guy?"

"That one who was talking to you the other day. When we came. The older guy with the sketchbook."

"Oh, you mean Henry Byler. I don't know. He might have

got enough inspiration that he doesn't need to come back. It's
the first time I've seen him down there."

"Do you know where he lives?"

"*Ja*. He inherited my—" *Friend's? Special friend's?* No, that
wasn't right, even though she and Joe were writing like special
friends did. *Boyfriend's?* Yes, that was better. Then maybe Eric
would pass it on to his persistent brother as a reminder. "My
boyfriend's Aendi Sadie's place."

"What's an ain-die?"

"Auntie. His aunt's place."

"Can you show me?"

Finally Priscilla understood where this was going. "You
want to see Henry again? Because of his sketchbook? Do you
like pottery?"

Under his shaggy hair, which always seemed to be ob-
scuring his face, his eyes held hers. They were green and
vulnerable and fierce with an emotion she hadn't seen much
before. Henry had it, though, when he was talking about his
pots. And Sarah had it when she was making something and
came out of herself enough to let it go.

Passion.

"*Ja*," she said in response to an answer he hadn't given in
words. "If you meet me down in the creek bottom where we
saw him before at quarter past two, I'll take you over to his
house."

The gratitude that flooded his eyes was a gift—made all
the more precious because it came from someone who had no
practice in being thankful.

# CHAPTER 10

Henry was bent over his recipe book, making notes on what he was calling his "sky and water glaze," which was inadequate shorthand for what he'd envisioned in that moment of clarity by the creek. When two silhouettes blocked the light from the open barn door, he lifted his head, momentarily disoriented by the sudden mental return to barn... farm... ordinary life.

He squinted against the light. "Who's that? Caleb? I thought you were helping your grandpa in the fields today."

"It's not Caleb, Henry. It's Priscilla. And Eric, who is staying at the Inn."

He put down the pen and closed the book. "Eric? That kid who was bugging you?"

"That was my brother, Justin."

So he did talk, this kid who had looked into his sketchbook as if it were the Scriptures or some ancient key to the meaning of life. He got up and held out a hand again, and this time, the kid shook it like he meant business. "Nice to see you again, Eric. What brings you and Priscilla over here?"

He looked at the girl, who was more likely to give him an answer. "He asked to come, so I brought him. And now I've got to be getting home. I have a week's worth of laundry to take in off the line and fold and iron."

"Thanks," Eric said to her.

She smiled at both of them, flickered through the barn doors, and was gone. Which left Henry with a teenager who suddenly looked very unsure of himself, now that he'd got what he asked for.

"I hope your parents know where you are," Henry finally said.

"We told Ginny we were coming. She'll tell them when they get back from the train."

That was good. Sensible. Very Priscilla-like.

Eric hesitated, as if debating whether to give up too much personal information to a stranger. "They went to Strasburg."

"Ah, that train. They should enjoy it. Now that you're here, what would you like me to do with you?"

To his surprise, the kid flinched. Just a tiny movement, but Henry immediately saw his mistake. "Not that you're not welcome," he assured him, and the kid stopped looking like he was going to bolt out the door. "I always enjoy talking to another artist. That is...I got the impression the other day that you were interested in art."

"I—I wanted to know what you were doing there. At the creek. With the sketches. And stuff." Each word came out as though he were regurgitating something. As if it was so hard for him to talk about this that he had to force himself to do it.

Talk was hard when something meant a lot to you. Henry got up. "I could use a hand, if you have a little time."

"With what?"

Eric followed him over to the wedging bench. "The thing about being a potter is that there's always something that needs to be done. And that usually means wedging the clay before you can work on it."

"I don't know what that means." The boy's avid gaze took in the bench, the block of clay covered in plastic, the cutting wire with its two wood handles.

"It simply means whacking the air out of it. Caleb usually does it for me—he's the boy from the next farm—but he's with his granddad today."

With Eric looking on, he cut a piece and began to wedge it, hitting it over and over and leaning his weight into the job. He explained about the bubbles and how they had to be worked out of it, then gave him a fresh piece with both hands.

Eric was tentative at first, then, when he saw that banging it on the bench wouldn't hurt it, he really got into it. The kid was strong for his size—he could put almost as much pressure on the clay as Henry could himself.

"You're a natural at this." *Bang—thump!*

"That's what Priscilla said"—*Bang!*—"this morning when we were"—*Whack!*—"making the beds."

"You helped her make the beds?"

"Yeah. Never did it before. Justin said he wanted to, but I did it."

"Does Justin make a habit of doing a lot of talk and not so much action?" *Whack!*

"He'd freak if he saw me." *Whump—flip—bang!*

Punctuated by the sounds of wedging, Eric began to talk, the way Henry remembered his female cousins talking as they did the dishes. There was something about repetitive shared labor that freed the mind—and the mouth.

"I want to do art—pottery, maybe, or sculpture—but I can't. At home, I mean. To practice stuff."

"Why not?"

A sidelong glance. "Do you know what Justin would do?"

"What, make fun of it? Consider the source. You'll have

to grow a thick skin sooner or later, Eric. When you show a piece, or even offer it for sale in a booth at a fair, people will feel free to give their opinions about it."

"I still couldn't. He'd probably break anything I made and say it was an accident that happened while he was admiring it."

"Is he really that small?"

"No. But he's the oldest. He's used to being the one who gets the attention."

"But you doing what you love doesn't take away anything from him."

"He doesn't have anything that he loves doing."

Henry got a picture of a black hole—those phenomena in space that sucked everything in their orbit into their own dense emptiness. "What about your folks? Wouldn't they be happy that you were doing something you liked?"

"All they care about is grades."

"That's reasonable. Good grades are important."

"But I'm only in eighth grade. Nobody cares what middle-schoolers do."

An idea flashed into Henry's head. "Art academy high schools might care."

"What?"

The banging and thumping stopped as Henry marshaled his flash of an idea into sense. "You're going to high school next year, aren't you?"

Eric nodded, and from the look in his eyes, he wasn't looking forward to it much. Who would, when your elder brother was probably a senior in the same school?

"What if you asked your parents if you could go to an art academy high school? Then you'd have lots of studio time, and you could keep your pieces there, not at home."

Eric stared at him. "Is that what you did?"

"I got serious about pottery later, in college. But that was me. There's no reason you couldn't start now, if that's what you want to do."

"I didn't even know there *were* art high schools."

"Ginny has a computer upstairs in the library—that place with the couch outside your room. You might do some research, and then bring it up with your parents. I don't know, but you might still have time to get in, and a—" He stopped. "Do you have a portfolio?"

"N-No. Just some drawings. I keep them under the bed so Justin doesn't find them. Manga, mostly. Comics. For fun."

"Nothing wrong with drawing. You saw my sketchbook— you'll need that skill. But you'll need a portfolio to show the admissions people you're serious. And if you're going for pottery or sculpture, that means a freestanding piece or two."

Despair flooded into Eric's face. "But how can I do that?"

"Summer classes?"

"We're supposed to go to California to my grandparents' place in two weeks. Me and Justin. For a month." His eyes filled with tears of frustration, and he banged down his third or fourth piece of wedged clay, leaving it in a lump on the bench as he turned away, fists clenched and shoulders hunched. "This is stupid. I wish I'd never said anything."

And then he bolted out of the workroom before Henry could say another word. A sound escaped the boy—a sob—a gasp—and in utter shame, he whacked the door open farther and fell through it.

Henry stood frozen in place, cool, forgiving clay under his own hands, as the boy's running footsteps crunched in the gravel—skidded—and then voices rose, one of them *Deitsch*.

Wiping his hands on a rag, Henry hurried to the door to find two boys outside. Eric glared at Caleb, who was blocking him with the air of someone trying to prevent a jumper going off a bridge.

"Get out of the way!" Eric wiped his nose, clearly desperate to make sure no one had seen him crying.

"I'm not in your way. You looked like you hurt yourself on the door," Caleb said reasonably. "What's the matter?"

"Nothing!"

With an internal sigh, Henry resigned himself to not getting much more work done that day. "Eric, calm down and come back inside."

"I've gotta go."

"To what? Your folks won't be back yet, and I could really use a hand with that forty pounds of clay that needs to be wedged. Caleb, I wasn't expecting you."

"We got finished early. Who is this, Henry?"

"This is Eric Parker, who's staying at the Rose Arbor Inn with his family. He's interested in becoming a sculptor or a potter. We were just discussing his options."

"*Ja?*" Caleb looked as though he didn't believe it. He swiped his straw hat off the ground where it had fallen, and jammed it on his head. "Does he know how to wedge clay?"

"Yes." Eric's tone was sulky, but at least he wasn't running.

"Then why aren't you doing it?"

Henry said smoothly, "Come on. Let's continue our discussion while we work."

A month ago, if someone had told him he'd be holding a pottery class for teenagers in his aunt's barn, he'd have said they were crazy. But two months ago, if someone said he'd be in Willow Creek at all, he'd have said the same.

The Amish would say it wasn't craziness at all, but the

hand of God at work. Henry was going to reserve judgment and simply take the day's twists and turns as they came.

This was quite a twist, in his opinion.

He brought Caleb up to speed with blithe disregard for any sense of privacy Eric might have thought himself entitled to, as they banged the clay on the bench.

"If you can't make something at home, then you'll have to make it here," Caleb said at last. "Unless you know someone in your town with a barn like Henry's, to make things in."

"No," Eric said. "What do you mean, here?"

"When did you say you were going home, Eric?" Henry asked.

"Wednesday."

"Morning or afternoon?"

"I don't know."

"What are you going to make?" Caleb asked him. He wrapped his piece of clay, set it on the worktable, and cut the next piece.

"I can't make anything. The closest I've gotten to clay is making a jewelry tray for my mom in second grade."

"I bet you've had ideas, though," Henry said. "Choose something simple, without too many additions like handles or lids. Go for shape rather than complexity."

Eric stopped wedging, his hands wrapped around the lump on the bench. "No way can I make a—a whatever, get it in the kiln, put that glaze stuff on it, and have something the day after tomorrow."

"Why not?" Caleb gazed at him.

"Because it's impossible, that's why not!"

"The only thing impossible is a portfolio piece that you don't make," Henry observed mildly. "At least get a start on something. You could make some sketches for something simple, and by Wednesday it could be at what we call the 'leather hard' stage. Then you'd need to do a bit of cleanup, and it would be ready to dry. Once that's done, I could give it its first firing with the batter bowls I'll have ready to go by then."

"What if my parents want to leave after breakfast?"

"Then you stall them," Caleb said. "But I guess breaking a piece of harness wouldn't work for you, *nix?*"

"*Nix.*" But Henry could see the gears grinding into motion in the boy's mind. And once they got started, well oiled with hope, he would bet they wouldn't be stopped.

Green eyes met Henry's gaze. "What about a vase? Can you teach me to do that?"

Henry bobbed his head from side to side as he considered it. "No handles. Shape is all-important. But it takes skill to create that shape—and I'm not sure anyone could develop that skill in the space of an afternoon."

"Aren't vases kind of ordinary?" Caleb wanted to know. "Isn't this like a contest?"

"Sort of."

"You should make something nobody else has."

"Like what?"

"I dunno. You're supposed to be the artist, not me."

To hide a smile, Henry rubbed his face on his shoulder as if he had an itch. Caleb's honesty left a man nowhere to hide— even in his own mind.

Eric banged his clay one last time and covered it next to the others. He straightened, and his gaze traveled around the barn, clearly seeking inspiration. Walls, beams, loft. Bench, stalls now empty of horses, wire enclosure that held crates instead of chickens. Lamps, green ware batter bowls, shelving, buckets of glaze.

Lamps. Batter bowls.

Henry's eyebrows lifted as he saw the moment an idea kindled in the kid's brain.

"We went to Williamsburg last summer," Eric said slowly. "They had these lanterns with candles in them, made out of metal with holes in it."

"Punched tin?" Henry asked.

"Yeah." He glanced around. "Do you have a piece of paper?"

"Right here." He handed the boy his sketchbook.

Eric's hand was sure, and in a moment he'd completed a sketch. "What about this? How hard would this be?"

It looked something like a round butter dish, with a domed top and a flat bottom. But the top was cut out so that the light from the candle shone through.

"This is doable." Henry took the pen and added a sketch below it. "You'd flatten a piece of clay, trim it, and drape it over a shaper of some kind—a mixing bowl, for instance. Then you'd cut out your design with a knife and let it dry. The plate for the bottom is easy. You could get the hang of it in a day or two. The trimming will be tricky, though, with all these internal edges. To say nothing of the glazing, when you get to that point."

"He could dip it," Caleb suggested. "Mammi dips fabric in dye when it isn't the right color for her quilts."

"Good point. Eric?"

"Is it—a good idea?" He looked from Henry to Caleb, as though inviting comment would net him criticism, or worse, laughter.

"The tourists would like it," Caleb said. "There's nothing like that at the market."

"It's straightforward, different, and useful," Henry said. "I can't see a committee turning it away out of hand."

"And we could get it started—enough to take with me— by Wednesday?" Caleb kept his gaze on Henry for confirmation.

"*You* could get it started. But you can't waste any time." Henry handed him the clay he'd just wedged, and dug a rolling pin out of one of the boxes under the bench. "So far today you've learned to make a bed and wedge clay. Ever tried to roll a piece of clay like a piecrust?"

# CHAPTER 11

The sun was barely up on Tuesday when Sarah pulled Dulcie to a halt in Jacob and Corinne's yard. The air felt moist and quiet, the crunch of the wheels in the gravel louder than usual by contrast. Her in-laws' horse and buggy had been lent to Zeke today, which Sarah expected. What she did not expect was only the one standing ready, the horse they usually took to church and on long errands quietly cropping the edges of the lawn.

If Zeke and Fannie King planned to do a little matchmaking between Amanda Yoder and Fannie's cousin Silas, they were going to have to do a better job than this.

She got down, tied up Dulcie, and found Corinne and Fannie in the kitchen putting a lunch in the big cooler, which would ride in the back.

"Isn't Silas taking Amanda over to Ruth's?" she asked in a low tone, in case Amanda was within earshot. "Why didn't you tell me you needed another buggy? I could have brought over Simon's courting buggy last night."

"I don't know if she'd want to go all that way in an open one," Fannie King said. "It looks like it might rain later."

"It has a cover, and it's nearly new. It's very comfortable."

"I don't know that Amanda would be willing to make such

a show, Sarah." Corinne screwed the lid on a thermos of lemonade and stowed it in the cooler. "It's better that she goes with Zeke and Fannie."

"The two of them scrunched into the back of the family buggy? Silas won't get much of a view of the country, will he?"

Fannie chuckled. "I don't know as it's the countryside he's looking at. No, Silas can go with you."

"Me!"

"And Amanda, too, if you want. You girls can fight over who will sit up front with him."

This was not funny. It was even less so when Amanda came out into the yard with her and saw how the seating arrangements had been set up. Or not set up, to be more precise.

"I'll go with Zeke and Fannie, Sarah," she said—but the only reply she got was a cheery wave as Zeke shook the reins and clattered off with his wife—and without anyone else.

"Never mind. You can ride back with them," Sarah said. Before Amanda could protest, Sarah had climbed into the back of her own buggy, leaving Amanda no choice but to take the seat on Silas's left.

"I'm a lucky man this morning." He untied Dulcie and got in on the driver's side as if he was completely unaware that the next best thing to a game of musical chairs had just occurred. "Sarah, you'll have to give me directions. It seems Zeke is in such a hurry to see Ruth and Isaac Lehman that he's left us behind."

Maybe this was better anyway. Sarah comforted herself with the thought that Amanda might not have liked being forced to be alone with Silas. Fifteen miles was a long way when you were as shy as she was. As it was, the three of them could talk as friends, and there was enough conversational fodder in the ups and downs of the road past the farms of the *Gmee* that there would be no uncomfortable silences.

It took a good five miles, though, before Amanda recovered from her embarrassment at being in the front seat enough to make any contribution to the conversation. Though her comments were short and soft, at least she was talking. Sarah sometimes had to chime in when the silences got too long, but Silas was good about supporting anything she said.

All in all, Sarah thought as he finally drew the buggy up in the Lehman yard and they all got out, it had been a good ride. Silas would see how womanly and modest Amanda was, and she herself would have the satisfaction of knowing she'd been there to witness the beginning of their romance.

Ruth Lehman was not a demonstrative woman, but her pleasure in seeing Zeke and Fannie so unexpectedly cracked even her self-control, and she threw her arms around Fannie in joy. "Why didn't you tell me you were coming?" she exclaimed. "Oh my, I'm not going to get a bit of work done today—Sarah, you should have sent me a note!"

"Maybe," Sarah said with a smile that held more than a little mischief. "But when else would I ever get a chance to see you all *verhuddelt* like this?"

"Never you mind, I have a recipe for you to make up whether there are folks come to visit or not. Come on inside, everyone, and we'll have a snack. Oh, and Silas, maybe you could go out to the barn and tell Isaac to come in. He won't want to miss a minute."

It soon became clear that, whether Zeke was the family prankster or not, he was also Ruth's favorite. Sarah had never seen her face so animated or heard her laugh so much as she did this morning, and it was difficult, after coffee and then after lunch, to settle down to anything approaching a lesson in herbs.

"I'm sorry, Sarah," Ruth confessed out in her compounding room when Sarah let herself in to see the recipe she was to make. "It's wonderful to see them, but I do feel bad that you and I haven't had our usual time together."

"There will be other times for us, but not for Zeke and Fannie. You go and enjoy yourself with them, and I'll ask Amanda to help me."

"You'll need to wait—I think she and Silas went out to the barn to see the little pigs."

"You have pigs?" This was new. And it wasn't even farrowing season.

"Yes, have you ever seen them? They're the potbellied kind. I don't see the use in them, myself, but the *Englisch* folks seem to love them. It's Christopher's youngest boy's project—but I think his Daed has as much fun with them as Jordan does." She leaned over the table to see what Sarah had compiled so far. "*Gut.* You have everything except the elder flowers, which you'll find up in the copse at the top of our hill."

"How much?"

"Two cups. This is for my daughter Amelia's middle boy, Elam. We think he might be developing an allergy to pollens, and this will help get his lymph system working again to clear it all out."

"I'll be back in a few minutes."

The copse of trees lay in a fold in the hill, where an underground spring probably bubbled up, the water forming a runnel in the spring but completely invisible now except for the extra verdancy of the grass where it ran. The early afternoon air smelled fresh, scented with something sweet that turned out to be both the elderflowers on the big, bushy tree, and a wild rose growing not too far away.

Sarah realized too late that she'd forgotten to bring a bowl for the flowers. Even a paper sack would have done the job. Ach, never mind. God had given her two hands, and she'd just fill them with His bounty and be grateful that He had provided a good cure for colds right here on this sunny slope.

Someone hallooed her and she looked over her shoulder as she broke off a cluster of the creamy flowers. Her mouth dropped open and she snapped it shut as Silas Lapp ambled up the last part of the slope and joined her under the trees.

"I thought you were in the barn looking at the potbellied pigs," she said, reaching for another cluster. With Amanda. Where had she gone?

"It's nice and cool up here," he said, though it was perfectly cool in the barn. Half of it was buried in the old-fashioned system that maintained a fairly constant temperature for the animals, summer and winter. "What are those?"

"These are elderflowers. We infuse them with other herbs to make a tea for colds and flu. These ones are for Ruth's grandson."

"Isn't it just as simple to take a pill from the drugstore?"

"That depends on whether you can get to a drugstore. But a walk up the hill, now . . . that you can do anytime, and enjoy the gifts God has given us in nature while you're at it."

He smiled to acknowledge that she was right, and turned to look out at the view. This consisted of the Lehman farm, the seam of trees growing down the side of the hill, and a good portion of the next farm over, which had been planted in oats that waved like an ocean under the weight of the breeze.

"Is Amanda on her way up, too?" Sarah asked. "She might

remember to bring something to carry these back in. Which is more than I did, I'm afraid."

"Do you need help?" Immediately, he stepped past a stand of spindly wild plums, and cupped his hands around hers. "Let me take these for you."

Warm hands, callused by hard work, the fingers shorter than either Michael's or Henry's, imprisoned both of hers, the clusters of elderflowers held between them like a bouquet.

Sarah jerked her hands out of his and the flowers fell into his palms.

Or they would have, if he hadn't jerked his own back, clearly startled that she was startled. Instead, they fell on the ground, which was littered with last year's leaves and stones and wild grass. Sarah knelt to pick them up, blushing.

"I'm sorry. I wasn't expecting—"

"No, I'm the one who is sorry. That was forward of me. I thought—" He stopped.

She had all the flowers now. Never mind. She didn't need anything to carry them in if she kept a good grip on the stems. Then his words and the way he'd cut them off penetrated.

"You thought what?" Straightening, she clutched the flowers with one hand while she looped her tied *Kapp* strings over her head with one finger so they hung down her back, out of the way.

"I didn't think it would startle you, having a man touch your hand. After all, you have been married."

It was a lucky thing she was standing on a level spot, or she might have tumbled backward down the hill in sheer surprise.

"It depends," she said lamely. What was he trying to say?

"Depends on the man? Sarah, I enjoyed very much talking to you on the way over today. I hope you enjoyed it, too."

"Well—yes, but—" He'd been talking to Amanda! Everything she'd said had been to help the *Maedel* out because she was so shy.

"Then perhaps we might talk again sometime. Alone together, I mean."

Oh dear, this wasn't right. He had got onto the wrong track, and it was up to her to steer him over to the right one.

"I talk too much sometimes. Amanda is very shy, but she has good things to say when she has a chance. She's an interesting girl."

"I'm sure she is."

"You should talk to her more, Silas. You'd like her."

"I do like her. But I like you, too. And how can you say a twenty-year-old girl is more interesting than you are, with your knowledge of plants and herbs?"

"I don't know much. Just enough to be dangerous. That's why I come to Ruth for lessons."

"What I see more than that is a heart with a care for the people of God, and that's more difficult to teach. I like that about you, Sarah. It tells me that you have a big capacity to love."

Oh, no. That word could not come into the conversation under any circumstances.

"I love my family, certainly. My sons. And my husband, still."

"Your husband?" he said gently. "Corinne tells me it has been five years."

"*Ja.* Six, in the fall."

"He was a good man."

"The best."

"But your youngest boy, I would think he needs a father."

Oh, now, this really was forward. "He is close to his Daed, and he has several uncles close by to stand in that place for him."

Silence fell, in which the breeze rustled in the grass and whispered restlessly in the leaves overhead. "Silas, I need to get these flowers down to Ruth before they wilt. I don't want them to lose their essence."

"Let me walk you back."

But she made good and sure that her steps were faster than his. By the time she crossed the yard, he had fallen far enough behind that when Amanda came out of the house, there was nothing in her gaze as she met Sarah's own but interest in the flowers and the cure they were making for little Elam.

She'd had a narrow escape. She'd have to remember not to put herself in a position where she was alone with him again.

She could not let people think she welcomed the attentions of a man who should be intended for Amanda.

# CHAPTER 12

When the men were backing the horses between the buggy rails later that afternoon, Sarah made sure that Amanda knew how much she wanted to visit with Zeke and Fannie on the way home.

"I may not get a good chance again," she told her in Ruth's compiling room, as she put packets of herbs and leaves in her small cooler and fitted the lid on top. "Especially if they go back to Mount Joy on Friday."

"*Ja*, I heard Zeke tell Ruth that," Amanda said, handing her a Mason jar full of the elderflower tea. "I hope you enjoy your trip home with them—though I'd enjoy mine much more if you came in your buggy with me. And…Silas."

Something in Amanda's tone—some deeper note that told her she was telling the truth and not just being nice—made Sarah look up.

Where was the calm Amanda who worked in the background seeing to other people's comfort? Who saw the funny side of life and made quiet jokes that you got three seconds too late because sometimes they went over your head? The Amanda standing next to her at the table looked almost panicked.

"Mandy? Is everything all right?"

Color flooded into the girl's face. "Oh, *ja*. I'm just being silly."

"*Silly* is the last word I'd use to describe you. What's wrong?"

"I—I don't—" She gulped and tried again. "What am I going to say to him?"

"To whom?" As if she didn't know. "Silas?"

Amanda nodded miserably. "He's so nice, and so kind, and—and I feel like such a child when I'm around him."

She cared. More than Sarah had realized up until now. This had gone past matchmaking and was in uncharted territory—where it was dangerous for people to meddle.

Guilt weaseled in under Sarah's breastbone for allowing the ten minutes she and Silas had spent up on the hillside. Thank goodness she'd cut it short. If she'd had any inclinations that way—which she didn't—the pain in Amanda's eyes would have put an end to them here and now.

"No one would ever say you were a child. That's the last impression you want to give him, *neh?*"

"But I can't help it, Sarah. Whenever he's around, I either fade into the wall or babble like a little *Maedelin*. No wonder he looks like he wants to pat me on the head half the time and avoid me the other half."

"He doesn't want to avoid you. No man in his right mind would."

Amanda stepped closer, so that their shoulders touched and she could lower her voice. "You've been married. You've been through this before. What should I do?"

"Shouldn't you be asking your mother these things, *Liewi?*"

"There are fifteen miles of talking between me and my mother right now," Amanda whispered, glancing over her shoulder as if Ruth or even Silas might step through the door to ask what was keeping them. "I need your help. If you won't come in the buggy with me, then at least tell me what to say."

She wouldn't say *come in the buggy with us* because saying *us* would be presumptuous and proud. As far as Amanda was concerned, there was no *us*, no matter how much her family had been angling over the last couple of days to make it so.

"You could ask him about his family. About his brothers and sisters."

"They're Fannie's cousins. I've met them before, at Old Christmas and at weddings."

"But do you know which sibling he gets along with best? Why his sisters chose to marry the men they did? Where his brothers are farming and why they bought the land they did?"

"No," Amanda said slowly. "I never thought of all that."

"A woman who is interested in a man is interested in his family, because they are the people she will be spending her life with," Sarah told her, also with an eye on the door. "And since he loves his family, he won't have any difficulty talking about them, and it will say something good about you that you're interested."

"Is that what you talked about up on the hill?"

Sarah stopped herself from jerking around just in time, and picked up the cooler instead. "On the hill?"

"*Ja*, when you were getting the elderflowers. I watched him hike up there after you—I thought maybe he thought you were cutting down the whole tree, not just picking flower clusters off it."

Sarah smiled, half in relief and half in appreciation of the picture. "I think he might be the sort of man who needs to get out in the fresh air once in a while, especially if there are a lot of relatives in the same room."

"I'm like that, too. I wish he'd told me. We could have walked up there together."

"I'm sure he would have enjoyed that. Now, *kummscht du.* They'll be looking for us."

In the hustle of saying good-bye and giving last-minute messages to those in their various households, Sarah felt very clever to find just enough time to climb into the back of the King buggy before Zeke and Fannie settled into the front.

"Three's a crowd, *nix?*" Zeke said as he shook the reins over Mercury's back and the buggy jerked into motion.

"*Warum?*" she asked pertly. "Do you want me to get out so you and Fannie can be alone?"

Zeke roared with laughter and even Fannie chuckled as they rolled down the gravel drive and out on the paved road. Behind them, through the open window in the back, Sarah could hear Dulcie's clip-clop pick up its pace as the horse realized they were going home.

The grinding of the bare wheels on the asphalt made it impossible to hear the conversations of anyone but those who were in the buggy with her—which was fine. Amanda would tell her all about her trip home with Silas, and in the meantime, she wouldn't look back to see if the two of them were talking. She'd do what she said she was going to do, and that was visit with Zeke and Fannie.

But Fannie had other ideas.

"So, Sarah, it has been good to see so much of you this visit." She raised her voice a little above the sound of the wheels.

"That's one of the good things about living on the acreage so close to Jacob and Corinne—Caleb and Simon and I walk over often to share meals and news and visits. I'm so glad you could come in the summer, when the evenings are longer and we have more time to enjoy our visit with you. It's a shame Simon isn't going to be home until the fall. He would have liked to have seen you, I know."

"So you are not lonely?"

"Oh, no, never."

Fannie directed a knowing look at her over her shoulder. "Never?"

Sarah knew what she meant, but such a thing could not be discussed in front of a man, even one's husband. "Hardly ever. My days are full—now more than ever, what with learning from Ruth and having people come for remedies."

"Not so full that you haven't had time to talk to people—Silas, for instance."

Amanda was the one talking to Silas, not her. "He is a very nice person."

"And well situated, too. He owns his farm, and his family is close around him to help out when he needs it. But the one thing he needs, he doesn't have. And time is marching on."

"It's in God's hands, Fannie wife," Zeke put in. "But I'd say he's doing what he can to move things along."

"I'm glad to see it, too. He's not a man to put himself forward, is Silas. He's modest, good to his parents, and works hard, just as a man should."

In other words, he was the perfect candidate for Amanda. "Even though they are related, the connection is distant enough that it doesn't matter," Sarah agreed. "People marry shirttail cousins all the time."

"But in this case, the connection is only by marriage," Fannie replied.

"By marriage?" Sarah tried to work this out in her head. "I suppose it is—you're her mother's cousin, and Silas is your cousin...no, the relationship is there. Or is there something I'm missing?"

"Her mother—" Fannie stopped. "Who are you talking about?"

"Amanda, of course. Why do you think I wangled it so that they rode home alone together?"

Fannie's mouth dropped open and she exchanged a glance with her husband, who grinned and shook his head. "You've been talking at cross-purposes, the two of you. Sarah, don't you know that my wife has had her eye on *you* for Silas?"

Sarah's whole face went slack with dismay before she got it under control. But it was too late. Fannie had already seen it.

Fannie cleared her throat. "It doesn't matter who I have my eye on. It's not up to me, it's up to God. But I have to say that you two did seem to hit it off very well. And there have been opportunities where the two of you talked alone."

"Completely accidental opportunities."

"It didn't look so accidental this afternoon, when he went up the hill after you."

"He thought I might need a hand." This was silly. They were building a romance out of nothing. Fannie should be focusing her considerable energy on Amanda, who would make Silas an excellent wife.

"That's the kind of man he is," Fannie said with satisfaction. "As I said—considerate, thoughtful, and on the lookout for chances to help, especially with a young widow who is also thoughtful and looking for ways to help."

Silas must have been talking to them, because he'd said something similar up there on the hill. "I'm sure he's not interested in me," she said. "I—I'm not looking for—" *Stop stammering.* "I'm not interested in anyone new right now," she said more firmly.

"But these things aren't up to us, are they?" Fannie said. "If God has revealed to us His choice of mate, it's up to us to be willing, isn't that so?"

"Yes, but we must have a conviction, too," Sarah countered. "The only conviction I've had is that I need to learn more about the healing path He has set me on, and that is taking all my time and thought. There is none to spare for—for men."

Zeke chuckled. "I never met a woman who couldn't make a little time for a man. Or a lot. It's funny how many things can be put aside when there's courting to be done."

Sarah thought a little guiltily of the evenings she'd spent walking over the hill to see Henry. But she'd always had a good reason—and there was no question of courtship there. In fact, if people had it in their minds that it was time for her to marry again, he was probably the safest person in the neighborhood for her to spend any time with.

"I had my time of courtship with Michael," she said firmly. "That season of life is past, and once my boys are grown and on their own, I'll be serving God's people with my herbs and remedies."

"Don't rule a good man out, Sarah," Fannie said in a tone that hinted she'd seen such things before.

"Oh, I haven't—and if one comes by, I'll point him in Amanda's direction. She's a wonderful girl—skilled in the kitchen and garden, gentle with the children, and faithful in her service to God. Silas would be foolish to overlook her."

"She's a little young for him, wouldn't you say?" Fannie said.

"She's twenty. He can't be more than thirty."

"He's thirty-two."

"Why has he never married, then?" It was a fair question.

"Most men his age have a wife and three or four children by now."

"He's been establishing himself on the farm, and..." Zeke exchanged another glance with his wife, the kind that asked a question and received an answer in less than a second. "And it's taken him this long to get over that girl."

"Ah," Sarah said. "Was he married before?"

"No, no," Fannie assured her. "But they were to marry, five or six years ago. She kept him waiting almost two years, and then on their wedding day, as they were upstairs with the ministers, and all their family and friends downstairs waiting for the ceremony to begin—she told him she loved someone else. Someone she worked with at the restaurant. She married him a month later—though it was a much smaller affair. It was difficult to convince the out-of-state relatives to come back again so soon when half of them weren't sure she'd go through with it."

This was news to Sarah. "How awful for him. Was she seeing them both at once?"

"Apparently. He has a tender, faithful heart, and it has taken him a long time to recover." Fannie shifted in her seat to look at Sarah directly. "If he is interested in you and you don't return it, Sarah, I beg you, be kind to him. If you had seen him that Sunday afterward, when he was supposed to have been sitting with the married men and was not—" Fannie's gaze faltered. "He is a good man. I wouldn't want him to go through that kind of sorrow again."

"I won't let it get to that point," Sarah blurted out. "If he doesn't learn to care, he won't be hurt."

"I think that once someone is hurt in that way, the least pressure on the same spot will cause it to ache," Fannie said quietly. "Just keep it in mind, Sarah."

She knew all about the ache of grief. Michael had been taken from her in the midst of the summer of their lives—but at least she had had a few years with him, and she could look back on them and still find the joy there.

Silas did not even have that.

Which was why he needed to turn his attention to Amanda, who was less capable of hurting someone than a baby chick.

# CHAPTER 13

Priscilla had to resist—and keep resisting—the temptation to walk over their back acres to the Byler barn. Her curiosity about Eric and his pottery project was practically buzzing in the air around her head. But if Dat found out she'd left the sewing lying on the table to go running off across lots, she'd be in *Druwwel* so deep she wouldn't climb out until she got married.

So, since today was Tuesday, she and Katie sewed new dresses for themselves and Saranne, and Pris did her level best to focus on it. Mamm had got a new sewing machine, so it was a race to see who would get to it first, and who would have to make do with the old treadle that Mamm and Mammi and probably even Grossmammi had used. Before he gave it to her, Dat had taken the new machine over to Eli Fischer in Whinburg, who removed its electric motor and made it run on compressed air instead. It took a bit of concentration at first to get the hang of making the stitches even without it getting away from her. Priscilla had lost control of it once and sent the needle practically galloping down the seam. But once she'd learned, its speed came in handy on the long borders of quilts. You could put those on lickety-split, as long as you kept a close eye on the needle and didn't let the fabric get twisted or bunched.

"I love this color," Katie said, stroking the soft gold poly-cotton with a loving hand. It had a real subtle ripple in it that made it look silky while still being sturdy enough to wear in the buggy or to town. "It looks like the sun does in the late afternoon."

"I'm glad we have enough for all three of us," Pris agreed. "Plain and Fancy Fabrics gets in such nice stuff—Miriam and Amanda really have a knack for ordering colors everyone likes."

"Everyone but the old ladies," Katie said, dropping her voice in case Mamm heard and thought she was being disrespectful.

"Miriam sells dark colors, too." Pris put the scissors down and began to pin the underarm seam of a sleeve. "See this? What I really want to do is put a couple of pintucks in at the bottom edge. Do you think Mamm would make me take them out?"

"Yes," Katie said, the fabric whirring under the needle, guided by her patient hands.

"Really? Malinda Kanagy had two tucks in her sleeves on Sunday, did you see? Right at the hem, like this. You could hardly notice them until you got up close to her."

"Just because Malinda got away with it doesn't mean you will. Come on, Pris. You're already in enough trouble over the fire. Don't push it."

Priscilla made a rude sound with her lips. "There were some girls at the volleyball game on Friday who had them, too—and little fabric flowers in between the two tucks. They were so cute."

"Now you're just being crazy. Flowers?"

"Sure. Made from the same fabric as the dress. Some were shaped like little daisies, and one girl had snipped hers all around, like a dandelion."

"You know what Mamm does to dandelions."

Sadly, Priscilla did, all too well. Mamm yanked them out of the ground and fed them to the chickens, because you couldn't compost them. They'd just grow back.

A couple of hours later, the dresses were finished. Priscilla put hers on and turned this way and that in front of the glass doors of *der Echschank*, the corner cabinet, where Mamm kept her wedding china. It was the only surface in the house large enough that you could see most of your reflection at once, since the bathroom mirror was only big enough to see your face and hair. The dress fit nicely and she liked the smooth touch of the fabric on her shins.

When she got ready for work on Wednesday, it was tempting to take the dress off its hanger and put it on, but that would be foolish. A color this light was meant for going to town in, or riding in a courting buggy on a Sunday afternoon.

She pruned up her lips. Talk about an opportunity lost— the only courting buggy she had a chance of riding in was sitting in Paul Byler's barn, unused now that Joe was out in Colorado.

Maybe she should have taken Benny Peachey up on his offer the other day. But no. That was too high a price to pay for the pleasure of wearing a yellow dress.

So she put on one of her work dresses, a dark green that didn't show dirt much. When she got to the Rose Arbor Inn, she found the place in an uproar, with suitcases and overflowing shopping bags standing in the hall, the bookcase Mrs. Parker had bought out in the parking lot next to their big SUV, and quilts draped on the banisters of the staircase and on the seats of the chairs in the sitting room.

"This place is going to seem very big and roomy when they're gone," she said to Ginny, who was dashing from stove to sink to refrigerator as she tried to get breakfast together.

"It wouldn't be so bad, but Mrs. Parker has lost track of some of her belongings, and they're turning rooms and car upside down trying to figure out what she did with them."

Poor Ginny. She needed more help right now than simply cleaning and dusting. "Why don't you let me make the gravy, and you can go and help them?" She wouldn't be able to get started on the cleaning anyway, if the guests weren't out of the bedrooms and bathrooms yet.

"That would be great." And a big plastic spoon was smacked into her hand as someone called down from upstairs and Ginny went to help.

Yum, sausage gravy. Priscilla breathed the heavenly scent. It took a bit of attention at first, but once it was bubbling, she'd throw the biscuits together and get them on the cookie sheets, ready for baking. She hovered over the pan, stirring and adding cream, when she realized she wasn't alone.

"Hey," Eric said, leaning around the door frame. "I mean, *Gooder merry-yah.*"

"*Guder Mariye,*" she responded with a smile, and then lowered her voice. "Well?" After a moment, when he didn't smile back, she had to ask. "Did you get it done?"

His face was pale and his eyes a little red, as if he hadn't got enough sleep last night, or had been crying. "No," he said a little desperately. "I don't know what to do. Dad says we have to be on the highway by nine, and it's eight fifteen already, and I haven't heard anything from Henry. I was there till almost eleven last night."

Eleven? She'd already been asleep for two hours. "What is left to be done?"

"I trimmed it last night and Henry was going to see if it

was hard enough to pack this morning, so I could take it with me. But if Dad wants to leave, there isn't going to be time for me to get over there and pick it up."

This was making no sense to Priscilla. She understood wanting to keep something to yourself, but not like this. "Can't you just tell your father about it? You must have said something when you got back last night."

"They didn't know I was gone."

For a moment she just stared at the boy in astonishment. "How could they not know? All they'd have to do is look in your room."

"They went to some play or musical or something, and I said I didn't want to go. I gave Justin the slip and went to Henry's, and got back just before they did."

"Oh, Eric." What was wrong with simply telling the truth? "You have to tell them. They won't be angry—they'll probably be happy you've found something you enjoyed doing on your holiday."

"No, they won't. They don't know about the art school and I'm not going to tell them. Not until we get home." His green eyes held hers desperately. "Priscilla, you have to help me."

What on earth could she do? Lie down in the gravel behind the SUV so they couldn't leave?

"Help you do what?" Justin strolled into the dining room and swiped an orange out of the bowl on the table. "You mess up again, Eric? Wet your bed and need Priscilla Rose to change the sheets?"

"Stop being so mean, Justin," Priscilla snapped before she thought.

"I'm not mean." Justin looked wounded. "He did wet the bed."

"When I was *five*." Eric vanished up the stairs, leaving Priscilla alone with Justin.

*Wunderbaar.* At least the Dutch doors were closed to the guests, so he couldn't invade the kitchen, only lean on the top of it and talk.

Talk didn't mean anything. Everyone knew that action really said what was in your mind. If the fruit of your lips gave praise to His name and your hands were busy taking food out of your brother's mouth, which one would God take most into account?

Exactly.

Even so, Priscilla braced herself for whatever nonsense would come out of Justin's mouth.

"Do you really think I'm mean?"

Of course he would want to talk about himself.

"I don't know you well enough to answer that." She stirred the gravy and inspected its color. "But bringing up something so personal in front of a stranger isn't very kind."

"I was just teasing him. He's used to it."

"There is teasing, and then there's meanness. One hurts, and the other doesn't." Maybe a little more flour. She sprinkled it in.

"Eric doesn't care."

"Oh? Is that why he ran out of the room?"

"He ran out because he's been so antsy he can't sit still. I don't know what's the matter with him. My parents were fine last night, and this morning everyone's all mad at each other." He leaned over the top of the door. "What is that?"

"Sausage gravy, to go on the biscuits I'm going to make."

"I thought you were the chambermaid."

"I am, but Ginny needs help this morning, and I can make biscuits. I do it at home all the time." Oops. Too much flour.

Now she'd better put in a little more cream. There would be no shortage of gravy this morning, that was for sure.

"Can I taste it?"

"It's not ready."

"When will it be ready?"

"When you stop bothering me and let me finish it."

"Now who's being mean?"

She flicked a glance at him. "Most people can tell the difference between being mean and being truthful."

"Sometimes they're the same thing."

"You can tell the truth without being mean."

"Depends on the truth, I guess."

"Depends on the spirit you say it in. I only meant that if you talk to me, I'll be distracted from the gravy. If it burns, all this meat and cream will be wasted."

"I'm glad to know I distract you."

"A fly in the room would do the same."

He shook his head at her. "I'm just not going to get anywhere with you, am I?"

"I don't know why you'd want to. You're going home today." Thank goodness.

"Not if my mom doesn't find her sunglasses."

Pris stopped stirring. "Is that why the house is upside down? They're looking for a pair of sunglasses?" How ridiculous. Mrs. Parker had probably left them on a restaurant table somewhere and they were long gone.

"They cost five hundred dollars. Mom is kind of attached to them."

Pris nearly dropped the spoon flat in the gravy. "Five hundred dollars! For three pieces of plastic and two hinges? How is that even possible?"

He shrugged. "It's what they cost. So yeah, she's turning

the house upside down. That's why I'm down here talking to you. It's not safe up there."

She turned down the gas under the gravy to let it simmer, and got out a bowl to make the biscuits. For once, Justin just watched, as though she were a television program, while she mixed the dough and rolled it out, then cut the biscuits with the rim of a water glass and put them in the oven.

"Don't you need a recipe?" he asked when she was done.

"No. I've done this a hundred times. Dat likes biscuits. Even my youngest sister knows how to make them."

Footsteps thumped on the stairs, and Ginny came bustling in. "How are we doing?"

"The gravy is simmering and the biscuits just went in."

"Perfect. I'll just do the eggs and we'll be ready. I think everyone could use something to eat and then have another look."

"No sunglasses?" Justin asked.

"Not yet. But we'll all look again, and if worse comes to worst, I can always mail them to your mother when we find them."

This plan, however, didn't seem to sit well with Mrs. Parker when she came down to breakfast. "I'm not leaving until I find them, and that's final," she said around her biscuits and gravy. "What if they get smashed in the mail?"

After breakfast, it was clear that Mr. Parker's plan of leaving by nine wasn't going to work, either. Eric's face lost a little of its tension, but every time the phone rang, he jumped a foot and dashed to the landing so he could listen to Ginny answer it.

Priscilla decided that since everything was upside down, she'd work backward, and begin with dusting the public rooms. After carefully piling Mrs. Parker's quilts in one chair, she dusted the bookcases, woodwork, and picture frames in the front sitting room and in the office, then moved into the family room, where the television was. And for good measure, she took the cushions out of the sofa and all the chairs and brushed them, just in case the sunglasses had fallen down between them.

The Parkers unpacked and repacked their suitcases and took them out to the car, which they turned out as well, looking under everything. Eleven o'clock passed, and Pris thought it would be safe to get started on the bathrooms. If she didn't do something, she wouldn't finish before three o'clock, and what if a walk-in guest came and found her on her knees next to a toilet?

She opened her closet and took out her basket of cleaning supplies. It would be a relief to get something, at least, back in order.

She pulled out a cleaning rag and frowned. It wasn't like Kate Schrock to ball the rags up in the bottom to get mildewy. They always left clean rags for one another. Pris shook it out and something black clattered to the floor.

Sunglasses.

A vein of something sparkly ran along the arms, and *Gucci* was spelled out on one side in what looked like diamonds.

Had Mrs. Parker come in here looking for soap or extra towels, and somehow dropped her glasses in the cleaning basket?

Not wrapped up in a rag, she hadn't.

But if a certain someone wanted to stall his parents' departure long enough, and knew where she kept the cleaning things—things that weren't likely to be disturbed by anyone but his secret ally—then it made perfect sense.

"What have you got there?"

Priscilla jumped and dropped both rag and glasses, which landed in the basket.

"Are those my mom's?" Justin fished them out. "Mom! I found them!"

Isabel Parker burst out of the Peace Room—which had not been living up to its name so far today—and snatched the sunglasses from Justin's hand. "Thank goodness! I *knew* they were in the house somewhere. Where were they?"

"Right there, in with the Lysol and the toilet brushes."

Priscilla was about to retort that there was no such thing in her basket, when she saw Mrs. Parker's face and the words dried up on her tongue.

"Why were my sunglasses in with the cleaning things?"

Why was she looking so angry again? She was supposed to be happy they'd been found! "I—I was—"

"You were what? Going to steal them?"

Priscilla's mouth opened and closed, the breath knocked out of her by sheer shock that this woman could believe she'd do such a thing.

"Well? Answer me, or I swear I'm going to call the police!"

# CHAPTER 14

The phone at the Rose Arbor Inn rang through to the answering machine a second time and Henry gave up. He couldn't leave a message, because then Eric's secret would be out. And the kid wasn't picking up when his own cell phone rang—goodness knows why. Maybe he'd forgotten to charge it, or an angry parent had confiscated it. In a normal world, Henry would take a photo of the kid's nearly dry project and e-mail it to him, but guess who hadn't charged his phone, either?

So there was only one thing Henry could do, and that was to mosey on over to the Inn and deliver his message in person.

It was another beautiful June day, though in the distance above the hills, he could see thunder-bumpers forming. They'd had a string of sunny days, but the downside to that was the humidity that kept on rising until a storm came up to break it.

Henry climbed down into the creek bottom to take the shortcut to the Inn. With any luck, he'd make it there and back home before the rain started. Sure, he could take his car, but he welcomed the opportunity to walk after wrestling clay for several hours, and he set a fast pace along the path.

A group of Amish teenagers were swinging out into the

creek on a rope swing and dropping into the deep hole, as kids had probably done around here for generations. A couple of boys hanging in the tree waved at him, and he waved back.

No reason not to be friendly.

He emerged from under the old covered bridge, and crossed the grassy slope that led up to Ginny's fence. After closing the gate behind him, he walked into the parking lot and saw a big SUV with stuff all over the ground around it.

And even from here, he could hear the shouting.

Ginny. In trouble.

He sprinted down the walk and through the open door. The voices were coming from upstairs—Ginny's—Priscilla's—and a number he didn't recognize.

As he climbed the stairs, the people gathered in the communal space off which the rooms opened came into view.

"I'm telling you, she stole my sunglasses and hid them in her cleaning stuff!" shouted a woman in artfully faded jeans, stabbing a lacquered fingernail at a basket full of spray bottles and rags that sat abandoned on the floor.

"And I'm telling *you* that it's impossible," Ginny snapped. "Priscilla is Amish. They. Don't. Steal."

The knowledge that anyone would believe Priscilla Mast capable of theft rocked Henry on his heels. He stepped out onto the landing and saw Priscilla huddled up on the sofa between two bookcases, crying silently into her apron.

"Then why were they in there?" The woman's voice rose again. "Huh? Why? Because I didn't roll them up in a dirty rag and stuff them in that closet."

In the door to one of the rooms, the kid called Justin lounged against the frame. And beside him, looking like a deer caught in the hunters' headlights, was Eric.

Eric, who had made them all promise not to tell his parents

about his pottery project. Eric, who had said last night as he left the barn that he would just have to find a way to delay their going home today, no matter what.

Henry had a very bad feeling about this.

"What's going on?" He crossed the room, and in doing so, separated Ginny and her guest, who were practically nose to nose with the claws about to come out. Then he sat beside Priscilla, who attempted to turn away until he put one arm around her and drew her into a hug. He could feel her thin body shake as she tried not to draw attention to herself by sobbing.

Poor kid. This had to stop. "What's the matter, honey? What's this about sunglasses?"

"Who are you?" The guy was obviously Eric and Justin's father.

"Henry Byler." And then he met Eric's panicked gaze. Well, keeping secrets was one thing, but when it hurt other people, it was time to come clean. "I'm a potter. I've been teaching your youngest boy here how to work clay."

The man's jaw dropped, and then snapped shut again. "He never said a word to us. What are you talking about?"

Rather than answer, Henry cocked an eyebrow at Eric. "Want to let your dad in on what's been going on?"

Eric shook his head.

"I think you're going to have to, if this is how you planned to stall them long enough for the clay to dry. Bad plan, Son. You owe Priscilla here an apology."

"What—what—" Eric's mother got her mouth under control. "Who are you and what business do you have talking to my son like that?"

"He just told you, Mom," Justin said.

"Stay out of this!" both his parents snapped at him, and he

drew his chin in like a turtle, clearly not used to being spoken to in such a tone.

Eric looked like he wanted to climb out a window, but Henry had had enough. Priscilla didn't deserve this. "Eric? Time to come clean."

Here was what one of his college professors used to call a *defining moment*. Either the kid would grow a spine and tell his family the truth, or he'd try to cover up his lie and let poor Priscilla take the fall. At which point Henry would step in, but by then the damage to both the kid and Priscilla would already be done.

*Come on, Eric. Stand up for yourself.*

His thoughts must have been plain on his face, because Eric lifted his chin and took a breath. "It's true, what he says. I've been learning about pottery in Henry's studio since Monday. I have a project that's drying and I needed us to not go home until I could go over there and get it."

His parents both stared at him as though he were a changeling and they were wondering where their real son was.

"Was there a reason you didn't just say to your dad, hey, Dad, I need a couple of hours until my project dries?" Ginny asked quietly. "Did you need to swipe your mom's sunglasses and hide them in Priscilla's things and get her in all this trouble for nothing?"

The kid's initial spurt of bravery began to dissolve. "I needed a place where they wouldn't look," he said miserably. "I thought I could get them back before Priscilla started work."

"So...you took my sunglasses? And hid them in there?" His mother waggled her fingers at the basket on the floor.

Eric nodded. "Sorry, Mom."

Henry cleared his throat.

Eric shifted his gaze to Priscilla. "Sorry, Pris. I didn't mean to get you in trouble."

Priscilla scrubbed her cheeks with her apron and didn't answer. And then Ginny stepped back into Eric's mom's line of sight and lifted an eyebrow expectantly.

The woman blinked. "What?"

Ginny tilted her chin in Priscilla's direction. Her meaning was clear: *Since we're apologizing, there's one left to go.*

"I hardly think—well, honestly, she was the obvious—what was I supposed to—"

"Mom!" Eric's face said it all: *If I can admit I was wrong, why can't you?*

Which was probably what caused her to huff and turn toward Priscilla. "I'm sorry," she bit out, and walked into the Peace Room. "I hope you're happy now." The door closed behind her.

Ginny rolled her eyes. "Now that that's settled, Henry, why don't you and Eric and Trent Parker go into the TV room and talk things over while Priscilla and I get started on these bathrooms?"

Priscilla started up. "*Ach, neh*, Ginny, *ich kann*—"

"It's okay, sugar. I feel a powerful need to take out some emotion on a dirty shower. That's one thing about housework. Sometimes it can be downright therapeutic."

# Chapter 15

The tomatoes were growing fast in the warm weather—the plants had bushed out and were already above Sarah's head as she knelt next to their hoops, weeding. And, she was very glad to see, the calendula planted as a border to her crazy-quilt garden was doing its job to keep the slugs away.

She would need to harvest the calendula flowers soon. Just a couple more days and they would be fully opened, ready to offer their healing power for tinctures and teas.

What a wonderful world the *gut Gott* had given His people. All things—even petals and the leaves in the field—really did work together for good to them who loved Him, and were called according to His purpose.

"That smile is like lemonade on a hot day."

Startled, Sarah lifted her head above the starry yellow tomato flowers, and got to her feet, dusting soil off the skirt of her black bib apron.

"Henry! I didn't know you were there."

He stood in the grass with his hands in the pockets of his jeans, in a relaxed posture that contradicted the pinched expression at the corners of his eyes. He must have walked over the hill from his place, because there was no car in the lane.

"That's why I didn't say anything. There is something soothing about a woman working in her garden."

"What you call *soothing* is really relief because you don't have to do it." She was glad to see him smile, so she added, "In the fall, you should turn over Sadie's garden. It always used to do so well and it's a shame to see it growing nothing but starts and weeds."

She had her opinions about a certain life that was like that, but she was smart enough to keep them to herself. If it was her place to say any more than she already had on the subject, God would prompt her in the moment and give her the words to say.

In the meantime, if he found her company soothing, then she would try to give him peace.

"Maybe I will," he said. "It looks like I'll still be here in the fall, so I should start thinking long-term instead of pretending I'm only a guest in Sadie's house."

"Is that why you need soothing? Because you're not sure you want to stay?"

He knelt on the other side of the tomatoes, outside the calendula border, and began to pull weeds. With the scented bushes between them like a screen, he said, "No, that's not it. I'm just feeling bad because of something that happened up at Ginny's."

What had happened at the Rose Arbor Inn? "Shouldn't you be talking it over with Ginny?"

"No, it's not safe yet. She might be annoyed with me."

He'd said *something that happened*. So it didn't sound like something personal between him and Ginny. "Is it that boy who's staying there? Caleb told me you were teaching him about making pottery—that he has a school project or something?"

"He wants to get into an art high school, and needs a piece for a portfolio." Henry yanked a dandelion up with its whole root—which took some energy. "I got him started, but the simple fact is that the project is going to take time. Instead of telling his parents what he was doing like a sensible person, so they could adjust their plans and leave a little later this morning, he took his mother's five-hundred-dollar sunglasses and hid them—in Priscilla's cleaning basket."

Shocked, Sarah sat back on her heels and craned around the tomato plant to get a clear view of him. "What happened?"

"Priscilla found them when she went to get started, and the kid's mother accused her of stealing them, and it got ugly really fast."

"Is she all right?" Oh, what a thing to happen to Priscilla!

"She wouldn't defend herself, poor kid, so it was a lucky thing I got there and could clear some of it up. The upshot is that they'll stop by my place on their way back to Connecticut. The piece won't be dry enough to move by then, but at least they can see his sketches and have an idea of what he's trying to do."

She gave up on the weeds altogether. "But why did it have to be such a big secret? Caleb says this boy was adamant that no one say anything."

"I think he was so afraid of being ridiculed for something that meant a lot to him that he felt forced to keep it secret. Not that I can blame him for that. The family dynamic is more about buying what you want than creating it. As though somehow if you make something, it has less value and you're free to laugh at it."

"No good comes of deception."

"I'll say. And I have a feeling that if they call looking for a reservation at the Inn ever again, Ginny will find a way to make sure all the rooms are booked."

"So if they aren't taking this clay thing with them, what will happen to it?"

Henry sighed. "I don't know. It's at what we call the *leather hard* stage. Eric trimmed it up last night, but it needs to dry completely and then get its first firing. I could ship it to him then, I suppose, but after all this, I wouldn't want the piece—it'll be a candle lantern when it's done—to arrive smashed and useless. They're fragile at the bisque stage."

Sarah was silent. How awful, to put Priscilla through such an experience for nothing.

Henry must have been thinking along the same lines, because he yanked another dandelion and said, "The sad thing is, that kid really loved working with the clay. His sketches were good, and you could see he cared about what he was doing in every line. Ten to one he'll go home now and never touch clay again, just because this was such a disaster."

"If he'd just told the truth, none of it would have happened."

"I know. Caleb told him so, but evidently the family isn't used to working that way."

That was her Caleb. He was so transparent himself that deception and trying to dodge around things instead of just facing them were foreign to his nature. He always took the most direct route, even when it might not be the most comfortable for other people. This boy Eric ought to spend some more time in his company. Maybe some of that might rub off.

Sarah sucked in a breath as an idea struck her.

"Henry, what more needs to be done on this piece—this lantern?"

"It'll need to dry some more, which will take a few days. Then like I said, I'll fire it with the batter bowls I'll have ready for the kiln by then. After that, it would be glazed and fired a second time, which takes several days more. It's a long process." He took his attention off the destruction of the dandelions and looked at her. "I see that face. The one that got me dragged off to the library to stalk people on the Internet. What's on your mind?"

Sarah tried to rearrange her expression into one of dignity. "I do not stalk people, as you say. God brought a family together, and if He used you and me and the Internet to reunite Oran Yost with his son, then it was all in His plan."

"Okay.... Go on—spit it out."

She stood, and so did he, facing her over the tomato flowers that would mean good fruit later in the summer. "What if I invited this boy to stay, Henry? He could finish his piece and be friends with Caleb, and maybe we could do him some good."

She'd surprised him now.

"A thirteen-year-old worldly boy loose in Amish farm country with no electricity, no video games, no iPod, no TV? Do you know what you'd be letting yourself in for?"

Sarah felt sorry for a child whose life consisted of trying to entertain himself. "There's plenty to do here when he's not working on his project with you. And he could go with Caleb and his friends to swim in the creek and play volleyball and baseball. He wouldn't have time to miss his TV and video games."

Henry gazed at her, thinking out loud. "Priscilla taught him to make a bed, and he learned how to handle clay a lot faster than I thought he would. Maybe you're right. Maybe he is different, and just never had a chance to show it."

"So you'll ask his parents when they come this afternoon?"

She was not merely offering this visit as a holiday, after all. This was something akin to prescribing herbs for a person with an illness. The patient had a lack, and a cure existed to fill it, or to fix the thing that was causing it. Surely God had prompted her to make the offer. If that was so, then she needed to heed that still, small voice.

Even if secretly, she wasn't sure having a worldly teenager in the house would be smart—or even possible.

"I'll ask them," Henry said. "If you think you can stand it if they agree."

"If the boy has a hard time adjusting to life in an Amish household, well, it isn't forever, Henry. We can all survive a week or two. And we don't know—maybe he will like it."

"Maybe." The pinched look around his eyes had slowly smoothed itself away.

"So do you feel better?" she asked softly.

His lips quirked up in a smile as he half shrugged. "How could such a crazy plan make anyone feel better?"

"When we do things for others, it often makes us feel better ourselves."

The smile became a real one, and her heart lightened. "I'll remember that when I go back over to face Ginny."

Suddenly Sarah felt the urge to yank up a few dandelions by the roots herself.

# CHAPTER 16

After she made lunch for herself and Caleb and he jogged back over to the Jacob Yoder farm to help his grandfather, Sarah harnessed Dulcie and drove over to the Peacheys' to see how Linda was faring.

Ella Peachey came out the kitchen door as Sarah pulled on the reins and Dulcie halted in the yard. "Why, Sarah Yoder," she said, wiping her hands on a dish towel. "This is a surprise, seeing you on this side of Willow Creek."

"I don't get over this way very often," she agreed, climbing out of the buggy. She looped the reins over the fence and hoped that Dulcie would be happy enough cropping grass there for the quarter hour or so that she planned to visit. "It seems to be as much as I can do to get into town to do the shopping, with people coming over more than they used to."

"For cures, you mean." Ella turned and Sarah followed her into the house.

"Yes." Linda was nowhere in sight. "Is Linda home? I hoped to speak with her and see how she's doing." As she crossed the kitchen floor, she stepped in something sticky, and the sole of her sneaker made a sound like adhesive tape coming off the roll.

"She took the men's lunch out to them in the field. She'll be back soon."

Rather than offering her a cup of coffee from the pot on the stove, Ella went back to doing the dishes. Sarah hesitated, then removed some kind of small engine—a sewing machine, maybe?—from the seat of the kitchen chair before she sat down.

If Crist and Arlon Peachey were working in the fields, that was a good sign. "Are they planting the third crop of corn?" Since Amish farmers could only harvest so much at a time with the horses and machinery, they staggered their crops. When one was ready to harvest, the next would be a week or two behind. The harvest season was longer and sometimes the weather didn't cooperate, but at least the system made the volume manageable.

"No, they're getting the first one in now. They planted the silage corn a couple of weeks ago."

The first commercial crop—so late! "They'll be watching the skies pretty closely during harvest then, won't they?" she said mildly. It would never do to say what she really thought, which was that the Peachey men were risking their crop and consequently their family's livelihood. It was so unnecessary. If a man could plant now, then why couldn't he have planted in May?

"I expect so," Ella said. She didn't seem concerned about the future of her livelihood—or about the sticky floors—or anything. Her face was round and open and interested, as though nothing were out of order.

At a loss for anything else to say, Sarah got up and discreetly brushed off the back of her dress. "Linda should be on her way back. I'll just go out and meet her."

Shaking off her wet hands, Ella went with her to the door

and pointed. "They're in the west field. Look, there's Linda now, just coming over the hill."

With a smile of thanks, Sarah made her escape.

Of course it would be difficult to keep things clean with two working men and three teenage boys in the house. But where were the girls? There was one twelve and one a little younger, wasn't there? It should have been their job to help their mother keep the house clean.

Linda saw her coming, and waved. Before long, the two met on the slope of the hill, which had either been planted in a hay mix, or had been left to go fallow. Sarah rather suspected it was the latter.

Linda wore a calico scarf over her hair, and perspiration glinted on her forehead. She wore no apron, just a dress and a pair of sneakers without shoelaces. You could never say that Linda was vain about her appearance. But she was certainly looking a little better.

"Hallo," Sarah said when she was close enough. "Ella said you were out this way, so I thought I'd come to meet you." She touched the spiky yellow flowers of the tall cluster of plants between them. "And look what I've found."

"Besides me, you mean?"

"You're flourishing as well as the buttercups—much better than the last time I saw you. But I was talking about this." She turned over a leaf and inspected the underside. No bugs, just healthy veins and stems, and lots of tender inner leaves. "This is mullein. The nicest clump of it I've seen around here. It's used for respiratory problems, and it also heals on the outside. Ruth just told me about a salve she makes for muscle and tissue pain, and since people are out of doors more in the summer and can get hurt on the farm equipment, I thought it might be wise to have some of that salve on hand. Do you think Arlon would mind if I harvested these?"

Linda laughed. "I don't think he'd mind if you brought a horse and mower over here and took the whole field. If someone needs something, Arlon will be the first to give it to him. Sometimes I think—" She stopped.

"What?"

"Oh, nothing. He has a giving heart and an open hand, that's all. Both of them do, and so did their Dat before them. Between that and what he and Crist have got going out in the barn, it's a wonder they don't just let the whole farm go to meadow weeds. You could invite every herbalist in Lancaster County to come and harvest it." The thought made her smile again, and made Sarah wonder what on earth was really going on here.

"What's out in the barn?" She hardly dared ask. Maybe she didn't want to know.

"Come and I'll show you."

"Just let me cut some of these plants first."

Sarah had taken to carrying a small knife and a plastic bag in her pockets, just in case she ran across a plant she could use.

But she'd put the mullein and a little water in the bucket she kept in the buggy, and then they wouldn't be wilted by the time she got home. What a lucky find! She'd have enough leaves to dry for teas, along with several jars of salve.

*Denkes, dear Lord, for bringing me here and showing me the gift of these plants. I pray that you would show me how I can help Linda, too. Use my hands, Lord, and help me to give her good advice.*

Linda held out her arms and Sarah filled them with leafy cut stalks of mullein. She filled her own arms, too, so that they probably looked like an advancing forest as they made their way across the field to the opening in the fence where the men came in with the horses.

"How are you feeling, Linda? I didn't really come here to harvest your plants—I came to see how you were."

Behind her armful of yellow flowers, Linda's face flushed. "You shouldn't have gone to the trouble."

"Well, there wasn't really an opportunity to speak of such personal things at church. You and Ella were busy."

"I feel fine."

"You're taking the tea three times a day? And the tincture?"

"*Ja.* But I was right—with all the water you're having me drink, I spend half the day in the bathroom."

"Better that than being dehydrated. Give it time. You'll find your body will adjust—we retain water because the body is afraid it isn't going to get enough. Once we keep it well supplied, it releases the stored water and the stress, too."

"I did find that," Linda allowed.

So small a proof, but if it led to faith in the larger treatments, then that was good.

They crossed the lawn to the buggy and stood the mullein plants up in the bucket. Some water from the hose would keep them fresh until it was time to go.

"So show me what your husband and brother-in-law have going in the barn, and then I'll be on my way."

"Promise you won't laugh."

"Laugh? Why, what have they got in there to laugh about?"

Linda said nothing, just smiled and motioned Sarah through the open barn doors. Half a dozen cats scattered when they walked in, and the buggy horse looked curiously over its stall at them as they passed.

Old Dan Peachey, Crist and Arlon's grandfather, had kept

dairy cattle years ago, but all signs of that in the milking parlor were gone except for the grates running along the floor to the unused manure pit. The cement floor had been power-washed and was so clean that for a moment Sarah wondered if Ella and Linda scrubbed this one instead of the one in the kitchen. And all over it, on shelves, and on workbenches, were pieces of machinery in various stages of construction or repair.

It looked like a well-organized junkyard.

"What...is it?" Sarah finally asked. "Are they doing appliance repair?"

"Here's where you're not to laugh," Linda said. "They're inventing."

Sarah's mouth dropped open. "This is why they've left planting their fields so late?"

"Part of the reason. They get so caught up in a project that a week can go by and they realize the work out on the farm has gotten away from them." Linda pointed to an apparatus that involved fan blades and a battery. "That's a solar fan. Most of what they're doing involves solar power and batteries. Have you seen the big bank up on the roof of the barn?"

Sarah shook her head. They'd come in on the house side, not the side that looked over the south fields.

Ah. The south side, where the sun spent most of the day.

"It powers the barn so that they hardly ever need to use the generator when they work out here. Except maybe in the winter, when the snow clouds set in. The batteries store the power and they use it at night."

Solar batteries cost a fortune. Was that where the money was going?

"So these machines..."

"This is a winch. This one goes on a washing machine—or it will. Mine is going to be the guinea pig, I'm told."

"And this?"

"Crist tells me it will power my sewing machine, but it seems awfully big. I think they need to work on that one. I'm glad you're not laughing."

"There is no reason to laugh," Sarah said bravely. "What a good idea—to use the light of the sun God made after dark."

"As Crist says, it's just a matter of tinkering until you get something to work."

*And meanwhile, your crops go unplanted and your children run wild.* "What about the boys? Do they help? And where are the girls? I meant to say hello but I haven't seen them."

"The boys aren't really interested in inventing, and neither of them have a knack for farming. The girls are over at Ella's sister's in Lititz for a couple of weeks for a visit."

"Why don't the boys have a knack for farming?" Sarah couldn't keep the question from coming out. "Is it because they haven't been taught? Because Arlon is more interested in his inventions?"

Linda turned away and began to walk back through the breezeway, past the horses' stalls. "I imagine so. It's not really my place to ask those questions—this isn't my farm, and they aren't my boys—except in my heart."

Sarah took the gentle reproof in the spirit in which it was meant. "You're right, of course. Well, I hope the boys find something they can do soon. Before you know it, they'll be courting. A girl will be thinking of a home of her own, and they'll need to think about supporting her."

"Is that what you think about Simon?"

Linda would never criticize, Sarah realized, but she certainly got her point across in the kindest possible way.

"I hardly had a chance to think about it before he up and left for Colorado. At least he's getting this travel bug out of his system while he's young. He'll be eighteen when he gets back, and it'll be time to settle down and get serious about a trade—whether it's buggy-making or something else."

"Benny is seventeen, and Leon is eighteen already, but I haven't seen any signs that they want to use a courting buggy. If they had one, that is."

"Do you think that's so? Didn't you see Benny teasing Priscilla Mast on Sunday?"

Linda shook her head. "Benny teases everyone. Even me. And his mother. I wouldn't use that as an indication that he's interested in her."

That was a relief. "Priscilla is writing to Joe Byler anyway. And before that, she was sweet on Simon."

"She's a nice girl."

They stepped out into the yard, and Dulcie lifted her head as if to say, *Are you finished? Because I've eaten all the grass I can reach.*

"I'm glad you're taking the treatment seriously, Linda," she said, and squeezed her hand. "I must be on my way, but when you run out of tea, please let me know and I'll make up some more for you."

"I will. And I told Crist to save you a few nice roasts and a backstrap from the hunting in the fall. But until then, do you need a gadget of some kind at your place? Crist could make you something."

"Believe me, between my neighbors and my in-laws, I have everything I need. But *denkes* for the offer."

She untied Dulcie and climbed into the buggy. It wasn't until she was well down the highway that she felt safe enough to laugh out loud. Even if she did need one of the strange solar-powered gadgets, the Peachey boys probably wouldn't remember to make it for months.

As Dulcie's hooves clip-clopped their familiar rhythm on the pavement, she sobered, her thoughts returning to all that was neglected in favor of the inventions. How could Linda stand living in such a precarious way, never knowing from one week to the next whether there would be food on the table? How could she bring a baby into that kind of home? Ella had done so, and look at the result—boys who would rather put off work until the playing was done instead of the other way around.

Sarah wasn't sure what she could do, but there was One who did.

*Oh, Lord, Your children have need of you and the provision of Your hand. Help me to know how to help them—how to speak a word in season, how to offer a suggestion when it's Your will that I speak up. Give me strength to do the right thing, Lord. And help me to know what that is.*

# CHAPTER 17

Henry heard the crunch of gravel in the yard through the open barn doors and for a moment wondered what was missing. And then it came to him—the *clip-clop* of hooves had been replaced by the purr of an engine, which meant either Ginny or the Parkers had just arrived.

He had a feeling that Ginny might still be a little upset about his involvement in this whole fiasco, so it was unlikely to be her Honda CR-V. That left—

*Slam!* "Is this where you've been coming every day when we're supposed to be vacationing as a family?"

The Parkers.

Henry stepped outside and walked down the ramp to meet them, wiping his dusty hands on a rag. "Hi, Mrs. Parker. Eric. Justin. Mr. Parker. Glad you could come."

"We might as well book another night in a motel somewhere," Mr. Parker said, locking the car with his key fob, though there was no one in five acres who would make off with it. "Even if we leave now, we won't make it home until the small hours tomorrow, and I'd rather not drive that late."

"We're leaving," Isabel Parker said tightly. "I am so done. When you get tired, I can take over. The way I feel right now, I can't get home soon enough."

Henry caught Eric's eye. "I had hoped that Eric would be able to take a few minutes to make some adjustments to his piece before it dries completely. That way, I can give it its first firing."

"We don't have time," Isabel said.

"What does that mean, *adjustments?*" Justin wanted to know.

"Come on in and I'll show you."

Henry led them into the barn, where Eric went straight to the bench and touched both parts of his lantern as if to say, *Everything okay?* The plate on which the carved dome would sit needed some trimming on the bottom, Henry explained to the boy's parents, but not much. Most of the work would be in smoothing the various edges of the carving in the dome.

"You did this?" Mr. Parker asked. He leaned over to inspect the dome. "What are these? Birds?"

Henry resisted the urge to act as tour guide. If Eric was going to stand up for himself and his art, let it be now, with Henry there for moral support. He nodded at him, encouraging him silently to take the lead.

"Yes," Eric whispered, then cleared his throat. "They're geese. They make a V pattern, like they're flying around the light inside. Toward where it's warm, like geese do in the fall."

Silently, Henry reached behind him for the sketches, and handed them to the boy.

"I drew it out first on paper." He showed his father. "Then before I draped the clay over a bowl to make the dome, I made a round paper template with cutouts, and cut the clay through it." He looked to Henry as if seeking confirmation that those were the right terms to use, and on Henry's nod, said, "I'm not good enough yet to do it freehand."

"You sketched these?" Mrs. Parker held the page torn from Henry's sketchbook.

Justin leaned in. "They look like pterodactyls."

But instead of losing his temper or fading out the door, hurt and angry, Eric looked his brother in the eye. "They're *stylized*, not drawn from life. Which you might know if you ever did anything but play rugby and video games."

"Hey!" Justin looked wounded. "I don't know much about art, but I know what I see. And those look like pterodactyls."

"It's perfectly clear they're geese, Justin," his mother said impatiently. "Stop antagonizing him." She turned back to her younger son. "So what is it you have to do this afternoon?"

"Not much," Eric said eagerly. "Henry was going to show me how to trim the plate so it doesn't wobble on a flat surface."

"And we do the smoothing on the dome with a flat tool and a bit of water," Henry said.

"How long will that take?"

"I estimate fifteen minutes for the plate, and maybe an hour for the dome." At Mrs. Parker's expression, Henry said, "Clay is a medium that trains a person in patience. I'm sorry that our process takes so long, but I'm not sorry that Eric got a chance to try it. I really think this would be a good direction for him."

"What, clay?" Again, she returned to the sketches of the geese. "Not drawing or painting?"

"He's good at that, too, and it's a necessary skill if he's going to be designing his own pieces."

Henry felt Eric's gaze on him, panicked, silently asking him not to say anything more. "I feel that once Eric gains some more confidence, he should discover what he's capable of. At the very least, he could use some training in the craft—and the sooner, the better."

"Training? You mean, like with you?" his father asked, picking up one of Ginny's completed mugs and blinking as he recognized where the one that was probably in his suitcase had come from.

"Not necessarily with me." It was time to tell the truth, and it looked like Eric hadn't mustered up the courage to do it. But instead of laughing and dismissing the thought, his parents were actually having a rational discussion on the subject. "There are a number of very good art academy high schools out there. I think Eric has what it takes to do well. After all," he added, "there's no motivation better than doing something you love."

"There's no money in it, though." Mr. Parker's tone was flat. Dismissive. In another life, he would probably be an art critic. "Why go to a special school unless you're a prodigy and expect to have a career? What kind of career can a person have…as a potter?"

*Look at you*, Henry heard. *You're one step away from poverty, out here on your tumbledown farm in the middle of nowhere. Making things that are useful and ubiquitous.*

"It's not a bad living," Henry said. "I just signed contracts to do a limited-edition series for D.W. Frith. My work will be in six of their East Coast stores. You might keep an eye out for it in the fall."

Isabel Parker had perked up at the mention of the exclusive store's name. "Your work? What work? I get their catalog."

He walked over and picked up a batter bowl. "These. And a collection of serving plates, and a place setting. In fact, Eric was with me when I got the inspiration for the glaze recipe I'm going to use."

"It's going to look like sun sparkling on water, Mom," Eric said eagerly. "Henry let me help him mix the chemicals. He said I was a good influence."

"D.W. Frith," Mr. Parker repeated. "In New York."

"And other places," Henry said mildly. "But getting back to Eric, even if he decided to do it only as a hobby, there's something to be said for the sheer pleasure of doing something well. And if it's useful, that's a bonus."

"A special school." Mr. Parker didn't seem to be going with the flow. "Where special means expensive."

"Or special needs," Justin threw over his shoulder, ambling toward the doors.

Henry ignored him. "Not necessarily expensive. The most immediate problem, if a person were to start in September, would be a portfolio. That's what Eric was making a start on here."

"Oh, so you two have already talked about it and made up your minds, have you?" Isabel sniffed, then sneezed.

"Clay dust. Sorry," Henry said. "Why don't you go outside while I show Eric what to do?"

"What's the point?" Eric had exhausted his small stock of courage. He took the sketches from his mother's hand. "They're not going to let me do it. It doesn't matter. Let's go home."

"Now we're talking," Justin said from outside on the ramp. "Hey, there's an Amish lady coming this way. And a kid in a straw hat. Better get in the car, Mom. Maybe it's Priscilla's mother."

That was a possibility, Henry thought as he walked to the barn doors, but an unlikely one. The better possibility was Sarah and Caleb.

And so it proved to be.

Caleb galloped into the barn right past the Parkers. "Hey, Eric! Is it ready? Can you take it with you?"

"Nope. Henry's going to show me what to do if my parents don't bug out right away."

"Will they?"

"Looks like it."

Their voices dropped too low for Henry to hear, and he turned back to the motley crew outside the barn.

"Hello," Sarah said, holding out her hand. She was dressed for town in a raspberry-colored dress, black cape and apron, and a crisp white organdy *Kapp*. No gardening clothes and damp skirts here. "I am Sarah Yoder, from next door. You must be the Parkers."

Mr. Parker recovered from his surprise first, and shook her hand. After a moment, so did Isabel. "How do you know our names?"

Sarah smiled. "My son Caleb—whose manners are suffering this afternoon, it seems—does odd jobs for Henry. He has told me all about Eric and his project."

"We just found out ourselves, this minute," Isabel said stiffly. "It would have been nice to know what he's been up to all these times he's ditched his family. After all—"

She glanced at Henry and clammed up, the mouth that had been relaxed at the discovery of her son's talent tightening up again.

"After all, I could have been an ex-con or something," Henry agreed. "It was my fault. I should have introduced myself long before this."

"Henry is completely trustworthy," Sarah said. "I hope you will forgive him. He gets"—she glanced at him and smiled, as though she knew a secret and was letting them in on it—"very focused and sometimes forgets the real world."

The apology seemed to leave Isabel with nothing to say, and Sarah seized her moment.

"Henry and I were talking about Eric, and we wondered…I wondered…about the project?" She looked to Henry for help.

"I told them about the art academy high school possibility," he said. "And why Eric was making his lantern. For a portfolio."

"Ah." Relief made her face relax. "So then I can ask them?"

"Ask us what?" Isabel tensed. "What are you people up to now?"

"Isabel." Her husband put a hand on her arm.

"I'm about done with not knowing what's going on with my own son," she snapped. "These Amish are supposed to be all honest and God-fearing, and I'm just not seeing it."

"Isabel!"

"Please forgive me," Sarah said, the light in her face quenched as though someone had blown out a flame. She clasped her hands nervously. "I did not mean to offend. I'll just get Caleb and we'll be on our way."

"Now look what you did," Trent Parker whispered to his wife as Sarah slipped through the doors. "You didn't even give her a chance to speak."

"What's she going to say?" Isabel hissed. "Is she going to tell me how to bring up my kids, like Henry here?"

What was wrong with this woman that she saw fault and ulterior motives in everyone around her? "She wasn't, actually," Henry said in as calm a tone as he could muster. "She was going to invite Eric to stay with her and Caleb for a couple of weeks later in the summer, so he could finish his lantern right here and not have to have it shipped unglazed and maybe broken."

Isabel's mouth dropped open.

Before more angry words could come out of it, Henry went on, "I think he would enjoy it. He and Caleb seem to have hit it off, and there's a lot for them to do when they're not here in the studio. Swimming, games, all kinds of healthy outdoor stuff."

"Our son," Trent Parker finally managed. "Stay on an Amish farm. With people we don't know. Are you kidding me?"

"You may not know them, but I do. Eric would be safe here. And well occupied. And goodness knows, well fed. Sarah makes the best pies on the planet."

"Absolutely not." Isabel opened the passenger door. "Justin, get in the car. Trent, we're leaving. Go and get Eric, please."

Henry knew when he was beaten. But Eric, apparently, did not. He went, but not quietly, and the SUV's tires threw up gravel when it accelerated down the lane, as though Mr. Parker thought the boy would jump out if he went any slower.

Caleb kicked at one of the stones that had clattered at their feet. "I don't know why they're so mad. It was a really good plan. We would have had fun—and maybe done him some good, wouldn't we, Mamm?"

Sarah watched the dust settle as the SUV accelerated away down Willow Creek Road. "I think there must be people in the world who don't believe in good," she said softly. "It must be a terrible way to live."

"I wish I could have said something to convince them," Henry admitted.

"What are you going to do with Eric's project?" Caleb asked. "It's still sitting in there where he left it."

"I don't know. It has to be trimmed before it dries any more. Maybe I'll do that for him, and box it up and send it to him. Ginny will have their address."

"I would have liked to have seen the lantern when it was finished," Sarah said.

"I would have liked to have seen Eric finish it."

"Maybe he will," Caleb said. "He took his sketches. I saw him hide them in his pocket."

# Chapter 18

The next morning after breakfast, Sarah sent Caleb out to weed the garden. There hadn't been a single moment yesterday to tend to the mullein she'd gathered at the Peachey farm, and if she wanted it at its best, she needed to pay it some attention.

She stripped the leaves from the long stems and took all but a couple of cups of them outside to the drying rack on the south side of the house. Then, working from one of the recipes Ruth had given her, she measured olive oil into a deep saucepan and tore up the remaining mullein leaves, adding them to the warming oil with chopped comfrey leaf, a palmful of chopped fresh mint, a tablespoon of rosemary, and a few whole cloves.

With the flame on the burner down as low as it would go, she mashed the leaves in the oil with the back of a spoon, and breathed in as the kitchen filled with a delicious aroma. It needed to cook slowly for two hours, but she had no shortage of tasks to fill the time.

She had just filled the sink to do the dishes when feet pounded on the porch, and Caleb burst into the kitchen. "Caleb! You're supposed to be weeding the garden! *Was tut sie hier?*"

"Mamm—the phone. It's Joe, and he needs you quick!"

*Simon!*

Sarah dropped the frying pan in the water with a splash and dashed for the door. It had been a long time since she'd run foot races at the little one-room school in her home district, but her legs hadn't forgotten how to stretch out and eat up the ground.

She swung into the phone shanty that she, her in-laws, and the Kanagy place across the road all shared and grabbed the receiver, out of breath.

"Hallo? Joe? *Ischt du?*"

"*Ja, ischt mir.*"

"Is it Simon? Is he all right?"

"Sarah, calm down. Simon is fine." He cleared his throat. "Mostly fine. *Wie geht's?*"

"Never mind how I'm doing, what does 'mostly fine' mean?" For whatever had happened must be serious, if Joe had had to find a phone instead of writing. And how many times had he tried the shanty number before someone had come close enough to hear it?

"We were taking care of the horses this morning and one of them stepped on him, is all."

"On him? What part of him?"

"His foot. The rest of him is fine, Sarah. He can't walk real well, though, which is why it's me down at the big house using their phone, and not him. It's a couple hundred yards' walk and the foreman wouldn't let him get up."

"Thank goodness for that. And it wasn't a thigh or an arm. How bad is it?"

"That big brown gelding got him pretty good. Simon was looking at his foot, thinking he'd picked up a rock—which he had—but it's a new horse and I guess he thought Simon was getting too familiar. Stepped sideways and Simon couldn't get out of the way in time."

"Did you get his boot off?"

"*Ja*, before the swelling got too bad. It's bad now. He'll probably lose the nail. It's looking pretty squashed."

"Is that what the doctor said?"

"Ain't no doctor out this far, and we can't afford to pay the clinic anyhow. The foreman is an EMT and is pretty good with injuries, but they asked me to call you even so."

"To do what? Do they want me to come?" Sarah's whole spirit quailed at the thought, but if Simon needed her, she would gird up her loins and go.

Other than a trip to Ohio for a wedding and a trip to Florida as a girl, she hadn't been outside Pennsylvania—and as majestic a picture as Silas had painted, she wasn't sure she was up to it alone. Would Caleb and Amanda go with her maybe? Could she ask Jacob and Corinne for the train fare for all three of them?

Joe made a huffing sound of astonishment. "Come all the way out here because a horse stepped on his toes? Of course you don't need to. Simon didn't even want me to telephone you. Said he didn't want to worry you."

"I'm glad you did, Joe. That's the mark of a true friend— doing the right thing." *Help me be calm, Lord. Help me to think what I can do, from my place right here.* "What does the foreman suggest for treatment?"

"Ice, elevation, some salve they keep on hand."

Salve.

"Do they have B and W out there in Colorado?"

"Ain't seen any. Mamm uses that stuff on us all the time, but I don't think she tried it on stomped toes."

Sarah might not be able to go out there herself, but she

could send something to help. "Joe, listen to me. If I send you some B and W and some herbs to put on his foot, will you see that it goes on and he doesn't argue?"

"Herbs? Aw, Sarah, I don't think—"

"*Neh, lauscht du.* I'll write out the instructions on what to do, wrap everything you'll need in a parcel, and send it out there overnight." It would cost a fortune, and maybe UPS wouldn't even go up into the mountains if it was so remote, but she had to try. "I learned what to do, Joe, so if I can learn how, then so can you. Expect it tomorrow. I'll put it together right now and be in town within the hour. All right?"

"If you're sure you want to do that."

"Ruth told me about a similar case, and what she did. A boy got an augur right through his toe. The toe was infected and swollen up so bad they thought the boy would lose it, but they put burdock leaf and B and W on it, and it healed up just fine. You'd never know he was injured, she says. So we're going to do the same for Simon, and no matter what kind of fuss he puts up, you tell him if he doesn't do what you say, I'm coming out there to do it myself. You hear?"

Joe laughed, and said something to someone over his shoulder. "I'll tell him."

"If you have questions, call Henry's phone in the barn and he'll come over and get me. Then you won't have to chance that someone will hear the ringing in the shanty."

"All right. Good-bye, Sarah."

"Thank you, Joe. Give Simon my love."

"I will."

Sarah's heart was still beating fast as she came out of the shanty and found Caleb waiting anxiously outside. She told him what had happened. "You're going to make him a cure, Mamm? What can I do?"

She didn't have one son to hug and comfort, but she did have the other. She took him into her arms and hugged him hard, much to his surprise. "You're a good boy and I'm glad I still have you with me," she said into his hair. "Now, I need at least three dozen fresh, unblemished burdock leaves from behind the chicken house. You remember where I showed you?"

"*Ja.* I'll get them."

He took off down the lane and she hurried into the front bedroom. Despite her best efforts to look on the sunny side, gruesome images of Simon's long foot all black with bruises and maybe even infection kept rising up in her mind's eye. No, she couldn't think that way. She had to focus on the healing, or she might forget something important and he would suffer.

She had several small tins of burn and wound salve, that Amish standby that seemed to heal everything from lawn mower blade cuts to burns from the stove. She chose a big one, because Joe would have to apply it every other day at least. Several lengths of surgical gauze and padding—though a foreman trained as an EMT would probably have some, she couldn't take the chance. And a roll of tape.

Caleb came in with the leaves and she took them from him gratefully. "*Gut*—these are just what we need, fresh and pliable so Joe can wrap them around the foot."

She layered them between wet paper towels and sealed them in a zip bag.

"Caleb, hitch up Dulcie. We're going into town to UPS."

He dove out the door. She turned off the burner under

the mullein—it would have to wait until later, when she was calm—then tore a sheet out of her recipe book.

Dear Joe,

Thank you for your call and for being such a help. Simon is lucky to have your friendship. Here is what you need to do:

Put a pot full of water on the stove and bring it to a boil.

Dip the leaves in the water to blanch them and make them pliable.

Let them cool enough to handle.

Take a gauze pad the size of the toe and spread B&W on it like peanut butter. Then tear up a burdock leaf and lay a couple of pieces on the pad and wrap it around the toe firmly with tape.

Change the dressing once every day.

If you see it getting red or a red streak runs up his leg, it's infected and he must see a doctor immediately.

Write and let me know how he does. I'm glad you're together and can watch out for each other.

> Your sister in Christ,
> Sarah

On a second sheet, she wrote Simon's name.

Dear Simon,

I've asked Joe to use the contents of this parcel to treat your foot. Don't give him a hard time, but let him follow the directions I've enclosed.

I love you and want to see you heal. Give the foot

time, and don't try to get up too early. While you're laid up, you could write me a nice long letter.

God be with you.

All my love,
Mamm

At the UPS office, the woman behind the counter assured Sarah that they would have the parcel on the ranch's doorstep by four o'clock the following afternoon. Simon's foot would probably be swelled to the skin's limits by then, but considering how far the package had to go, it was the best anyone could do. Sarah watched the woman take it into the back, and sent a prayer with it. The parcel was in God's hands now...and the extra money she had hoped to put toward the mortgage was in the UPS till.

But Corinne and Jacob would understand. In fact, she and Caleb should go over there now and tell them what had happened. If Joe got it in his head to call his mother on the phone they kept in the garden shed, figuring his dad would be out in the fields, it would never do for Corinne to hear what had befallen her grandson from Barbara Byler at the sisters' day quilting tomorrow.

"*Kommst du*, Caleb," she said as they left the counter. "We're going to Mammi and Daadi's."

"Can I drive?"

"I would be happy if you did."

Delighted, Caleb took the man's place on the right side of the buggy. Usually she or Simon drove, but her younger son was the man of the family now and he never missed a chance to take the reins.

When they pulled up in the Yoder yard, Corinne came

out, her forehead creased with concern. "Jacob says he saw you heading into town as if a barn was on fire," she said, reaching up to pat Dulcie's neck and loop the reins over the fence while Caleb and Sarah got down. "Is everything all right?"

There weren't too many ways to give bad news, but Sarah did her best to tell Corinne what had happened with a spirit that wouldn't worry her any more than necessary. And when she finished and they were seated at the kitchen table with Fannie and Amanda, Corinne actually smiled.

"You've sent a cure and told Joe Byler how to handle it." She laughed in delight. "You never know. That boy might find he likes making cures and take up the work himself."

"He wouldn't be the first man to do it," Fannie said, and blew gently on her mug of hot coffee. "There's that man out in Indiana who's in the papers all the time for curing people—even folks whose doctors have despaired of them."

"Who's despaired of whom?" The men came in, having obviously seen Sarah's buggy outside. Jacob's gaze found Sarah's, full of concern.

She told the story again, with more fact and less emotion this time, and Jacob's face relaxed. "Joe is a good boy. He'll follow your instructions to the letter, and it will be just like you being there."

"Without the kisses and the pillow plumping and the mother-hen clucking," Zeke put in.

"If I could have sent myself UPS, I would have, clucking and all," Sarah admitted. "But the foreman is an EMT, apparently, so Joe has someone to help if he needs it. Between *Englisch* medicine and mine, Simon will make a good recovery, I'm sure of it."

She wasn't afraid, not after that first rush of panic at the sound of Joe's voice. She had done what she could, and the rest was up to God.

"It's like we heard on Sunday," Silas said in his quiet way. The preaching had been on the subject of faith. "Didn't the preacher say we must have faith in the strength of God's hand around us?"

Sarah smiled at him gratefully for the reminder. That image of her boy in God's mighty hand would calm her when she woke in the night, worrying about infection and whether the parcel would get there in time and whether Joe would skip a line in the instructions and forget to—

Sarah took a deep breath.

"No matter how old they get, we still worry," Corinne told her, and squeezed her hand. "That doesn't mean we lack faith. It just means we're mothers."

# CHAPTER 19

Corinne asked Sarah and Caleb to stay for supper, even though the next day was Friday and they'd be back again as usual. But Sarah was glad. While the fear had subsided, her spirit was still unsettled and she couldn't think of anything that would help more than Corinne's warm gaze and Amanda's steady shoulder at her side as they peeled potatoes and shredded carrots and red cabbage for a colorful slaw.

"The taxi is coming tomorrow morning to take Zeke and Fannie back up to Mount Joy," Amanda said. "I'm glad you could stay so we can all be together this last night."

Something she said snagged Sarah's attention the way the cleavers on the hillside did her skirt. She rinsed the potato and picked up another one. "Zeke and Fannie? But Silas is going with them, isn't he?"

"Apparently not," Amanda said in a low voice. "Miriam and Joshua invited him to stay another week—more, if he wants. Joshua has been planning to remodel the old bathroom in their house for ages, and with another pair of hands he could get the job done this month."

"Is that the only reason he's staying on?" Sarah asked carefully, focusing completely on the smooth movement of the peeler.

Amanda blushed. "I don't know. I hope—I mean, it would be prideful of me to think that—that—" She stammered to a stop.

"Has he said anything to you?" Sarah's voice was nearly a whisper now, since the men were washing up just outside at the double sink.

"That's the trouble—we talk all the time," Amanda said in a rush. "But there is nothing to it. He remarks on the weather. I say how the garden is doing. He wonders if Dat will get the third planting done before it rains. I say I'm working on a quilt to go in the auction in the fall. But nothing about—about—nothing personal."

Poor Amanda. Sometimes, before a boy finally decided that a girl might be the one for him, he spent more time hemming and hawing and making conversation than he did courting. When Michael had come along, all thoughts of other men had fled from Sarah's mind. Conversation with Michael wasn't difficult. It was a joy—two souls who couldn't wait to discover each other, to peel back the layers of their characters to reveal the hidden fears and hopes inside. Conversation with Henry was a little bit like that—though why that should be was a mystery. She seemed to have jumped right into his life and learned some of his secrets—and he hers—without even trying. Sometimes she'd even made those discoveries in anger, which was even stranger.

"Maybe some men have a gift from God," she said to Amanda. "Conversation isn't easy for everyone, you know. Just be patient and make it easy for him to come to you. Be the listening ear and the welcoming smile, and you will be the one he wants to tell things to."

"I try," Amanda whispered. "But I don't want him to think I'm forward."

"Nobody could think that of you," Sarah assured her.

The men came in, and Corinne bustled over to take the roast out of the oven, and the time for confidences evaporated.

After supper, Caleb and Miriam's boys went with their grandfather to the barn to muck out the dairy and carry milk cans while Zeke and Jacob milked the cows. Jacob didn't do it by hand anymore, but used a pair of portable vacuum milkers with hoses for his small herd. Still, it was a two-person job, and three was even better. The older boys carried the buckets of fresh milk to the big holding tank that was emptied by the milk truck driver every other day, and Miriam's and Amanda's job was to wash the buckets and equipment in hot water and detergent once they had been used.

While they were doing that, Sarah got busy in the kitchen, putting the food away and filling the sink with hot water. To her surprise, instead of heading out to the barn as well, Silas took a dish towel out of the drawer and leaned on the counter next to the drain rack.

"You don't have to do that," she told him, thinking quickly. "Not here, at least. You could help Amanda in the dairy with the cans, and send Miriam back here to help me clean up."

"Knowing those two, the job is probably half done already," he said with a smile, and Sarah knew she'd been outmaneuvered.

Well, she would just have to keep the conversation friendly and light, and hope that with all the help Jacob had in the barn, the milking would be done so fast they'd be back before she knew it, and the cows would wonder what had happened.

She got busy with the piles of dishes. "Fannie and Zeke

have had a good visit, haven't they? My in-laws will be sad to see them go tomorrow. We all will."

"Myself included. You've heard I'll be staying a little longer?"

Sarah nodded. "You'll enjoy staying with Miriam and Joshua. He's a wise man, and loves a good joke. Not as much as Zeke, though! Miriam will be glad to see the new bathroom finished, too. She's had to put up with leaky pipes and a cracked sink for too long—it's a big project to take on when time and money are short."

"I'm glad to help. I've had a little experience with plumbing at my own house, which was painful at the time, but now I'm glad to have had it, if it helps Joshua."

"Is your house old?"

"Yes—two hundred years or so. Which is probably why I was able to afford it."

"Two hundred years!" She'd never lived in a house that old, but she'd visited plenty. They took a lot of upkeep, from what she'd heard folks say.

"Everything works, despite its age, though it could use a woman's hand. It feels an awful lot like a bachelor place, and needs a change."

*Oh dear. Oh dear. What needs a change here is the subject—and quick.*

She scrubbed a plate with energy. "I'm sure there are any number of girls in your district who would take on a job like that with pleasure."

Another plate. And another.

"There might be, but some are easier to have around a home than others."

An opening, she thought with relief, rinsing the plates and putting them in the rack, then plunging her hands in the hot water for the next one. "Amanda is very easy to be around, isn't she? There is something about her calm spirit and loyal heart that makes you want to be in the same room with her, no matter where in the house she is."

"You are a good friend to her."

"She is a better friend to me. I have three sisters in Mifflin County, but I count her as my fourth. She might be only twenty, but she's mature, a member of the church, and ready to care for a home of her own."

There. Hints didn't come any broader than that.

He took the stack of dry plates to the cupboard. "If I didn't know better, I would say you are trying to point me in her direction, Sarah Yoder."

"And why not? I've seen many a man who doesn't know better. Sometimes they have to be pointed, for their own good."

He smiled and began to dry the silverware. "I admit that sometimes we miss what's right under our noses. But I don't think that's the case here." The drawer closed with a sound like an exclamation point. "Sarah, I want to stop beating around the bush and ask if you would be interested."

If she could have run from the room, she would have. Instead, she prayed that someone—anyone—would come.

"Interested...in what?"

"In me." Color washed into his face. "I know there are many better prospects, and maybe you already have your eye on someone, but I wanted you to know that on my side, I'm very interested."

She could hardly gather her thoughts together, between watching the door hoping someone would come through it, and hoping Amanda was not that someone. "I told you— Michael—I—"

"I have to confess that I engineered the extra week with Joshua just so I would have a reason to stay. Hoping that there might be some opportunities for us to get to know one another better."

She had to settle this once and for all, with no more stammering.

"I would value those opportunities, Silas, to become better friends. But friends is all we can be." Oh dear. That sounded blunt. Unkind almost, and she didn't mean it to be. But she couldn't think of a way to soften it so he would not misunderstand.

He gazed at her, his towel going around and around inside a glass. "You sound very definite. Have you made your mind up so soon, without even giving me a chance?"

"I...had hoped that you might give Amanda a chance," she said into the soapsuds.

"And I think I hinted before that while I like Amanda a lot and respect her very much, it is not she who fills my thoughts and makes me walk up the hill three and four times a day, and turn back before I get to the top."

"Is that what you've been doing?" Could her face get any redder? Maybe someone better not come in right now. What would they think?

"It's a sad confession, but it shows you my state of mind."

"I'm sorry," she whispered. This was awful. How was she going to tell Amanda this? They told each other nearly everything.

"You're sorry about my state of mind, or you're sorry you can't return my feelings?" His tone was gentle—but she still didn't dare look up and meet his eyes.

"Both."

"Then I am sorry, too. And you're sure?"

She didn't know whether she was standing on her own feet, or upside down, or was just plain going crazy. "I'm so *verhuddelt* right now I don't know what to think. But mostly I'm disappointed for Amanda's sake. She—" Oh, no, she couldn't betray Amanda's feelings for him, and she had come within a word of doing so! She gulped. "She would be worth getting to know, Silas."

"And I'm sure I will—as friends. We'll all be friends." But his voice had a note of disappointment in it. "No matter what, you are still my sisters in God."

"And that is how you must think of me. Silas—I'm sorry. I don't think I can face everyone just now." She drained the water from the sink and wrung out the cloth. "If you could tell Corinne I've had to go home, and tell Caleb I'll see him there…"

"Sarah, don't—I don't want to chase you away."

"You haven't. I just need a little walk and some breathing time. You'll tell them?"

"Of course. Be prepared for Zeke to say something about it in the morning, though."

Zeke always had a joke for every situation. But as Sarah slipped out the kitchen door into the soft summer night, she doubted very much whether anyone could find anything amusing in this one.

# CHAPTER 20

After the debacle with the Parkers, Henry wouldn't be surprised if Ginny decided that their friendship should end.

The moon was on the wane, but between its remaining quarter and the brilliance of the stars in this part of the country where there wasn't a lot of electric competition, there was more than enough light for him to stroll along the creek bottom on the shortcut over to the Rose Arbor Inn. In the light backpack he used for day hikes was a carefully wrapped mug of a new design. He'd meant to bring it over earlier in the week, but now he was glad he hadn't.

It would make a great peace offering.

Something glimmered in a break after the maple copse where the *Youngie* had been using the rope swing, and after a startled second, he realized it was an Amish woman carrying a flashlight.

A woman of a size and shape that was familiar. At this time of night, when most Amish women were tucking in their kids?

"Sarah, is that you?" he said in a gentle tone, the kind you'd use on a frightened horse. Even so, she turned with a gasp and dropped the flashlight. Luckily, she was well over on the path, so it didn't land in the creek.

"It's me. Henry. I'm just on my way over to Ginny's. Is everything all right?"

With a shaky laugh, she retrieved the light and then shone it on him, as if to make sure it was really he and not someone else. Then she snapped it off. Twinkles danced in front of his eyes before they adjusted to the moonlight again.

"Henry. I thought it was—never mind. *Wie geht's?*"

"I'm well. But are you? What are you doing out here in the dark? Have you lost a hen?"

"A hen? Oh. No, I was just walking. Trying to...what do the *Englisch* say? Clear my head."

"Has something happened? Caleb said Simon had suffered some kind of mishap. Is he all right?"

"I hope so. A horse stepped on his foot, so I sent a care package this morning. I'm hoping that Joe can doctor him."

"That was good thinking. No doctors that far out of town?"

"None that the boys can afford, apparently. So between the two of us, we'll do the best we can for him."

"So now you're walking, trying not to worry." It didn't seem like her, though. "I would have thought you'd be out in the garden, picking something to make yourself a calming tea."

Her white *Kapp* bobbed in acknowledgment. "I need to finish up a salve I started this morning and haven't got back to. But somehow I needed air and space and the sound of the water more. I'm grateful God gives us these helps in times of trial."

There was more to the tone in her voice than worry about her boy. And when he'd greeted her, she'd thought he was someone else.

"Is something trying you? Other than what happened to Simon?"

She moved away, to where the stones and clumps of sedge formed a narrow barrier between path and water. "It's not something I can talk about with you."

Heat flooded his face at the reproof. "Oh. Sorry. I suppose there are some things you'd prefer to keep between you and your women friends, like Amanda. I didn't mean to pry."

"Amanda." The breath soughed out of her. "That's just the trouble. I've made a mess of things by not speaking up sooner, and if her feelings are wounded, I'll never forgive myself."

Did she want to tell him or not? Or had the dark and the rush of the creek that covered the outside sounds worked its magic and given her a sense of privacy?

"Speaking up to whom?"

With a groan, she scrubbed at her cheeks with her empty hand. "Oh, to Silas. He told me this evening that he's interested in me, and would like to court me."

Henry felt as though she'd slapped him. He actually took a step back to regain his balance. "*Court* you?"

"You sound as surprised as I felt. He's been here visiting with Corinne's cousins all week, and I thought he would be a wonderful prospect for Amanda. I did everything possible to get them together, and come to find out, Fannie and Zeke have been doing everything possible to get *him* together with *me*."

Thoughts flapped around in his head like a bunch of startled sparrows, and he couldn't catch a single one in order to reply.

"And now he's arranged to stay another week to help Joshua remodel the bathroom at their place—but underneath it all, it's so he'll have time to get to know me better. Except I told him we could only be friends, because it's Amanda I thought he was interested in. Now what am I going to do?"

What was the matter with him? He needed to get a grip.

"Seems—it seems you've done it. Said you wanted to be friends, I mean."

"Well, yes, but in the meantime, it's going to change things between us. And how can I tell Amanda that he was staying for me when she's the one who's interested and will hope he's staying for her? It would hurt her horribly."

"You can't tell her," he said instantly. The fewer people who knew about this, the better. Including him. What had possessed him to walk tonight when he could have driven over to Ginny's like a rational man?

Ginny's. He needed to get over there. If he dillydallied here any longer, she might go to bed, and then when she had to come down and answer the door, she'd be even more annoyed with him.

"We don't keep secrets from one another," she said on a sigh. "Not since Michael died. She and Corinne helped me through that time, and ever since, we've had complete confidence in one another."

"Well, you'll have to. Nobody wants to hear that the person they care about is interested in somebody else. Look, Sarah, I have to go. Let me walk you back to your place."

Even in the dark, he could feel her recoil in confusion at his brusque tone and the sudden end to confession time. "You don't need to do that. I'm not ready to go back."

"Then you're okay if I leave you? I need to get over to Ginny's or she'll be even madder at me than she already is."

"Oh," she said. "Well, you don't want that. I'll be fine. I was walking this creek path for years before you came, you know."

"Good night."

"Would you like my flashlight?"

"No. Thanks. Good night." He didn't need anything from

her. He set off along the path at twice the speed he'd begun with. Not a flashlight, not a herbal cure, nothing.

And nothing, evidently, was exactly what he was going to get.

Ginny hadn't gone to bed yet, and looked very fetching in a pair of shorts and a Seton Hill alumni sweatshirt. Also very fetching was her smile of welcome as she let him in and led the way back to her private sitting room, where guests didn't go and the Amish girls didn't clean.

After a brief stop in the kitchen for a couple of glasses of iced tea and a plate of chocolate chip cookies, she put them on the low coffee table and curled up in the armchair.

"So, did everything get resolved with the Parkers?" He might as well get that off the table right away.

"Oh, yes. No further apologies were forthcoming for poor Priscilla. Have you seen her? She says she's all right, but she's so humble that I don't know if I can believe her."

"I think she is. I don't know about Eric, though. He left his project behind when they practically dragged him away, and who knows if he'll ever be able to finish it. I wanted to ask you for their address so I can send it to him, at least. After that, it will be up to him."

She gazed at him over the rim of her glass. "You should have told his parents about the pottery lessons, Henry."

On a sigh, he said, "I know. There is a whole raft of things I don't know about kids, and how much their parents get involved in their lives is one of them."

"I don't think those two are super involved in the boys' lives. But after the initial heads-up, they would have gone about their holiday and been happy he was occupied. As it was, they felt hard done by and deceived. I tried to tell them you didn't have ulterior motives where their son was concerned, but you could tell that's what was in their minds."

This had never occurred to Henry, not even once. "You must be joking."

A single shake of her head made her curls dance all around the yellow cotton bandeau she wore in her hair. "It's a nasty world out there, in case you didn't notice."

"I know that, but not here in Willow Creek."

"I don't think evil pays any attention to social demographics. And besides, even though they weren't the best parents I ever saw, they have a right to know who their kid is with. I did my best to tell them you were all right, so you can relax about that."

"Do you think I should write and apologize?"

"I think you should send the package and chalk it up to a learning experience. And be glad Sarah doesn't have the same kinds of feelings about Caleb working for you."

Henry felt a jolt in his solar plexus at the mention of Sarah's name so soon after a similar jolt down there in the creek bottom. He took a long drink of tea, the cold liquid splashing into his stomach and giving his nervous system something else to think about.

"Speaking of work, I have something to show you." He took the new mug out of its wrapping—an old jacket he'd used as packing material during his move. "What do you think?"

She turned the mug over in her hands. "Henry, it's beautiful. It's like those old—oh, what do you call it—back at the turn of the last century when artists made things look like plants."

"Art Nouveau."

"That's it. And this is a . . . rosebud?"

"Exactly."

"But it's not quite. It's a mug obviously, but these lines here, they suggest petals, and the way they unfurl at the top, and then the glaze does the rest . . . it's beautiful, Henry."

"I'm using the same style on the mugs I'm doing for D.W. Frith, and maybe just a hint of a leaf shape on the handles of the batter bowls. This was an experiment. I wanted your opinion."

"My opinion is that I want you to change what you've been doing for me and make the house mugs like this from now on. No one else is going to have anything like them." Then she looked up. "Oh, but they'll be more expensive, won't they?"

"They will, but you can make up the difference in the room rate if the guests choose to keep them."

"Or I can trim costs out somewhere else. Can I keep this? I want to drink my coffee out of it."

"Sure. I have more at the studio, but I thought you'd like the pink."

She put the rosebud mug on the coffee table and unfolded herself from the chair. She dropped a kiss on his cheek as she snuggled up beside him on the couch.

"You're getting to know me well enough to know that I like bright flower colors."

"I've noticed that." Though she didn't seem like a flower, not the way the Amish girls did with their graceful long skirts and crisp *Kapps*. She seemed more exotic, like a bird of paradise in a garden where hummingbirds typically lived. "Are you happy in Willow Creek, Ginny?"

She leaned away a little to examine his face. "Most of the time. I like what I do, and I love my house. My neighbors are far enough away to give me privacy when I want it, and close enough and nice enough that I can walk over and get a cup of sugar when I run out. I have friends here, and interests, and I just joined the quilting guild, though when I'm going to have time to sew is a mystery. Why do you ask?"

"It's a nice place to try to be happy in."

"My house, or Willow Creek?"

"Your house is great, but I meant Willow Creek."

"So you're settling in, are you?"

"I think so. I'm finding my groove, as you would say, with the clay and the things I can do with it here. And like you say, friends and interests. If it wasn't for you and the Inn, I wouldn't have gotten that contract with D.W. Frith. I should pay you a finder's fee."

"Or make the new mugs for the same price as the old ones."

He laughed, and she adjusted her position against his side. It seemed natural to move his arm around her shoulders, and she tucked her bent knees up against his thigh.

"You drive a hard bargain."

"I have to, a woman alone running her own business."

"Don't push the damsel in distress routine too hard. I can see right through it."

"Hey, if it saves me a couple of bucks, I'll do what I have to." She grinned at him and leaned over to swipe a couple of cookies. "Here. Have one. I just made them this afternoon. A peace offering for being so cranky the other day over those people."

"Your crankiness was on Priscilla's behalf, so I don't blame you—or take it personally." He had, a little, but he wouldn't tell her that.

"I do get cranky over stuff, Henry," she said. "If you're going to be around, I want you to know that. I have a bit of a temper, but the good thing is, it always blows over fast."

"I'm the opposite," he admitted, since she seemed to be in the mood for confidences. And she did feel really good against him. It had been a long time since he'd sat and cuddled with a woman and had the kind of intimate conversation that cuddling led to. "My temper is the kind that simmers for days and then blows up over something completely unrelated."

"That's worse."

"Don't I know it."

"But there's a cure for it, you know—communication. How about we make a deal. If we get mad at each other, I'll stomp and yell and you make sure you stand up to me and say what you have to say. Then I'll simmer down and you won't withdraw and it'll all get resolved."

"You're such an adult. Where's the fun in that?"

"It ain't fun, believe me. I was married, remember? There's nothing harder when two people can't say what's on their minds. I need that now, so consider yourself warned."

What a difference between this woman and the Amish woman he'd just left in the creek bottom. Ginny talked things out beforehand, like a blueprint of what to do once they got there. With Sarah, things just happened and she managed to say what needed to be said and so did he—sometimes awkwardly, sometimes clumsily.

And why was he comparing the two of them? Talk about a pointless exercise—unless it was to show Ginny in the best light. Which she was quite capable of doing on her own.

She was looking up at him, soft and curvy and smart and probably the best *Englisch* cook in the entire countryside.

None of which mattered a bit as he lowered his head and kissed her smiling mouth.

# CHAPTER 21

An inn with no Parkers in it was a clean and happy place to be.

Priscilla left the Rose Arbor Inn on Friday afternoon with the sound of Ginny's singing in her ears. It was one of the fast songs she sometimes heard on Ginny's radio, which she called "contemporary worship," but to Pris's ears it sounded like rock music most of the time. Ginny was in a very tuneful mood, and her voice was pretty—husky and melodious at the same time.

She wouldn't say what she was so happy about, but Pris's sharp eyes hadn't missed the rosebud-shaped mug on the kitchen counter that hadn't been there Wednesday, nor the initials pressed into the bottom of it.

She could add one and one to make two as well as anybody.

It was none of her business if Ginny was divorced and Henry was ex-Amish. They had no *Ordnung* to tell them that courtship or even marriage was wrong, and so Ginny added up the accounts in her office while she sang, and no doubt Henry was in his studio making some other beautiful thing for her.

And meanwhile, Pris was free and her week's pay was in her pocket and town was just a short walk down the road.

At the fabric store, she discovered that Amanda and Miriam had received some pretty new fabric, which Amanda was busy draping in the window.

"Hallo, Pris, *wie geht's?* Are you here for dress fabric so soon?"

"Hi, Amanda. *Neh*, not this time. I need some fat quarters. It's Mamm's birthday soon and I want to make her some pot holders. I just saw a picture of a log-cabin quilt, but each square was a chicken. The quilter made triangles at the top of each block so they look like a chicken's comb."

Amanda laughed. "How cute! Miriam even has some little black buttons on the button rack that you could use for eyes, if you wanted. Help yourself to the basket on the counter—she just filled it yesterday and the weekend tourists haven't got to it yet."

At the cash register Miriam was ringing up Evie Troyer, the bishop's wife. "Hallo, Pris. Is this what you're looking for?" Evie pushed the basket toward her. "What's this about pot holders and chickens?"

Quickly, Pris described what she'd seen in one of the brochures Ginny kept at the Inn for the quilt hunters. "I thought I could use the same idea of the squares to make pot holders." She unrolled a quarter. "Doesn't this black-and-white look like a Barred Rock's feathers? And this red one with the paisley could be her Red Stars."

"What a good idea." Evie's keen gaze took in the contents of the basket. "You could shade the logs in the cabin block from bottom to top, so it looked like wings and breast feathers."

Evie was so smart. There was a reason she had a countywide reputation as a quilter. Her designs were simple, but she put colors together in combinations you'd never think of, and they came out looking incredibly complicated. Her quilts were always the first to go at the auction, and brought in the most money, too.

"I like that," Pris said happily. "These will be fun for me and Katie and Saranne to make, and Mamm will love them."

"Why don't you make a few extra, and I can sell them at my booth at the Amish Market?" Evie said. "I bet you could get ten dollars apiece for them."

"Ten dollars!" Pris fumbled some butter-yellow cotton that would be perfect for beaks, and caught it before it dropped. "Nobody would pay ten dollars for a pot holder."

"You would be surprised. Make up a couple, and I'll see if they sell. If they don't, I'll mark them down to half price and then they will."

Half her pay went to Mamm for household expenses, but that still left Priscilla with enough to buy quite a few fat quarters, some tiny black buttons, and a length of ribbon to cut up for hanging loops. And she still had enough to go to the Amish store tomorrow to order a couple of fresh new *Kapps* from the Grossmammi of the lady who ran the store, who made them in all sizes.

She was standing at the corner outside the fabric store with her bag of purchases, waiting for the light to change, when a horse and buggy rattled up beside her.

"Hey, Pris," Benny Peachey said through the open door.

She turned in surprise. "You have a buggy." It was second- or maybe even third-hand, and it didn't look like there was a shade in the back window anymore, but it had wheels and axles and Benny looked as pleased with it as could be.

"Me and Leon found it and fixed it up. Looks pretty grand, don't it?"

*Found* it? "How do you find a buggy, Benny?"

His face was as open as a daisy. "You'd be surprised what you find back there in the woods. Looked like someone got stuck in the mud out there and never got back to get their rig. It'd been there over a winter, looked like. Say, your light's green. Need a ride?"

"I—"

Behind his shabby rig, a shiny *Englisch* car with a bunch of kids in it not much older than themselves rocked forward and back as the driver gunned the ignition and braked immediately after.

"Benny, get out of the way before they run you over."

"Not until you get in."

*Vroom.* "Benny!"

The driver laid on the horn and Benny Peachey didn't move, though his horse tossed its head and skittered and the buggy rolled into the crosswalk.

There was going to be an accident unless she did what this crazy boy wanted. Priscilla dashed around the horse's head and leaped into the passenger side, hanging on to the bench while her shopping bag slid to the floor. Benny flapped the reins and the horse leaped away from the noise behind it. The horn blared as the car passed them and flew down a side road and over a hill.

"Good grief, Benny. You could have hurt your horse."

"Naw. He's steady as a rock." He grinned at her, sunburned and freckled and completely careless about causing a scene and making people stare. "What'cha up to in town?"

"Buying fabric for Mamm's birthday present. And trying not to be killed at traffic lights."

"You take life too seriously, Pris. You've gotta have more faith." He held the reins loosely, his body relaxed and one foot outside the door on the running board. Benny Peachey, it was clear, had faith to spare, while she felt rattled and upset.

"I don't like being forced into things. You can drop me at the end of our lane, *denki*."

"Aw, c'mon. Let's go for a ride."

"I don't want to go for a ride. I want to preshrink this cotton and get it drying on a line in my room so I can sew tomorrow."

"Plenty of time. Besides, I have something to show you."

"Show me?" What could he possibly have to show her? Another abandoned buggy?

"It's on the way to your place, Pris—simmer down."

At the pace he was driving, she couldn't very well jump out, and at least he was going generally in the right direction. When he took her down Twelfth, curiosity finally got the best of her.

"Are you taking me back to work? Because I just finished for the day."

"Close."

He guided the horse into the parking lot of the Rose Arbor Inn, where a pair of weekenders were just getting out of their car. "Honey, look, an Amish buggy," the man said to his wife, who looked to be about six months pregnant.

As Benny and Pris got out, the man gave a friendly wave, but he didn't ask to take their picture. He must have stayed here before. Pris waved back and they disappeared from view under the climbing roses over the gate. Benny tied up the horse and pointed toward the creek with his chin.

What on earth could he want to show her? A nest of baby birds? Had a fawn lost its mother? Was some *Englisch* movie star down there having a swim?

Priscilla gave up and followed him down the slope to what

Ginny laughingly called her boathouse. It was more a storage shed on the bank for an ancient canoe that Priscilla wouldn't trust if she were caught in a flood, some coiled-up rope, and a jumble of those rigid Styrofoam noodles that children used to swim with.

Benny opened the door and whistled softly.

A lost puppy. This was what he'd dragged her across town for? He couldn't have just taken it home himself?

Benny stepped back and the door opened wider. A dirty sneaker appeared, then a skinny leg in jeans.

A boy stepped out of the shed and lifted his head to meet her gaze, his eyes defiant and scared and slowly filling with tears.

Priscilla completely forgot how to speak English. "Eric Parker!" She lost her breath and started again. "*Was tutsch du hier? Sei du narrisch?*"

His face slackened with incomprehension, and she gathered what few brains she had left and tried to remember the words she needed. The polite ones. "What are you doing here? Did your parents come back?" Their big SUV hadn't been in the tiny lot, but with Eric's ability not to be where he was expected, that didn't mean anything. They could be parked outside the Sleep Inn in Willow Creek.

"Do you have anything to eat?" he said.

Her heart melted. "Benny, go back up to the buggy and bring my cloth bag. I have half a sandwich in there and some pickles."

When Benny was gone, she took the boy in from head to foot. His T-shirt looked as if it had been slept in, and his hair hadn't seen a comb that day, at least, and maybe the one before. One side of his face was dirty, and his eyes were red. "What happened to you?"

"I—I ran away."

Pris drew in a shocked breath. "Why?"

"Because they wouldn't let me stay here. With Henry. And Caleb and his mom."

"But Eric, we have to obey our parents. I'm sure they meant what's best for you."

"No, they didn't. They just care about what's best for them. As soon as we got home, they said they were sending me and Justin to our grandparents in California, like, this week. I told them I wanted to come back here and they said no. So I left."

Left from where? "Where is your home, Eric?"

"Connecticut. I bought a train ticket online with my Christmas money and then took a bus to the station. Then when I got to Lancaster, I didn't know what bus, but a bunch of kids was there with a church group and they were coming to Intercourse, so I went with them on their bus. And then Benny drove by and I remembered seeing him down here, so when he stopped at the light, I asked if I could get a ride here."

He ran out of breath, while she tried to take in the magnitude of this journey—and the sheer courage and stubbornness and disobedience it had taken to go through with it.

"When did you leave?"

"Yesterday, right after they told us. Justin is probably in California by now."

"With you gone? Eric, do you know your parents are probably frantic and have called the police?"

He just shrugged, and then Benny slid down the last of the slope and thrust her bag at her. She gave Eric all the food she had in it, and he wolfed it down as though he hadn't eaten since... well, he probably hadn't eaten since he'd left, unless he had money for something out of a vending machine.

"This is terrible. The police will probably arrest Benny for helping you."

"They'd have to find me first." Benny stole a pickle and crunched it, apparently unconcerned. "These are good, Pris. Did you make them?"

She ignored him. "We have to tell someone, Eric," she said. "An adult. An *Englisch* adult. You can't stay here in Ginny's shed."

"Can't I go to Caleb's? His mom invited me. She won't mind."

"Maybe not, but your parents are going to mind a lot, no matter what you think. We can't go to Sarah Yoder's. It's better she doesn't know you're here."

"What about Henry? He wanted me to stay and learn about pottery. I need to finish my project."

Henry was *Englisch* now. "And he's got a phone in the barn." She gathered up the empty plastic containers and stuffed them back in her bag. "That's where we'll go. The first thing to do is let your parents know where you are."

At the mention of his parents again, Eric's face closed up in an expression so stony and stubborn that for the second time in a few minutes, Priscilla was shocked.

"No. I won't. I'll run away again."

"You can come and stay with—" Benny got out before Priscilla rounded on him.

"You stay out of this!" she snapped. "You've already got yourself in enough trouble for bringing him back here. If Eric won't come obediently, pick him up and put him in the buggy like a sack of potatoes."

"Aren't you the bossy one," Benny said mildly as Eric

backed away, glancing from shed to creek as if looking for a way of escape.

But Priscilla was having no more of this nonsense. "I'm not bossy, I'm the only one down here who has the sense to do the right thing. Now, come on before I have to go and tell Ginny—and you can just imagine what she'll say."

Eric looked as if he were imagining it then and there. "But can we go to Henry's?" he asked, sounding less truculent than he had a moment ago.

"To use the phone. And for you to get your project, if he hasn't sent it away already."

"Sent it away!"

"To your address, you big silly. Now, come on."

# CHAPTER 22

Carefully, patiently, Henry drew his thumb along the soft, damp curve of the clay that would become the handle of a batter bowl, this second depression next to the first forming a ridge in the center like a vein or a stem. At the terminus of the curve, the clay splayed outward, clinging to the body of the bowl in the shape of a peony leaf, a sample of which he had found in Sadie's garden and pressed between the pages of his sketchbook as a model.

There. Henry straightened with satisfaction.

The classes he'd taken in historical pottery methods, and the hours of research he'd done on the Art Nouveau and Arts and Crafts movements, were beginning to pay off. Already his sketchbook had taken on a different character, full of natural forms instead of the abstracts he'd been working with without success in Denver.

This landscape around the farm abounded with natural forms. From the curves of pine needles to the flutter of poplar leaves, from the angle of a chicken's tail to the swirl of an eddy in the creek, his eyes had been opened to what the D.W. Frith rep had called the "inspiration in the flowers and fields."

He wasn't the first to have done so, but with the "sky and

water glaze" adapted with different tints to suggest the light coming through leaves and petals, he was definitely on to something. And with each piece, he refined it more. With each stroke of the brush, he found his joy again.

Along with his art, he had found a measure of joy in other places, too. Ginny's smile flickered in his memory, as did the warmth of her arms around him and the soft brush of curls as she laid her head on his shoulder. It had been a long time since he'd held a woman like that—well, if you didn't count that brief embrace with Sarah in the garden a few weeks back, which wasn't the same thing.

No, that one had ended in a push and a denial, and this one had ended in a kiss and a promise. Two totally different experiences, and he'd tell anyone which he preferred.

Gravel crunched under the wheels of a buggy outside the studio, and he grabbed a rag and wiped his hands. Not for the first time, he wondered if putting up that ARTISAN sign at the end of the lane hadn't been a mistake. There was far too much traffic around here for a man to focus on his work. Though the Amish typically didn't drive down to watch him. Maybe someone needed a hand—or a car or a phone.

Shapes appeared in the wide swath of sunlight between the heavy barn doors and he blinked.

No. It couldn't be.

Priscilla Mast gave Eric Parker a push in the small of his back while a skinny teenager wearing an Amish hat and broadfall pants leaned on the door with his hands in his pockets.

Henry didn't care who the second boy was. He stared at Eric in astonishment.

"Did your family change their minds?" he finally asked. "Are you going to stay with Caleb Yoder after all?"

Eric gulped and looked at Priscilla for help, but she merely raised her eyebrows at him and folded her arms.

This didn't smell right. He didn't have much experience with kids, but he had a whole lot of experience with guilty consciences.

"Eric? Where are your parents? Ginny didn't mention that she had another reservation for them so soon."

"At home. In Connecticut. I guess."

It took him a second to absorb this. And the look of the kid—wrinkled, dirty, and eyeing the plate of chocolate chip cookies Ginny had sent home with him way too avidly even for a thirteen-year-old boy—told him something he didn't want to know.

Priscilla could hold her peace no longer. "He ran away. He took a bus and a train and a buggy and here he is, without his parents knowing a thing."

"They can probably guess," Eric mumbled.

"You ran away? From Connecticut?" Henry repeated. "Are you kidding me?"

"I wish he was," Priscilla said. "So we're here to use your phone, please, to call his parents."

"Yes." Good plan. Excellent plan. One that would no doubt bring Trent and Isabel Parker back into his life with a screaming sound like a jet coming in for a landing. "I can't believe it, Eric. What were you thinking?"

"I wanted to come here, not go to California." He wouldn't raise his eyes from the floor, but Henry saw his gaze dart to the bench once or twice. Looking for something.

"Your lantern is in that box over there, ready to ship to you," he said.

A little of Eric's tension drained away. "You didn't throw it out."

"Of course not. It's not mine. But what is mine right now is a boatload of responsibility for you, and I'll tell you right now, I don't appreciate it."

The kid wilted, and Henry's conscience twinged, but it had to be said. "I thought more of you, Eric. We pursue our art with passion, not deceit and defiance."

"I couldn't think of anything else to do."

"I bet you could have, if you tried."

"You heard my parents. What they said."

"What I heard was a dad who was willing to consider a change in your academic future, if he got a chance to have a rational conversation about it. I'm thinking that probably isn't going to happen now, is it?"

Mumble.

"Well, go on. Call them. The phone is on the wall there, right next to—"

"Benny Peachey," said that individual cheerfully. "I gave him a ride to Willow Creek from Intercourse."

"Did you, now? Thank you for not letting him sleep on the street anyway. Eric, call. Now."

"Can't you do it?" he whispered, looking so beaten down and exhausted that Henry's heart melted the rest of the way.

With a sigh, he said, "What's your dad's number?"

The kid gave it to him, one reluctant digit at a time, and Henry braced himself as the call rang through.

"Parker. Did you find him?"

He must think this was the police. "Yes. He's safe. I'm—"

"Isabel!" Trent shouted into the background. "Pick up the phone! They found him!" Then into the receiver, "Where?"

"Mr. Parker, this is Henry Byler, in Willow Creek, Pennsylvania. Eric is here, in my studio."

A receiver clicked, and a breathless female voice said, "Eric? Honey, is that you?"

Henry repeated what he'd just said, to the same shocked silence. Then he thought he'd better elaborate while he could. "Apparently he took a train to Lancaster, a bus to Intercourse, and a buggy to Willow Creek. I'll say this for your boy—he's got guts."

Someone was making inarticulate sounds that finally resolved themselves into speech. "Guts?" Trent Parker roared. "You put that kid on the line right now!"

Henry felt a little like a kidnapper as he stretched the phone cord out to provide proof of life. "Your dad wants to talk to you."

But Eric didn't get to say more than a few mumbled words of apology before the volume on the other end got so loud that Henry took the receiver from his unresisting hand.

"All right, all right, I understand that you're upset, and you have every reason to be. But Eric is safe and I'll see that he gets a square meal and a good night's sleep, so he'll be fine by the time you get here tomorrow."

"What are you talking about?" Isabel snapped, since Trent appeared to have run out of steam.

"I assume you're coming to get him?"

"How can we do that? I've got flight reservations to California tomorrow, with Justin," Isabel said. "Does that child have any idea how much it would cost us to cancel?"

"But Trent—Mr. Parker—"

"Has to go back to work. Oil companies don't run themselves, you know. Some people can't just work when they feel like it—they have *responsibilities*."

"In my experience in the corporate world, it's the executive assistants who run most things. But all right. Do you want me to drive him up there?" The bowls would take a couple of days to dry anyway, before he could give them their first firing, so the timing could work.

"Mr. Byler, I just told you, Justin and I will be on a plane, and Trent will be in New York City. He's staying at the company suite while we're gone. It's not going to be much fun for Eric—he hates it in the city and the company isn't all that excited about kids in the suite, either."

Now, wait just a minute. "Mrs. Parker, do you think you could take twenty-four hours out of your busy life to pay some attention to the boy who loves his art so much he crossed three states by himself to come back to it?"

"The boy who ran away, you mean." Trent Parker had found his voice again. "The boy I'm half tempted to leave there, since clearly his parents' and brother's feelings don't mean a thing to him. He probably didn't give a single thought to us, or the cops crawling all over town, or his grandparents in California, who practically had a nervous breakdown when they heard he was missing."

Henry took a deep breath and committed himself. "You know, my offer still stands. He's welcome to stay with Sarah Yoder and Caleb, and take lessons in clay with me for a couple of weeks. That way, Isabel and Justin can get on the plane, and you can stay in the city and focus on business."

"I can't believe you'd bring that up again when—"

"Trent," his wife interrupted. "Listen. It's the perfect solution. Even if I did drive up there to get him, I'm not sure I can be trusted not to do some damage, I'm so angry and relieved and horrified that he'd even do this to us. In two weeks everyone will have settled down, Eric will have gotten what he wanted—again—and we can go on with the rest of our summer as planned."

"I'm not going to reward that boy for his bad behavior!"

Henry wasn't sure being abandoned in a New York apartment would teach the kid much, either. "We'll take good care of him—and you know, there's no disciplinarian like an Amish mother. It won't be any picnic for Eric, I can tell you that." He glanced at the boy, who was watching him like a baby bird getting ready to fling itself off a branch if he moved too suddenly. "But if he can stick it out, I think it will be worth it, for him and for you."

"If that woman touches my son, the police are going to hear about it," Isabel snapped.

"Izzy, would you relax? He's thirteen. Nobody spanks a thirteen-year-old. All right. Fine. Between the two of you, you've got us over a barrel," Trent said. "Eric stays there for two weeks, and then I'll drive up and get him. But you can tell him from me that the whole art high school idea is off the table. He can't behave like this and expect us to just give him whatever he wants."

"That's not my department," Henry said. "But I'll tell him."

After making arrangements to send clothes and whatever else boys needed these days for a two-week stay, Henry hung up.

"They're not coming?" Eric whispered.

Henry couldn't tell if the boy was devastated or glad. "Does that upset you?"

"No. I hoped they wouldn't. I hoped they'd just go and let me stay with you and Caleb."

"Well, they have. Your dad isn't happy about it at all, and once he simmers down, I recommend a phone call to apologize. You might not like it, you know, staying on an Amish farm."

"It ain't so bad." The boy leaning on the door had been listening the whole time, no doubt wondering what on earth kind of parents would find out their kid had run away—and let him stay where he'd run to. "But you can always run away to Connecticut if you don't."

Eric shook his head so vigorously, his shaggy skater-boy haircut whipped back and forth.

"Mind telling me who you are, exactly, Benny?" Henry inquired of the strange boy.

"I'm Arlon Peachey's Benny. Our farm's on Stickleback Road. I'm courting Pris here." He tilted his head in the girl's direction.

Priscilla gasped and flushed as cherry-pink as her dress with embarrassment and indignation. "You are not! What fibs you tell." She grasped Eric's hand. "Come on, Eric. I'll take you over to Sarah's and get you something decent to eat." She glared at Benny Peachey. "And no, we do *not* need a ride."

# CHAPTER 23

Sarah saw the little parade coming down the side of the hill between her acres and the Byler place—Henry, Priscilla, Benny Peachey, and...she stared. Then she shook the soil off the last handful of baby carrots and salad greens she and Caleb were pulling for supper, put them in the plastic bowl, and got to her feet.

"Mamm, that can't be—is that Eric Parker?"

"His parents must have changed their minds." She dusted off her apron and went to meet them.

It took about ten minutes for her and Caleb to understand what had really gone on since the Parker vehicle had roared out of Henry's lane on Wednesday. The thought of what the boy had done staggered her, and helplessly, she spread her hands as if trying to get the measure of it.

"Ran away. From Connecticut. To come back here. How is that even possible for a boy who's only thirteen?"

Since Eric looked to be falling down from hunger and weariness, she didn't really expect an answer from him. But he gathered himself together to reply.

"I wanted to be here. To stay with you, ma'am. And Caleb. And to learn stuff from Henry."

Now was clearly not the time to teach him that what a person already had was very often what he really wanted. So all Sarah said was, "Please don't call me ma'am, Eric. We don't use honorifics, and that word meant *my lady* in the old days—something you'd call someone of higher status than you. We don't believe in that—we're all equal in the eyes of God." She smiled and brushed the dirty hair out of his eyes. "My name is Sarah."

"Yes, ma— Sarah."

She glanced at Henry. "And his parents have really allowed him to stay with us?"

"I talked them into it," Henry said. "It seemed like the best plan for everyone, since the family is traveling tomorrow—Trent to New York City, and the other two to California."

This just beggared belief. Simon had done the next thing to running off, that was true, but he was a man grown, and had a friend with him to share the adventure. Eric had nothing but whatever was in that scuffed black backpack—and a will of iron.

The next two weeks could be very difficult. Offering hospitality with the parents' blessing was one thing. But offering it under duress was very different. She breathed a prayer for wisdom, and then a brief postscript of a prayer that Caleb would not be infected by the same willfulness.

"Come inside, all of you. Caleb and I are having sliced ham, salad, and macaroni and cheese for supper. Would you like to join us?"

"*Denki*, Sarah, but I need to be getting home to do my chores," Priscilla said.

"I'll give you a ride," Benny said promptly.

"*Neh*, I would rather walk. It's not far. Good-bye, Henry. See you soon, Eric and Caleb." And without another word, she cut across the lawn and into the orchard, where a path led between the Mast and the Yoder farms.

"Guess I'll collect my rig, then." And Benny loped off in the direction of the hill and the path Caleb had worn into it going to help Henry.

"You'll stay, won't you, Henry?" Eric said, looking about ready to faint.

"We don't bite," Caleb told him. "Come on and wash up." Eric went with him, looking back only once over his shoulder at Henry before they disappeared into the house.

"He looks scared to death," Henry observed, watching them.

"He should be. Imagine doing such a thing. He's right here in my yard and I still can't believe it. Or that his parents didn't have you drive him home immediately." She walked over to the edge of the garden, where the big plastic bowl sat.

"I offered, but they said no, and then I offered to keep him here. I think it would be good for the kid, Sarah. Some decent family life."

"Two weeks in someone else's family isn't going to fix the problems in his own."

"No, but he might learn a thing or two that would help him handle things better."

Sarah couldn't imagine what—he was far too old to be taught to obey, which was probably the best thing to help a child "handle things," but she was going to have to do her best.

Henry followed her around to the outside sink, where she dumped out the vegetables and turned on the cold-water faucet to rinse them. They had parted on slightly chilly terms the other night because he'd been in a hurry to see Ginny, and slightly chilly was no way to be with one's neighbors.

"I hope you will stay for dinner, Henry," she said, scrubbing the carrots vigorously. "I think Eric would feel more comfortable with you here."

He ran water into his side of the sink, then took the lettuces and began to wash them. "You might be right. And considering the alternative is boiled eggs and bacon, I'd be happy to."

"You're not having dinner with Ginny?" came out of her mouth before she even realized the thought was lurking in her mind, ready to spring like a kitten upon any wisp of passing common sense.

"No." The pile of lettuce and spinach on the counter grew. "We don't see each other every day. About as often as you would see Silas, I suppose."

"I'm not seeing Silas, as I told you." She dropped her voice so it was nearly inaudible. "And you're not to say things like that out loud where Caleb can hear." Then in a more normal tone, she said, "It was interesting, Benny Peachey being the one to bring Eric back to Willow Creek. I wish he hadn't left quite so soon—his mother said she would have him collect some herbs for me and I wanted to talk with him about them."

"With no Priscilla, there would be no point in his staying. He says he's courting her."

The carrots were clean, so she returned them to the plastic bowl, along with the clean greens and some cucumbers. "What a man says and what a woman thinks can be two different things. She's writing to Joe, don't forget. That means something to a girl like her."

"I think it's all in Benny's mind—that, or he just says outrageous things to get her to blush. I wouldn't put it past him."

"All the same, I won't mention it when I write to Simon. If Priscilla has something to say to Joe, she'll say it herself."

"She has no trouble saying what needs to be said, I'll give her that. Here, let me carry that in for you."

She relinquished the bowl. "I'll just be a minute. I want to get some nasturtiums to put in the salad. If Eric is going to stay here, we'll start him off properly."

As it turned out, Eric did not appreciate the nasturtiums. He did not appreciate salad either, or pickles, or anything remotely resembling a vegetable. He cleaned up every scrap of ham and macaroni, and asked for seconds, but when he asked for thirds, Sarah shook her head. "Not until you eat your salad. Look at Caleb's plate. He knows that God gave us vegetables to help our bodies work properly."

The boy looked at the plate, then at the bowl of macaroni that she had prudently removed to her end of the table. "But I'm *starving*. I haven't had anything to eat in two *days*."

"Then you'll find the salad very satisfying."

He pushed his chair back. "Mom never makes me eat stuff I don't like."

"No wonder your body is starving, then," Sarah said imperturbably. "It is not getting what it needs."

"Eric," Henry said, buttering another slice of her homemade bread, "we have a deal. You get to stay here instead of all by yourself in your dad's company apartment in the middle of New York. And in exchange for that, you fit in. I'll tell you this—a man can't wedge clay forty pounds at a time if he doesn't get his nutrition. Look at the difference between your arms and Caleb's."

Caleb looked at his own forearms, below where his shirtsleeves had been rolled up, as if he'd never seen them before. Her boy worked hard and without complaint, and he had the tanned, strong muscles to show for it, even at fourteen. There was a reason the Amish didn't bother to go to a gym or jog, Sarah thought with an inward smile. After the kind of day she and Caleb put in, who would have the energy?

Eric looked from Caleb's to his own pale, skinny arms. Then at the salad bowl, conveniently located next to his elbow.

"I'm not eating those yellow flowers. They probably have bugs in them."

"I'll eat them," Caleb said, removing the last two and popping them in his mouth. "Try the green goddess salad dressing Mamm made. It's really *gut*."

Sarah felt a sense of satisfaction at seeing the vegetables go down. If nothing else, the boy would go home with two weeks of nutritious meals and exercise under his belt. And then maybe he'd have the emotional stamina to deal with his family. Perhaps that was what Henry had meant.

After the prayer at the end of the meal, Caleb cleared the table. "Come and help me wash the dishes."

"Is it as hard as making a bed? Priscilla taught me at the Inn, but it was a lot to remember."

"*Neh*. Much simpler. They go in dirty, they come out clean. Do you want to sing a song?"

While Sarah swept up the kitchen floor, Caleb taught him the Noah song and how to wash dishes, both of which her boy had learned when he was hardly taller than the tabletop. Eric picked up the song quickly, and she smiled at the sound of two boyish voices in her kitchen once again.

Henry rigged up the Coleman lamps in the living room, and when the sweeping and the dishes were done, Sarah settled into her favorite chair next to her mending basket, while Caleb got out the English Bible.

"What are we doing?" Eric wanted to know.

"At night, before we go to bed, Caleb reads a little from the Bible so that we go to sleep with God's words in our minds," Sarah explained. "Especially since tomorrow is Sunday. We do not go to church until next week, but we'll still spend some quiet time together in the morning."

Eric seemed less concerned about tomorrow than tonight. "Before we go to bed? It's only eight o'clock." He looked around. "My superhero cartoons come on at eight. Where's your TV?"

Caleb grinned. "No electricity. No TV. No radio, no computer. But tomorrow we have lots of cows to milk at Daadi's place, so you'll be glad to go to bed."

"At eight o'clock? I don't think so."

"That gives you eight hours of sleep, Eric," Henry pointed out.

Eric did the sum in his head. "You get up at *four in the morning?*" Eric's dismay seemed to be deepening with every word they said. "I don't have to, do I?" He appealed to Henry.

Sarah kept silent. This was the moment where Henry needed to back her up. Henry had been the one to allow— even request—that Eric stay. If Eric were to do so, he would need to learn their ways for two weeks. If Henry backed down so that the boy would become merely a special guest who did not participate in family life, then she would gently suggest that Eric stay at the Byler place instead of at hers.

Her heart went out to Eric, getting ready to step into the world so wholly unprepared with even the smallest knowledge of how a household worked—or of what responsibility meant, or how it felt to be valued as a part of something bigger than himself. It would be good for him to stay. She could pack lots of lessons into two weeks. He had crossed three states to come here and work with Henry at the pottery studio. If he was willing to do that, he would be willing for the rest.

"I'm afraid you do," Henry told Eric with gentle firmness.

Sarah's back relaxed into the cushions of her chair.

"Sarah has agreed to feed you, keep your clothes clean, and give you a bed to sleep in. I've agreed to teach you as much as I can in the two weeks we have. We're both giving something. What are you giving?"

It was clear that, as determined as he was to learn and despite all he'd done to get here, Eric was used to thinking in terms of getting, not giving.

"This is what you can give in return for the gifts we're giving you," Henry said. "You can help Caleb with his chores. You can work in the garden, picking the vegetables you're going to eat at dinner—and yes, you'll eat them. And I'm sure there are other things you can help Sarah with when we're not working in the studio."

"I would love to have the beds made as nicely as the ones at the Inn," Sarah said wistfully, as if this possibility had been denied her all her life. "And the boy who helps whip the frosting for the whoopie pies is the boy who gets to lick the beaters afterward."

"No fair," Caleb protested.

"There are two beaters," she reminded him, playfully lowering her voice as if it were their secret.

"So that we don't have to have this conversation again, do you agree that it's fair and right that everyone pitches in?" Henry asked.

After a moment of thought, Eric nodded his head, once. Then he nodded again, several times.

"*Gut*, then," Caleb said. "We're reading from Matthew this week, Eric." He handed him the Bible and pointed out the verse where they'd left off the night before. "It's in English. Start right there."

Dear Priscilla,

Well, I just had my first experience at doctoring someone and I don't know how Michael's Sarah does it. I suppose you heard that Simon got his foot stepped on by a horse, and since we got no way to go to town except by begging a ride, or to pay for a doctor except by begging for an advance against our wages, it was up to us hands here to look after him.

Walt the foreman is an EMT but he couldn't do much but ice it and give Simon a couple days off. Then Sarah's package came last night and you should have seen Walt's face when I started putting old burdock leaves in the pot he uses to boil water for his instant coffee. Anyhow, I did what Sarah's instructions said so now we have to wait and see.

Simon's pretty upset about not being able to work but Walt told him to quit it. Everybody gets stepped on and he has a whole list of tasks that a man can do sitting down while he mends. Ha ha. Simon's learning how to patch jeans and ain't he thrilled about that. He already knew how to peel potatoes and shuck corn, which is good because we eat those a lot and it saves Teresa the cook having to do it. She parked him at the big table in the kitchen today and he works with his foot up on a chair. Course, he gets treats but I guess you have to have something to make up for missing out on rides and men's work.

We been here a whole month now and I still miss home. I don't know how them fellows who leave the church manage it. We haven't got down to visit the

Amish church yet but we hope to soon. I'm glad you like working at the Inn. Me and Jake helped Dad do some work around there a while back. Ginny is a nice woman. Her sticky buns are real good.

I hope you'll write back soon. I like the sound of your voice in the words.

Your friend,
Joe Byler

# CHAPTER 24

On Monday, after Sarah had done the washing and hung out their shirts, pants, and dresses to dry on the line—with the underwear hung discreetly inside on the drying rack in Simon's room—she harnessed Dulcie and set off in the buggy for the Peachey place.

Linda had been on her mind a lot since the last time she'd seen her, and after a couple of weeks of her patient drinking the tea, Sarah was anxious to know if she was seeing a change. With any luck, Benny would be at home, and she could take him into the fields and show him the kinds of herbs she needed for his aunt's health.

But mostly, she was just glad to get away by herself. That Eric, he was a strong-minded one. She'd known it going in, but it was one thing to hear about his epic journey, and another to see that same stubbornness in her own house.

Luckily, Caleb was not the kind to mimic bad behavior. He had less patience with it than she did—she supposed because he was not prepared to let Eric get away with anything he couldn't do himself.

Yesterday morning, her father-in-law had set the *Englisch* boy to simple tasks in the milking parlor, and sheer awe of his size and his beard and the way his kindly gaze still managed to pin you down had apparently made Eric decide that obedience was the only way he'd survive the experience. And to give him credit, he'd made the beds after breakfast. All of them, much to Sarah's surprise. But he'd had a hard time sitting through the Sunday reading and singing, there in their own living room, and after lunch Caleb had finally taken him off to Henry's, where he stayed until supper.

Dulcie slowed for a cross highway and Sarah carefully looked both ways before they made the left turn toward the Peachey place. Bringing up boys was no easy matter. She had been lucky that Michael was such a good father—and that his father had stepped in to fill that place when Michael had been taken from her. She was surrounded by good men.

Even Henry had not completely forgotten the upbringing of his childhood when he had stepped up to support her without her needing to say a word. Someday, she hoped, he would see that he belonged in their world still. After all, his reactions to others were Amish reactions. He took the place of authority when it was needed—such as with children—and the mantle of *Uffgeva*, or humility, when it was needed. He wasn't proud about his art, and other than the little sign at the end of his lane, which was no more and a lot less than any Amish craftsman might put there, he was very close-mouthed about it.

The Peachey place came into view and Sarah turned in. At least the garden was coming along well, given that it had to feed the family when all else failed. It needed a good weeding, though. She left Dulcie cropping grass and crossed the yard.

The door opened and Linda stepped out. "Sarah, *ischt gut* to see you. Are you giving me a checkup?"

"I am." She pretended to give Linda the once-over, and

then looked more closely. "Your skin looks better. You're getting more sleep, aren't you?"

"*Ja*, I am. I never would have believed it. By the time I take the last cup at night, I'm ready for bed and fall right to sleep. Come into the kitchen and let me see what I can fix for us while we talk."

She brought out a coffee cake that had a few slices left from breakfast, and poured two cups of coffee from the pot on the stove. It was bitter, but Sarah swallowed bravely and poured in some extra milk without saying a word.

"Isn't the weather beautiful?" Linda said, gazing out the kitchen window. "I'm half tempted to be like Benny, and go have a swim in the creek."

"Is that where he is?"

"He and Leon said they were taking their youngest brother fishing, so I hope they catch something. Arlon and Crist went to Whinburg to get some crates from the pallet shop there, and Ella went with them. So I'm home all alone and it's very tempting to play hooky."

Sarah made up her mind. "Why don't we? I'd love to take a ramble through your woods to see what I can harvest."

The Peachey acres included a wooded stretch along a shallow bend in Willow Creek across from the Esh farm, one of the largest in the area. Through the trees, Hiram Esh's neatly planted acres stretched into the distance, reminding Sarah again of the contrast between the two families. Linda seemed as much at home in the woods as she did in the kitchen, but that could be because both places were one step removed from a wilderness.

No, that was unkind. She must stop being so critical. But, Sarah told herself, the only reason these thoughts came was because she wanted to help. Linda's condition and her inability to conceive would be improved by some peace. Some security. Her own home. But how?

The local swimming hole was below the Rose Arbor Inn, but here, upstream from the splashing and play, was where the fishermen tended to congregate. As Sarah and Linda walked the path trodden smooth by generations of people who knew the secret of the pools and logs where the trout fanned themselves, she debated how to bring up the subject.

"Look." She bent to a clump of plants that bore white flowers. "Feverfew."

"I thought those were daisies."

"They belong to the daisy family, it's true. Ruth uses them for migraine headaches, so I'm going to try a tincture." She picked a number of stems with lots of healthy leaves and flowers, and walked on. "I was hoping to see Benny. If he runs across any more mullein plants in the fields, I could sure use those, too."

"I told him, but Benny—he has a memory like a sieve. He and Leon found pieces of an old buggy out in these woods and they've been busy fixing it up. I hardly see them."

Sarah kept her mouth shut. *It's not my place. It's not my place.* But Linda's health was her place. "I know we've spoken before about you having a peaceful home of your own."

Linda nodded, and stretched up to pick a stem of orange daylily from a clump growing on the bank above the path. Her slender figure looked as though it was gaining a little weight. No wonder her face looked more relaxed, between the lady's mantle tincture and the tea. "We have. And I said I didn't know how we would manage it. Or that we would want to." She glanced at Sarah. "It's not so bad, you know, what God has given us. There is enough on the table, and when there isn't, our families are happy to help out."

"I know, but I honestly feel that you would bloom better in a field of your own."

"But how? Just for the sake of discussion. There are no places to rent around Willow Creek."

"But there might be. What about Sadie Byler's place?"

Twirling the lily between her fingers, Linda walked on down the path. "But that *Englisch* potter has it now. Her nephew."

"I know, but he doesn't farm it. His cousins and uncles do. What if Crist went in with them, and you rented the house?"

Now incredulity fought with politeness in Linda's gaze. "Would you have me turn a man out of his home?"

"No, of course not, but he's seeing a woman in town—Ginny, who has the Rose Arbor Inn. If they were to marry, it would make sense for him to move to the Inn, and then the farm would be available. And even if they don't, it's a big house, and he spends most of his time in the studio in the barn. He might be convinced to rent it to you, and just keep a room for himself. I know he appreciates a woman's good cooking."

They crested a little rise, and below them could see the Peachey boys on the wide, sunny bank on the far side, casting lures into the water. Up- and downstream, boys who did not have the work of men to do gathered to exclaim over one another's catches, clearly delighted to have something to bring to the supper table.

The few seconds of watching the boys seemed to have given Linda a chance to organize her thoughts. "Thank you for thinking of me, Sarah, but Crist would never agree to move in with an *Englisch* man."

"He hasn't fixed up the house with electricity. In many ways, he still lives according to his upbringing."

"But he is not Amish. We don't even know him, and even

if we did, we couldn't be in fellowship with him." She turned to take Sarah's hands, her eyes gentle and earnest. "I appreciate your care for me, I really do. But you must turn your mind to your other patients. I—I do not want to move off Arlon and Ella's place."

Disappointment and concern hit Sarah hard, right below her heart. "But Linda, surely you must want a home of your own. A baby—"

"I'm content, Sarah. And so must you be." With a squeeze, she released Sarah's hands and began to climb down the bank to the creek. Sarah scrambled after her.

"What if Henry were to offer his place to you?"

"Why would he? He doesn't know us."

"He would if I brought up the idea, and introduced you."

"Sarah."

"*Ja?*"

"*Neh.*"

Sarah got a grip and reined in her galloping imagination as she reached the water. "I'm sorry. You're right. I'm interfering in a matter that should only be between husband and wife. Please forgive me."

Linda smiled her forgiveness over her shoulder, and stepped out on a flat rock in the water, one of many that were scattered over a submerged gravel bank where the creek took the bend. This was how the boys got to the flat meadow on the other side, but it had been a long time since Sarah had crossed a creek by hopping from rock to rock.

She made the last jump into the sedge and her sneaker slipped. With an exclamation, she teetered, and Linda turned just in time to grab her hand. "Careful!"

They pulled each other up into the grassy meadow and Benny waved.

"Aendi Linda! Sarah!"

"How are they biting?" Linda called.

"*Gut*—we'll have fresh brook trout for supper." He lifted the wriggling brown body he'd just unhooked from his line, and gaffed it with quick efficiency.

"We've come to find herbs," Sarah said. "Have you seen any mullein—the tall, spiky plant with the yellow flowers—that grows on the side of your hill?"

"There's lots in the back pasture." He baited the hook and the line sang as he cast it out into the water again. "That's where we found the buggy."

"Well, next time you go back there, you might pick me some in trade for your *Aendi*'s treatment."

"Happy to." He grinned at her, and then his bobber dipped and he whipped his full attention back to landing another fish.

"We'll leave them to it," she said, and then spotted Caleb and Eric upstream. "I'll just go see my boy and then we'll head back. I don't think you should be out in this hot sun."

Linda rambled back to the water's edge where the stepping-stones were, and Sarah made her way over to the younger boys. "Hallo. Any luck?"

Caleb grinned. "Eric's caught one and I've caught one."

"If you catch two more, I can fry them for supper with sliced potato chips."

"Really? We'll eat these?" Eric said. "These ones we caught?"

"We sure will. If God directed them to your hook, He clearly meant us to eat them."

"Or they just swam there by mistake."

She laughed. "Either way, we will not waste them. Do you have a ride home?"

Caleb nodded, watching the water carefully all the while. "Benny said he'd give us a lift. I think he wants to go bug Priscilla after."

Poor Priscilla. Being energetically courted by Benny Peachey couldn't be easy on a girl—especially if he didn't seem to be able to recognize *no* when he saw it.

Sarah recognized no. She just didn't agree with it. For Linda's sake, there had to be something she could do.

CHAPTER 25

Henry had to admire the kid—he didn't give up, whether that meant trekking across the country or showing tricky bubbles who was boss.

Once he'd learned how the kick wheel operated, Eric sat hunched over it, working a lump of clay into a round saucer shape, then into a cylinder. He'd already made three, but of course they were off center, or the walls were uneven, or they wobbled back into blobs before he could get the pressure of his hands right.

But he didn't give up.

He kept pressing, and pulling, and trying, and trying again.

They'd fallen into a rhythm during the first few days. Eric was up on Amish time, unlike Henry, so he'd do the milking with Caleb and then have breakfast, either with Sarah or at the Jacob Yoder place. From what Caleb said, Eric thought that Jacob Yoder was some human incarnation of an Old Testament prophet, and hardly had the courage to speak at all in the same room in case he got zapped by lightning.

Henry would get up at seven, eat, and they'd meet in the studio for the morning's lesson. While Eric practiced—rolling coils or slabs, or using the wheel—Henry would apply himself to his natural forms, experimenting with ideas or perfecting what he'd done the day before. He always answered questions, and when Eric got himself into a knot he couldn't get out of, Henry was the one to start him over.

Frustration at one's inability was hard enough. He'd have plenty of mistakes to correct when he was on his own.

Meanwhile, the cutout lantern had been trimmed, dried, and fired. Tomorrow, when the kiln was cool, they'd pull it out and see how it looked.

The boys had gone fishing yesterday, and Henry had had a moment, wishing he'd gone with them and then enjoyed the dinner that Sarah had made out of their catch. But instead, he'd gone to Ginny's.

For the second evening in a row.

As if their thoughts had connected across town, his cell phone rang and her name appeared on the screen.

"Glutton for punishment, are you?"

"I'm'a have to talk to you about this self-esteem problem you ex-Amish have," she said with affection. "Are you coming over tonight?"

"I don't want to wear out my welcome."

"No chance of that. A girl can get addicted to actual conversation after all this time alone—and I'm not talking about post-divorce, either."

"Ginny, you have people there constantly, and when they're gone, you have Priscilla and Kate. You're never alone."

"Socializing for work is different from conversing for pleasure."

She had a point. And so later that day, after Eric had gone back to Sarah's, he found himself wearing the river path a little deeper on his way over to the Inn. And not for the first time, reminding himself that he had a car and knew how to use it. He shouldn't be squeamish about leaving it in the parking lot, no matter how late it got when he finally went home. Ginny might want to go to Strasburg or even Lancaster, to see a movie or enjoy a dinner out. Surely, deep down, he couldn't really believe that anyone would care how long his car was parked over at her place?

Paul and Barbara didn't have much reason to come this way, and other than Sarah and the Yoders, they were the only people he really knew in this neighborhood.

Sarah would never say anything. But she would think plenty.

*Is that the reason you leave your car at home? So she'll think you're home and not with Ginny?*

Sarah Yoder was nothing more than a friend—despite that odd moment the other night when she had done a very Amish thing and yielded the man's place to him in dealing with Eric. It had been a very long time since he'd experienced that very feminine submission—and since he'd left the church at nineteen, he hadn't had a chance to experience it much to begin with.

It had felt strange, and a little scary, as though she were thrusting him into a role he had no preparation for—that of parent. But the strange thing was, he had stepped into it naturally and with only the briefest of hesitations, as if he'd known instinctively that taking the lead in teaching a boy was indeed his place, and not hers.

Not that he had much to offer in the parenting department. But he had Eric's respect, and by supporting Sarah and showing her his respect in turn, his example would teach the worldly boy that she was the one he would have to listen to.

Henry allowed himself a brief moment of amusement at what Eric's parents would think of all this. But since they'd flown off on their own business and abdicated responsibility to him and Sarah, they couldn't complain much, could they?

When he shared some of this with Ginny, she just shook her head. "I never got the chance to raise a family," she said, offering him a second rack of barbecued ribs that were better than anything he'd ever had in the Denver steakhouses. "But even I can't imagine just dumping your kid on people you didn't know hardly at all because it wasn't convenient to come and get him. How does poor Eric feel?"

"To be honest, I don't think it bothers him all that much. I mean, he took off from Connecticut without a whole lot of concern for how his parents would feel when he came up missing, right?"

"I suppose," she admitted, and took the last of the salad, heaping it on her plate.

She didn't make it with nasturtiums, but it was still a really good salad, and he was enjoying it.

"I guess that's just how they are, as strange as it seems to us," she said at last. "How does Sarah feel about her houseguest?"

Hearing her name on Ginny's tongue gave him a jolt. "She's adjusting. You know how the Amish are about obedience. I don't expect Eric has had a lot of practice at that."

"I'll say. Mostly he just did his own thing when they were staying here." She paused, and then said, "But aside from that, it's classy of her to take him on."

"She offered."

"But he could have stayed with you."

He smiled at the thought. "We might have killed each other at the end of the first day. I haven't had any experience with parenting—my sisters are still in the church, so I wouldn't see much of them, and my brother died a few years ago. I send cards to my nieces and nephews on their birthdays, but other than that, I haven't been around kids in years."

Her eyes softened, then she lowered her gaze to her salad. "Do you ever want a family?"

"I've never given it any thought. After Allison—after she died—I pretty much concluded that family life wasn't going to be my thing."

"But that was, what—ten years ago? Twelve?"

Ten years, six months, and a few days. "Something like that."

"You could have found someone in that time."

He would have reached out to touch her hand, but he had barbecue sauce and coarse-ground pepper all over his fingers. So he let his gaze fill with affection and touch hers.

"I think I might have."

"And what if I haven't completely given up hope?"

"Of having a family? I hope you haven't. You'd make a fantastic mother."

Her dusky cheeks colored, and her lashes fell again. She was enchanting. He wanted to wash his hands and take her into his arms, but by the time he got back from the sink, the moment would have passed. So he said, "You might have to cut back on the innkeeping a little. Or at least share it with an assistant manager."

"Well, that's the advantage of this line of work." She recovered quickly. "Babies can sleep in the kitchen as well as their rooms. Toddlers can play in the study. And kids can certainly have a whale of a time on the hill and down in the creek. This is actually a pretty good place to bring up a passel of kids."

"You sound like you've given it some thought while you weren't giving up hope."

"A woman does, you know, while she's waiting for the right baby-daddy to come along."

What a crazy expression. "Is that slang? What does it mean?"

"It's what you call the father of your children if you're not married to him."

A little frisson of alarm ran through him. "Oh, you'd want to be married to him." He paused. "Wouldn't you?"

"I've been married, Henry. I liked it... but I like not being married, too. If children were involved, though, you're probably right. Marriage would be the right thing to do, though when the divorce was going through, I swore never again." She dipped a piece of her roll in the salad dressing. "What was that you said a second ago? About how you might have found someone? Did you mean that or are you just flirting with me?"

He swallowed the last of his rib with difficulty. "Do I strike you as the flirting kind?"

With a smile of acknowledgment, she pushed his water glass toward him and he drank. "No. It's refreshing to talk with a man who says just what he thinks. No games, no stories, no sarcasm."

"I meant it." This time he did get up, and on the way to the sink to wash his hands, he took both their plates. She followed with the salad bowl and the other serving dishes, and they both began clearing up the kitchen as if it were the most natural thing in the world. "See how easily we work together? And we'd talk all night if we got the chance. It's been a long time, like I said. And kind of a miracle, really, to find a woman like you in a town this size."

"My ex would say it was God's will."

He believed in God, he supposed, but not the God he'd

grown up with—that watchful, frightening being who cared so deeply about the widths of hat brims and the shapes of buggies and the truth of every thought that flitted through a boy's mind.

"I'm not sure God concerns himself with bringing people together, though my mother would have said the same as your ex. She always told my sisters that God had a specific man in mind for them, and the only way to know who he would be was to pray. It always seemed to me that was a risky way of going about finding your mate. What if you got it wrong? What if you misinterpreted a sign?" He took the dishcloth from her and wiped down the counter. "Just one of many things that didn't add up for me."

"So you don't think you'll ever go back?" Her sure movements in restoring her domain to order stopped as she turned to him. "You're *Englisch* for life now?"

He dried his hands and took her into his arms. "I have many more reasons to stay than to go back," he told her, and that was the end of the talking.

# CHAPTER 26

Mamm opened Priscilla's bedroom door and leaned in. "You're just going to have to tell him the truth, *Liewi.*"

Pris had dashed upstairs to hide in her room when Benny Peachey's awful buggy had come rattling down the lane after supper, and now he was outside visiting with Dat, who for some inexplicable reason had not sent him packing.

"I have," Priscilla moaned. "I've told him that I'm writing to Joe, but he doesn't seem to get it. Can't you ask Dat to tell him to go?"

"To hear the two of them, you'd think Benny had come to see him." Mamm twitched the quilt straight, though there was hardly enough room for the two of them in Pris's little bedroom. "Here's an idea. How about we go out and sit together on the porch swing, and if Benny wants to speak with you, he can, and I'll be there to help if you need me."

Relief swept through her. "I've had enough of being alone with boys. Joe was the only one who felt like a friend. I can't figure out what Benny wants, and as for Justin—"

Too late, she snapped her mouth shut.

"Justin? That *Englisch* boy?" her mother said carefully.

Priscilla thought fast. She didn't want her mother to worry about someone she would probably never see again. "*Ja,* the one from the Inn—the older brother of that boy who ran away and is staying with Sarah Yoder."

"It was his parents who thought you were stealing. Were you alone with him? Was it all right, *Liewi?*"

Mamm looked so worried that Priscilla got up off the bed and hugged her. "*Ja*, it was all right. He thought he deserved the attention of every girl in the county, and when he didn't get it—well, I was never really alone with him. And he's gone now anyway. It doesn't matter."

Her mother gave her a squeeze and released her. "But Benny is not gone. Come downstairs and we'll take out some lemonade and cookies and have a nice visit."

When they came out onto the porch, they found Benny's horse tied up and he and Dat talking easily, Benny on the step and Dat in the wicker chair beside the door. Mamm put the laden tray on the little table between the chair and the swing, and offered Benny some lemonade and cookies.

"What brings you out this way?" she asked as he took them.

"I came to see Priscilla…and you folks." He bit into a lemon shortbread cookie with relish. "These are real good."

"That's good of you," Mamm said. "Especially when we'll see you on Sunday. How are your folks?"

"Mamm and Dat are well. Dat and Crist are up to something these days—but we don't know what. They went to Whinburg to get a crate to pack something up in. Me and Leon think they finally hit on something that works, and they're sending it away to someone who wants to buy it."

Priscilla usually didn't pay much attention to what the Peacheys did over there in their woods and unkempt fields. "What do you mean, something that works?"

"Aw, they make stuff in our barn. Inventions—you know, like if you wanted to make your stove run on solar power."

"Why would we do that?" Mamm wondered aloud. "It works just fine on propane."

"But some things don't. And Dat and Crist like to tinker until they do. That's why I think whatever went in that crate must work."

"But you don't know what it is?" Pris asked.

Benny turned to her eagerly, as if he was happy that she'd noticed him taking up space on their porch steps. "*Neh*, it could've been anything. But one of these days they'll think up something good and everyone will want one, and then me and Leon can have a new buggy."

"Seems to me you'd get there sooner if you put in some long days in those fields of yours," Isaiah Mast observed. "Better to depend on the crops God brings out of the earth than on the efforts of man with machinery."

"That's true," Benny allowed, "but Dat and Crist, they want to do good for the *Gmee*. Some of these things have worked—the solar panels on the roof work real well."

"I hear all the money from last fall's potato harvest went for those panels."

Which might be why everyone on the Peachey farm was extra skinny now.

Benny nodded. "But they save on gas for the generator. It keeps going up, but the price of sunlight stays the same." He grinned at his own joke. "Say, Pris, want to go for a drive?"

Any boy but Benny would have found a way to ask quietly, privately, at a get-together or after singing or any other place but on the front porch, right in front of a girl's parents. Priscilla waited half a second for Dat to tell him that no daughter of his was going anywhere with him, but when there was no sound except for Saranne upstairs, laughing at something Katie had said, she realized she was going to have to do this herself.

"I can't, Benny. I have the rest of my chores to do yet tonight."

"Ain't got 'em done yet? It's near dark."

"I worked yesterday and I have to work tomorrow, but I still have to do my share at home." When was Dat going to conclude that she wasn't about to get into any more trouble? She thought he might relax about his rule after the Parkers had given her such a hard time, but he hadn't. There was always hope, though... which was why she didn't pull against the traces very often.

"Another day, then? Say, Sunday afternoon after church? We could go for a drive. Leon could ask your friend Rosanne."

"Leon's a bit old for Rosanne," Mamm finally put in. "Isn't he close to twenty?"

"*Neh*, only eighteen. He's too shy to do anything by himself, but if we double dated, it would be okay."

Priscilla had had enough.

"Benny Peachey, I've told you before that I'm writing to Joe. That means I don't go for rides with other boys behind his back."

"You could write and tell him if you want. I've known Joe all his life—he's a Woodpecker same as you and me. He won't mind."

"*I* would mind." Did she really have to say this in front of her parents? No, she couldn't. "Benny, let's go for a walk in the orchard and get a few things straight."

Another grin, nearly as bright in the twilight as the first

flickers of the fireflies dancing over the lawn. "You're a pushy one, ain't you?"

She didn't dignify this with a reply, merely got out of the swing, smoothed down her dress, and walked down the steps right past him.

"Thanks for the cookies and lemonade, Lillian," he said to Mamm, and wished Dat good night as if he and Priscilla were going into town for an ice cream and wouldn't be back until midnight.

Boys, honestly.

The grass was soft under her bare feet as she crossed the lawn and made her way under the branches of the apple trees. To one side, she heard the soft murmurs of the chickens as they roosted up for the night in their shed, jostling for space and insisting that the pecking order be observed, even in sleep. The air was soft, still humid but cooling now that the sun had gone down.

It was the perfect evening for a walk. What a shame Joe and Simon were a thousand miles away, and all she had to share this beautiful evening with was Benny Peachey, who wouldn't recognize romance if it fell on his head like a windfall apple.

Not that she wanted him getting ideas along that line.

"Nice evening," he said, catching up to her with his longlegged stride.

She didn't waste time on pleasantries. "Benny, I'm not going to date you. I've told you time and again that I'm writing to Joe, and it's just too bad of you not to listen to me."

"I ain't planning to kiss you, if that's what you're worried about."

As if she'd ever allow it in a million years! "Why did you tell *Englisch* Henry Byler we were courting, then?"

"Aw, I was just trying to get your goat. I can see you're stuck on Joe."

She stopped dead in the grass and put her hands on her hips in exasperation. "Then what did you come over here for, pretending it was for me? Dat is probably wondering what on earth is going on."

To her surprise, the bravado fell away and he reached up with both hands to grip an overhanging branch, as if he planned to lift up his feet and swing on it like a monkey. But instead, he just hung on, stretching his arms. "I don't have any girl friends, you know."

"I can see why, if you tell everyone you pass on the sidewalk that you're courting them."

"*Neh*, I mean friends who are girls. To talk about things with. To ask things of."

That took the wind out of her sails good and proper. "What things? Can't you ask your Mamm?"

"She wouldn't understand. And maybe she'd even get mad." The bravado and humor had leached out of his voice, and in the dusk it sounded uncertain. Young.

Did he have a crush on one of her friends? Did he want to know if someone in her buddy bunch liked him back? But why would that make his mother upset?

"Why don't you tell me," she suggested at last, mystified.

After a few seconds, he said, "There's someone—what if—what would you do if someone was thinking about doing something…and other people thought it was the right thing, but you thought it was wrong? Would you speak up? If it was none of your business but you still had feelings about it?"

How was she supposed to answer that? She fell back on what she knew to be true. "If something is the right thing, how can it be wrong?"

"Things can be right to some people, and wrong to other people. It depends where you're standing, like whether the creek is running toward you or away from you depending on which way you're looking."

"Benny, just tell me what's going on, otherwise I don't know enough about it to help you. Is it one of the Woodpecker boys? Is he thinking about jumping the fence?"

In the twilight, his head jerked up, like a horse surprised by a gopher. "Jumping the fence? *Neh*, not that. At least, that I know of. It's *Englisch* Henry."

If she had been confused before, it was nothing to what she felt now. "Why should you be concerned with what *Englisch* Henry does? He's not one of us anymore. He doesn't have to follow the *Ordnung*. And besides, deciding that someone is doing something right or wrong is prideful. Who are you to judge him?"

She couldn't see his face all that well, but the outline of his head against the last of the light in the sky bobbed up and down in agreement. "All that you say is right. But…well, I heard Sarah Yoder talking with Aendi Linda, and it seems *Englisch* Henry is engaged to your boss."

It was a good thing she was leaning on the old Pink Lady's trunk, or she might have fallen right over in surprise. "That's not true. She would have told us."

But would she? True, Ginny had been awfully happy lately. She was a cheery person to begin with, but Pris had never heard her singing over her breakfast pans until recently. Or doing her hair in pretty ways, with braids and things. But it didn't follow that there was a man involved, did it? Couldn't an *Englisch* woman sing and do her hair differently for no other reason than she felt like it?

But if Sarah said it was so, then it must be, mustn't it?

"Maybe, maybe not. But if it is, and he moves off the farm to be with her, I'm afraid Aendi Linda and Uncle Crist would move there, and our family would be all in pieces, like it was before Linda came."

Pris said nothing, which was good, because Benny was rolling now, like a hay wagon gathering speed down a hill.

"Linda and Mamm are good friends. That's not to say that Mamm and Dat don't get along. Sometimes they don't. Sometimes it's me and Leon's fault, though. But since Crist married Linda, it's just been better. We don't have a lot, but it's home, and I don't want it to change."

"There's nothing wrong with them wanting a home of their own."

"I don't think they do. That's the problem. I think that Sarah has been working on Aendi Linda, and now she's thinking about it, and Uncle Crist will do anything in his power to make her smile. I'm afraid that if she goes to work on him, they'll really do it."

Priscilla tried to untangle all this and get to the bottom of what he really wanted from her. "So you think that while the *Gmee* would believe it's right for them to move out, it isn't really?"

"I don't know what I think," he admitted, his voice low. "That's why I needed to talk to somebody. Leon's no good for this stuff. If you need to bait a hook or fix something, he's your man, but not for talking things over and trying to figure things out."

Priscilla girded up her loins. "You want your aunt and uncle to be happy, don't you? If it's God's will that they move out, and they obey Him, then they will be."

"But maybe we won't," he said miserably. "How can it be God's will for them to be happy and not the rest of the family?"

But figuring out God's will was a task far greater than Priscilla could ask or think. "I don't know. But Benny, this isn't your business. Whether you think it's right or wrong what Sarah's doing, or what they're doing, it's got nothing to do with you. Just hoe your own row and don't look over at anyone else."

"But it's our *family*."

"And they're married and church members and whatever is God's will is what will happen."

From his silence, Benny didn't seem very satisfied with this for an answer, but Pris couldn't imagine what other answer she could give.

"What if I talked to Henry, and asked him to bring Ginny to the farm instead?"

With a sigh, Priscilla said, "This is grown-ups' business, and nobody will thank you for stomping into their row. You know what, Benny? You should be glad you don't have a dad like mine. If he heard me talking this way, he'd give me even more chores to do, to keep my nose where it belonged. That's my advice. Go back to the farm and find work. Do something to help your family with your hands instead of—of this."

"Will you do something for me? Will you ask Ginny if it's true that she and Henry are getting married?"

"She'll tell me to mind my own business. They haven't known each other but a couple of months."

"You know old people. He probably wants someone to cook for him, and she probably wants a man around the place."

Priscilla had never seen any evidence of Ginny wanting any such thing, but again, what did she know?

"If it comes up, I'll ask. But if it doesn't, I'll mind my own business. And now I'm going back to the house. I'm making some pot holders for Mamm's birthday and to sell at the Amish Market, and they won't sew themselves."

When they passed the porch, in the warm light from the lamp in the dining room Priscilla saw that Mamm and Dat were now rocking contentedly in the swing, Dat's arm around Mamm's shoulders. Marriage was a mystery. Her parents had sought God's will for their lifelong partner, and He had shown them both the one person in the world that He had chosen. But presumably this work had gone on in Arlon and Ella's lives, too.

Why, then, did Benny feel the family was "in pieces" without Linda's influence? Should Arlon have married Linda? But she came from a different district altogether, so that didn't make sense. God had arranged for her and Crist to meet, not her and Arlon.

Priscilla held Benny's horse's head as he climbed into the buggy. This whole subject of courtship was a puzzle, for certain. At least she was feeling fairly settled about Joe. She had no idea if he was The One, but she was perfectly content to answer his letters and hear his news about the strange new world out West. As for Simon, she was well over him. She'd been concerned to hear about the horse stepping on him, and hoped that in his next letter Joe would tell her Simon was recovering, but her heart didn't make that leap of anticipation at the sight of his name that had been her experience before.

Joe didn't make her heart leap—or only a little anyway. It was his steadiness she appreciated. And he liked the sound of her voice in her letters. Which wasn't even something she could control, and yet he still liked it.

It was nice to be liked just for being yourself.

"Well, good night, Pris," Benny said, picking up the reins. "*Denkes.*"

"I don't feel I helped much other than telling you what you already knew."

"Sometimes that's all a person needs to hear."

"You'd be better off finding out what *der Herr* wants you to hear."

"*Ja*, maybe. Tell Joe hey when you write next."

"I will."

"Tell him he's a lucky fellow, and if he's not careful, I'll still steal you away."

"I will not."

Chuckling, Benny flapped the reins over the horse's back and the ancient buggy with its peeling top heaved itself into motion.

Boys, honestly.

Dear Joe,

Thank you for your letter. It sounds as though you did real well doctoring Simon—I probably wouldn't have kept my head nearly as well. How is he doing? I haven't seen Sarah to ask her. Tell him hello from me and I hope he mends up quick.

I suppose you heard your cousin Henry on Sadie's farm is engaged to my boss, Ginny Hochstetler. I didn't hear that from her, but then, she's not obliged to tell me her personal news. She sure seems happy lately, and I was talking to Benny Peachey and he says it's true. He says to say hey, by the way. I always thought he was a harum-scarum kind of boy, but it seems he thinks about things, like whether something is right or wrong. I wish he'd think a little harder about helping out on the farm, him and Leon. I don't know what they do all day but fish and swim and find girls to bother.

If you hear anything of him and me, it's not true. I'm writing to you and that's that.

We've been having real fine weather and the garden is going crazy. We even have tomatoes already. Dad has a healed-up ankle though that tells him when the weather is going to change, and he says it's been bothering him. We'll have to see which is right—Dad's ankle or the back page in the paper!

I'm making pot holders with pieced fronts that look like chickens for my mother's birthday. I made about a dozen extra because Evie Troyer said she could sell them at her stall at the Amish Market. I hope that's true, and that Dad lets me keep the money. It will pay for paper and postage, ha ha.

I'll let this do for now.

                              Your friend,
                              Priscilla

# Chapter 27

The most exciting part of pottery, after creating a shape that satisfied his hands, was glazing it in a way that brought out its beauty and allowed light to give it that extra dimension that satisfied the eye as well.

Henry wondered if artistic philosophy might go over Eric's head, but then said it anyway. Fellow artists needed to discuss what they loved about their craft, no matter at what stage they found themselves.

To his surprise, Eric nodded. "It's the glaze that I look at first, and then the shape, and then I figure out what something is used for. Mom took us to a craft fair once and I spent the whole time talking to the potters about what makes brown, or blue, or that shiny stuff."

"Shiny stuff?"

"Like when it rains and there's oil on the puddles."

"Ah," Henry said. "That's called *iridescence*, and it's part of what I'm using in my sky and water glaze."

"Can I use it on my lantern?"

Here was a poser, where a man had to tread the fine line between using the resources at hand and using someone else's creation to get credit for his own.

"Can you justify to the admissions panel that you conceived and mixed the glaze as well as applying it?"

Eric stopped peeking into the five-gallon buckets of minerals and mixtures that were neatly labeled and lined up under the workbench. "Would I have to do that?"

"Probably."

The boy gazed into a bucket, but Henry got the impression he didn't see the contents. "Dad's not going to let me go, you know. He calls every night, and even when I tell him what we're doing and how much I'm learning, all he cares about is if I'm being a pain in the neck to Sarah."

"Nothing wrong with that. Are you?"

Eric made a face. "One false move and Caleb's grandpa will take a pitchfork to me."

"I doubt that very much. The Amish don't believe in violence."

"Then how come they spank their kids?"

"People have been spanking their kids for thousands of years. It's only lately that it's gotten political. But getting back to your dad, the way to show him you're serious about the school is to show him you've changed. That you're prepared to do what it takes—even if what it takes is boring stuff, like helping out around the house and making beds like you do at Sarah's."

Eric raised his eyebrows in an *Are you kidding me?* face. "Making beds is going to help me get into an art school? Ri-i-i-ght."

"Making beds is going to show your parents you're willing to work hard and make their investment worthwhile. That you're not just sitting there with your hand out, expecting them to cough up the cash."

"They have the cash."

"Not the point."

"But what if—" The sound of crunching wheels in the gravel stopped him, and he swiveled to see out the doors. "You've got a customer. In a big van."

"It's probably an Amish taxi." That many Amish folks in a van probably meant customers, a welcome interruption, so he washed his hands quickly and tucked his shirt into his jeans. An old straw hat hung on a nail next to the door, so he slapped it on his head—not so they'd think he was like them or was giving respect to their traditions, but because it was hot and bright outside the barn, and he had no idea what had become of his sunglasses.

Two guys were standing on the barn ramp, looking around the farm with their hands on their hips, like Realtors sizing up the value of a place. In the open doors at the back of the van, a girl with tattoos as thickly applied as sleeves on both arms was heaving on a metal box of the kind that musical instruments or other high-end equipment came in.

"Good morning," he called, and the two guys swung to face him. "What can I do for you?"

"Are you Henry Byler?" The older one came forward, his hand outstretched, and Henry shook it.

"I am."

"Great." His face broke into a smile. "I'm Sol Edwards, and this is Kyle Madison. We're the film crew that Dave Petersen from D.W. Frith sent to do the video segment."

Henry distinctly felt his jaw sag in astonishment. "What?"

Kyle dug in his jeans pocket for his phone. "We got the date right, didn't we? Thursday the twenty-fifth?" He scrolled through his e-mail and showed Henry the screen.

It was a message from Dave Petersen confirming the date and saying that while he hadn't yet spoken with Henry about the exact time, they were good to go.

Dave Petersen hadn't yet spoken with Henry because...
well, other than the ones from Ginny, he hadn't picked up
any of his calls. He knew there were messages on his phone,
but he'd been so consumed by his work and Ginny and
dealing with Eric that nothing else had seemed very important.

Except that D.W. Frith was important if he planned to
have a career. What had he been thinking, ignoring Dave
Petersen's number? Was he setting himself up to fail before he
even started?

"Sorry," he said, pasting on a smile that he hoped was re-
assuring. "I've been pretty busy and it completely slipped my
mind. Can you brief me on what we're doing?"

At the van, another box of equipment thumped on top
of the first one. Why was the girl doing all the heavy lifting
when there were two perfectly strong and healthy men standing here? He took a couple of steps toward her. "Can I help
you with that?" he called.

"No," she said. "Do I look like I can't handle it?"

"Don't mess with Carmen," Kyle said. "The cameras are
her department, and she will tear your head off if you get a
fingerprint on them."

Too late, Henry saw Eric emerge from around the back of
the van and reach inside.

"What do you think you're doing?" the girl snapped, her
red, angular haircut swinging as she whipped around.

"Helping you." Eric froze in mid-motion, his hands
around a box about two feet square.

"Did I ask for help?"

"You shouldn't have to ask. If a person sees work that needs
to be done, he should pitch in and do it."

Henry distinctly heard the echo of Caleb's voice and, behind that, Sarah's, but the urge to smile was buried in the need to save Eric from having his head torn off.

The girl regarded him. "You aren't Amish."

"Nope. But I still want to help. Is this all camera equipment?"

"Yes. Break something and I break you."

"Okay. Where do you want it?"

"Here for now. I want some establishing shots. Maybe you can be my guide. You live here?"

"No, I'm taking pottery lessons from Henry. But I can show you stuff."

"Deal. Watch that, it's heavy."

Sol exchanged a glance with Kyle. "That's a first."

"I heard that," Carmen called.

Henry began to revise his assumptions about exactly who was in charge here. "So what is your plan, Sol? Eric and I were about to start glazing, so if we're talking hours here, that's going to affect our schedule."

"Not hours, I hope," Sol replied. "A couple maybe. And I know you Amish are sketchy about having your photo taken, so mostly it'll be shots of the farm and the surrounding area, which we won't need you for. For the interview, maybe we could—"

"I think there might be something lost in translation here," Henry interrupted gently, before the error went any further. "I'm not Amish."

"You're not?" Sol looked him up and down, and Kyle began to look worried. "You look Amish."

Henry pulled off the straw hat, and ran his hands through his distinctly non-Amish haircut. "It's just a hat that was hanging in the barn. I thought Dave was clear on this. We already talked about it."

"That's not what we were told," Kyle said. "This video is for the home page of the D.W. Frith website, introducing your line of pottery, right? The marketing department is going crazy about the Amish stuff—back to the land, simplicity for your home, made by hand, all that. They're thinking fifty thousand hits a day."

"I suggest they think about the pottery, not about their marketing slant, then."

Sol adjusted his weight, as though he were digging in for some serious persuasion. "You know as well as I do that the marketing brings the customers in, and the product sells them. The creative brief said you were Amish."

"I used to be. And I explained to Dave that I'm not now. It wouldn't be honest to market me, as you say, as something I'm not. The people buying my pieces aren't getting anything more than the piece itself. They're getting a Byler bowl, not an Amish bowl."

Again the exchange of glances between Sol and Kyle. "That's what you think. Because what marketing is selling is a shared experience of Amish life, my friend, not just a bowl."

"How do you want to play this, then?" Kyle finally asked his colleague, when it was clear Henry—who had run through a dozen things he could say and decided against all of them—wasn't going to speak. "Because this isn't how the script reads."

"There's a script?" Henry managed.

"Talking points," Sol said, and then raised his voice so the woman at the van could hear. "Yo, Carmen, better cancel the establishing shots of the women and kids in the garden with the bonnets."

"Sarah's probably in her garden," Eric put in.

"Never mind Sarah," Henry said hastily. "Bad enough I

might have to do this. I'm absolutely not allowing my Amish neighbors to sell the *experience* by appearing in a video."

Sol looked as though a lightbulb had gone off in his mind. "But that's how we can get around it," he said. "The magazine copy is all 'Amish fields and flowers' so the outdoor shots can be about that. Your house. Your neighbor's garden. Bonnets in the distance, you know? No identifying shots or faces—oh yeah, they briefed us on that. Can we do close-ups of you in the hat?"

"It's an Amish hat. It says something about the man who wears it—primarily that he belongs to the church."

"Yeah, I know. Do you have any suspenders?"

"No." Henry was getting more than a little concerned. "I'm not dressing up Amish for this. It would be a lie. I left the church two decades ago and have no plans to go back."

Sol looked crestfallen. "No on the hat. And the shirt's just a plaid shirt, not a solid like those guys in town were wearing. So how are we going to shoot you?"

Carmen had finished unpacking her equipment, and hefted a video camera the size of a suitcase onto her shoulder. "Okay, kid. Show me some fields and flowers. And a few bonnets would be good."

Henry started forward. "No, you can't—"

"Mr. Byler, do you want those fifty thousand hits or not?" Sol demanded, clearly coming to the end of his allotment of persuasion. "Either I get this segment filmed today or I don't get paid, and D.W. Frith is one of my best clients. They're probably one of yours, too. Now, do we make them happy using whatever means we have available, or don't we?"

If he refused, Henry had no doubt that whoever wanted those fifty thousand hits on the website would make good and sure his pieces were relegated to the bargain basement, and that would be the end of his career outside the confines of the Amish Market in Willow Creek.

Eric and Carmen were nearly to the top of the hill behind the barn. "Eric, if Sarah is outside, run down and ask her if it would be okay to film her garden. If she's not, only go to the fence. I won't allow trespassing."

"Great." Sol brightened, clearly taking this as permission to go ahead with whatever Plan B was. "Kyle, get busy with the lights in the pottery studio so Carmen doesn't have to stand around waiting when she gets back. Meanwhile, Henry, if you don't mind, we'll wire you up with a mic so we can do some voice-overs. Any chance you can sound more Amish?"

Henry didn't even reply to that one. Instead, he allowed Kyle to hook a battery pack to his belt at the back, and run a microphone wire up under his shirt to clip on his collar.

"Now, if there's anything you don't feel comfortable answering," Sol said, "just say, 'No comment.' Picture yourself talking to a customer who's stopped by your studio. Be relaxed, breathe, don't be afraid to pause and think before you answer. We're going to scrub everything in post, so any slips of the tongue will be taken out, too. Be natural."

*Be natural.* "That's an un-Amish concept. The natural is something to be overcome in favor of the spiritual."

Sol nodded at Kyle, who nodded back, and Henry realized he was being recorded.

"So in one way, I'm going against my upbringing when I focus my work on natural forms, but in another way, I'm celebrating the shapes and curves that the Amish believe God made, and turning the lily of the field into something that can be used in home and kitchen."

There. That wasn't so hard.

As Henry talked, he thought less about the man he used to be and more about the man he was now. He talked about his process, and the more he told Sol about the forms he created and the glazing method he'd discovered down in the creek bottom, the more Sol drew him out until his philosophy of art was articulated in full.

When Carmen came back, Eric was still in tow and Caleb was with him. "Who's this?" Sol wanted to know. "Do we have a release to film him?"

"No," Henry said quickly. "This is Caleb, and he's under-age."

"It's all right, Henry," Caleb said. "This lady already filmed Mamm and me from the top of the hill. She promised she wouldn't show our faces. I wanted to come and see. I've never seen a film before."

"Caleb, I want you to go home." He wouldn't put it past any of this crew to sneak a few shots of the boy without anyone being the wiser. That's all he would need, is to have Caleb's face seven hundred pixels wide on fifty thousand computer screens.

"But Henry, I just wanted to—"

"I know, and I'm sorry. Take Eric with you."

"Henry!" they both complained.

"Now, please. Eric, I'll come over and get you when I'm ready to start on the glazing."

Slumping, dragging their heels, the boys slouched out of the barn and their voices faded as they climbed the hill.

"That was a shot for a different commercial," Carmen remarked. "Did I really just see two teenage boys do what they were told?"

"Never mind," Sol said. "Come on over here and we'll film Henry working. Tight focus on his hands, and Henry, if you'll just wear the hat, we can do some three-quarter shots from above with the voice-over."

Pointedly, Henry hung the hat on its nail near the barn doors, and took his seat at the wheel. Sol sighed and turned away to give Kyle some instructions about the lighting.

Maybe the key was to be very un-Amish and not cooperate much. The sooner he did that, the sooner he could get this crew out of his barn and get back to work.

# CHAPTER 28

Sarah set off for sisters' day at Corinne's with a couple of jars of face cream for Amanda in her basket, a letter for Corinne in her pocket, and a heart lighter than it had been for some time. The prospect of actually sewing had always been a daunting one for her, and her family seemed to have determined by mutual consent that she should be the one in the background of a quilting frolic making everyone comfortable—seeing that there was enough coffee made, preparing the snack for after the work was done, and sweeping up the cut threads around the quilting frame.

As long as no one put a needle in her hand and expected ten stitches to the inch, it was a place she was happy to fill.

Corinne's delight at the sight of the letter warmed Sarah's heart. Her mother-in-law wanted for nothing, so it wasn't often Sarah could give her a gift that made her as happy as sharing a letter from Simon.

Dear Mom,

I'm sitting at the kitchen table in the big house with a few minutes to spare before Teresa the cook gives me my next job to do. I wanted to thank you again for sending the leaves and things so fast. They seem to be working. Joe—who is a pretty good doctor—changes the dressing every night before we go to bed, and while it's a messy business, it's better than losing the toe, or at least the nail. It's still pretty ugly, but the swelling is going down fast. The foreman wants to know what's in the leaves that does that. Maybe you could tell him when you write next. And probably send another big jar of B&W because this one is only going to last another week.

They keep me busy in the kitchen. I've peeled more potatoes than I ever knew existed in the world, mixed biscuits, kneaded bread, dropped cookie batter on sheets by the hundreds, and even mixed up a cake or two. Teresa says I'm real handy in the kitchen, but I'd sure rather be out on the trail with Joe.

He's gone again this week, with a family group from some big city in the Midwest. There are probably seven girls around our age in the group, plus four guys our age and a little younger, plus a bunch of kids and all the adults, so he and the trail boss are going to have their hands full.

One of the girls was making eyes at him. Don't tell Priscilla. He carries Pris's letters around in his pocket. Don't tell her that, either.

One thing about being laid up is it gives you lots of time to think. And while they're real nice here and are treating me like I'm actually doing the job they hired me to do, it's not home. I don't know what Joe's got in his mind, but I'm thinking that when the snow flies in October, I'll get back on that train and come on home. I miss you and Caleb and Grandma and Grandpa and the family. Even if I was walking properly, we probably aren't going to get down to the Amish settlement until September, when things start to slow down here at the ranch. It feels funny not going to church. Guess I'm not cut out for Rumspringing and the English life the way some people are.

I hope you are keeping well. Please share this with the family.

Love from your son,
Simon

"That is such *gut* news," Corinne breathed, passing the letter on to Amanda, who read it eagerly while Miriam did the same over her shoulder. "I know you didn't want him to go out there and did everything you could to stop it—but Sarah, if it makes him realize his need for God and the church, then it has all been for the best." Corinne took her seat on one side of the new quilt, a Flower Basket that she and Amanda had pieced and was now neatly pinned to its batting and backing and rolled up on the frame, ready for its first stitches.

"I see that now," Sarah said, "but if I had it all to do over again, I'm not sure I could stop myself from trying to do the same."

Amanda handed the letter to Barbara Byler and went out of the room. When the door closed to the bathroom down the hall, Sarah pulled up a chair next to Corinne and said in a low tone, "What has happened to Amanda? She's so pale. Is she sick?"

"Lovesick," Miriam murmured, threading her needle with a long skein of black thread.

A niggle of worry swam through Sarah's stomach. So much had been happening in her own life and that of her patients that she had not given a single thought to Silas, who had been staying with Miriam and Joshua. "What happened?"

"I wish I knew," Corinne said. "She hasn't confided in me. She just keeps refusing dessert and half her dinner and won't say what's on her heart."

"She talks to you," Miriam said to Sarah. Down the hall, the toilet flushed, and she said quickly, "See if you can get her to tell you what the problem is. Because she's not acting like the usual girl in love."

Amanda wasn't like other girls, so that wasn't surprising. Then again... lack of sleep and weight loss weren't so unusual if you were staying up late with someone and trying to slim down a little. But as Sarah moved between kitchen and dining room, stealing glances at Amanda's face and downcast eyes as her dutiful needle rocked through the layers of the quilt, she realized that the girl hadn't been using the skin cream she'd given her, either.

A woman who wanted to bloom for her man by losing weight would not skip the skin regimen that would add to that bloom.

Something was wrong.

There was nothing to do but bide her time until the quilting was done. The quilters spent the morning anchoring the layers of the quilt, beginning in the middle and stitching in the ditch along the flower basket blocks. They managed to anchor about half the queen-sized quilt before sore hands demanded that they break for snack time and coffee. Even then, Amanda did not seem inclined to take herself off alone so that Sarah could corner her. It wasn't until Miriam and Barbara had gone, taking their oldest sister and her two nearly grown-up daughters with them, that Sarah and Amanda finished doing the dishes and Sarah saw her chance.

"Amanda, maybe you could come out to the garden with me? Corinne said she has a big crop of dock leaves out behind the springhouse, and I want to send Simon another batch. Between him and the little boys around here this summer, mine are nearly all used up."

Amanda hesitated, but her giving nature overcame whatever had briefly held her back. "I'll get the garden scissors."

Fed from the spring that bubbled up out of the ground and ran down a dip in the property that led to the larger body of Willow Creek, the dock leaves were luxuriant and bursting with the curative agent that God had put in them.

When she said this to Amanda, the girl smiled, a poor replica of her usual twinkle and humor. "Are you going to tell that to Simon's foreman, who wants to know what's in the leaves that heals so well?"

"I just might. It's the truth—and while I might look up what the curative compound is in my herb book, it doesn't hurt to give a word in season."

She slid her sister-in-law a glance. "What's wrong, *Liewi?* You're pale and thinner, and you're not taking care of your skin like you have been." She wouldn't even mention the dark circles under her eyes. That would just heap more on a soul that was probably already far too aware of her own imperfections.

Amanda snipped at a clump of leaves, the sound sharp and artificial under the soft rustle of the breeze in the trees behind them, and the melody of a pair of wrens circling the bark looking for insects. Off in the field, a bobwhite asked his eternal question, calling for a mate.

"I can't talk about it with you." Her voice was nearly as soft as the rustling leaves.

Sarah knelt next to her, struggling against the ambush of

pain. There was nothing they couldn't tell each other, except maybe details of marriage and childbirth that weren't fitting for an unmarried woman to hear. But when God changed that, Sarah had no doubt that she could share those things freely, too.

And then the last few words sank in. "With me? Why not with me?"

But Amanda just shook her head, and tears beaded on her lashes.

"Is it Silas? Has something happened?"

Amanda straightened and turned away, the scissors dangling from her hand. Finally she tossed them to the ground and wrapped her arms around herself—a protective gesture that Sarah didn't miss.

"Have you been seeing something of each other?" Sarah asked softly.

"*Ja.* I've been over to Miriam and Joshua's a number of times to see the progress on the bathroom. It's done now. As you probably noticed, Miriam is as happy as if fifty Christmases were all rolled into one."

"I did notice when we were talking around the quilting frame. But if the renovation is done, does that mean Silas will be going home?"

"That... is the problem."

"If you care for him, I can certainly see that it would be."

"*Du versteht nichts*, Sarah."

"Help me understand, then, *Schwechsder*." Sarah slid an arm around her hunched shoulders and gave her a squeeze. "Whatever it is, I want to help you. This pale face and these unhappy eyes hurt my heart, and I don't think that any of my teas and tinctures will cure it."

Amanda nodded. "I should know better than to keep anything from you." Still hugging herself, she raised her face to the sun, its late-afternoon light turning the curves of her face a buttery gold. "You remember when Zeke and Fannie were here and I told you that Silas spent most of our ride home asking questions about you?"

Sarah did, all too clearly. "*Ja.*"

"Well, over the last several days we've had other things to talk about—the renovation and how it was going, the latest edition of the *Budget*, what we heard in church, and lately, that funny *Englisch* boy who is staying at your place. Silas was quite concerned about that."

"Why? He's just a boy."

"I don't know. But he seemed quite exercised about it. Anyway, the renovation was done and I walked over to see it, and after supper, he hitched up the buggy and gave me a ride home."

"That was kind."

"And he said that he was ready to go to *his* home, but if he had a reason to stay, Miriam and Joshua had made it clear that he could use the guest room at their place as long as he wanted to."

"Doesn't he have his own farm?" Sarah tried to remember the details. "All I can think of is that cellular phone tower in his field and how Zeke disagrees with him for allowing it to be there."

"I gather the farm is mostly in hay because of it. His bishop might have something to say if too much money comes in and he risks becoming proud or complacent, so he didn't plant his fields with a cash crop."

"Silas doesn't strike me as a proud man." Hay took care of itself; it didn't have to be weeded or even watered much. A month's absence by the husbandman wouldn't bother it a bit.

"So during your ride, then, did he ask you to give him a reason to stay?" She hoped so. Oh, how she hoped that he would finally have seen Amanda's wonderful qualities and realized he mustn't miss his chance.

"He did. And I asked him a question in return."

"That must have taken courage. What was it?"

"Whether he was staying for me, or because he still had some hopes of you."

Sarah's heart gave a great thump and she pulled in a couple of deep breaths to steady it. "Me?" she managed.

"He told me that he had asked to court you first. And that you said you were not ready for courtship because you were setting yourself apart for the work of a *Dokterfraa*."

"That's all true."

Amanda whirled on her. "Then why didn't you tell me, Sarah? All this time, we've been having family dinners and sisters' days and going to church together, and you didn't say a word—you just let me like him and have my silly dreams and all the time he wanted *you*—had spoken to you so you knew he did!"

"I didn't—I—"

But Amanda plowed on, the lid blown off the pressure cooker at last. "The last thing I want you to think is that I'm proud, or offended. But Sarah, it would take a much better woman than me to be happy about being a man's second choice." She choked. "Is it so much to ask to be a *gut* man's first choice? Will I ever get that chance? And if I don't say yes to Silas, will I ever get a chance of any kind?"

The corners of her mouth pulled down as the rain followed the storm on her face, and she yanked up her apron to scrub the tears from her cheeks.

"Amanda. Oh, *Liewi*, I never meant to hurt you so." Sarah

pulled her unwilling body into her arms and let her cry, shaking with sobs and gripping Sarah's dress as though it would hold her up. Sarah eased her down to the grass and simply held her, letting her get it all out before she tried to speak.

Amanda gasped for breath and hunted blindly in the pockets of her dress, but Sarah beat her to it with a hanky. When she'd blown her nose and quieted a little, Sarah sat back on the grass and let the warm breeze flow between them for a few moments.

"The whole time he was talking to you about me," Sarah said gently, "I was talking to him about you. Every chance I got, I put the two of you together. I found out that Fannie and Zeke and even your Mamm were planning to try their hands at some matchmaking between him and me, and I put a stop to it before it could even get started."

"And yet...he hoped."

"It's what we frail humans do, don't we? Even in the face of sure disappointment, we think that if only we try hard enough, or argue long enough, or come again faithfully enough, the person will see it our way. I have to give him credit. After our second discussion on the matter, he finally accepted that what I said was what I meant, and after that it seems he focused his attention on you, where it should have been in the first place."

"He thinks he's too old for me." She blew her nose again.

"Do you think so? Have you heard his story?"

Amanda nodded. "Miriam told me he'd been deserted by his fiancée on their wedding day—just as the ministers were upstairs with them before the service started. And that it has taken him years to get over it. He's a little bit like *Englisch* Henry in that way. And maybe even you."

Sarah resisted being linked with Henry in anyone's mind,

even though it seemed to happen no matter what she did. "When you love, you don't stop with the person's death—or marriage to someone else," she said. "Some days, it seems as though I've just lost your brother. Other days, our wedding day seems so far in the past that it might have happened to someone else. But on both kinds of days, the love is still there. Still strong." She paused. "If Silas has come to the place where God is prompting him to find another to share his life, then it's *gut* he's obeying that prompting."

"By asking you if he could court you," Amanda said glumly.

"*Ja.* It was a step. Whether it was in the right direction is up for debate."

Amanda tried to smile, and failed. "But what should I do? The feelings that had been in my heart have just... died. As though a frost has settled on them and killed them."

"Is there any hope that they might come up again in a different season?"

"I don't know," the girl whispered. "I may not have a season to find out. He may just go home and court someone else."

"Will it bother you if he does, is the question."

But Amanda just shook her head. "Poor girl. She would be third best."

"It's not profitable to look at it that way, *Liewi.* Instead, think of it like this—his feelings for me must not have been that deep if he could turn to you so soon and see all your good qualities. Which is what I wanted him to do with all possible speed."

This time the smile perched on her lips, swaying, before it fell away. "What should I do, Sarah? Tell him to stay? Or let him go?"

"I don't think you should tell him anything. I think you should be your usual self, and he won't want to go away. Let your smile come when it wants to, and sing if you feel like it. Use my skin cream and eat blackberry pie when you want some. Get some sleep and think on what God says in His Word…and like a bee coming again and again to a flower, he won't be able to leave. And then you'll know he's staying for the real you—and that you are first among women."

Amanda patted the last of the salty tears from her cheeks. "You make it sound so easy."

"These things are not up to us, you know. If Silas is the man God has chosen for you, you'll know it—and so will he."

"I—I hope he is," Amanda whispered. "Maybe there is a green shoot or two still surviving under the frost."

"Then wait for the sun to come and thaw it out," Sarah advised her with a smile. "Now, come and gather up these dock leaves with me, so it doesn't get back to Silas that I was neglecting the health of the *Gmee* while we sunbathed in the grass—after I told him I was dedicating myself to that purpose."

Amanda retrieved the scissors and they finished harvesting the leaves. As they carried the green armfuls back to the house where Sarah had left her basket, she wondered again at just how much Amanda saw in people that they didn't realize themselves. It was a little like diagnosing an illness—and in some cases, there was no cure.

Like loving those who were lost.

Not for the first time, she gazed over the cornfield that climbed the hill behind her five acres. The hill that stood between her home, filled with life and good food and noisy boys, and Henry Byler's solitary, shabby house, filled with silence.

# CHAPTER 29

Henry snapped open the latches on the heavy lid of the kiln and glanced down at Eric, who shifted with a mix of impatience and anxiety next to him. "Ready?"

"What if it broke? Then what?"

"Let's take one thing at a time. You did everything right. The likelihood of breakage is no greater on your lantern than it is on any of my batter bowls. Come on. Let's have a look."

The lid swung up and Eric gripped the top edge, gazing into the cooled kiln as though it were a wishing well. The pieces they had stacked in here for the firing made a riot of color against the drab brick walls. Henry removed the cones, which melted when the kiln reached the correct temperature, and discarded them. Then he began to lift out the pieces.

On the top level were four batter bowls, two with the peony-leaf handles and glazed in a tawny green and gold, and two with handles that ended in a flourish like a wave curling against a shore, painted in his new sky and water glaze.

"Look at that," Eric breathed. "Did it come out the way you wanted it to?"

Henry held up the bowl, which gleamed with iridescence

along the rim and handle, the gentle lines his thumbs had made suggesting water and the movement of air. He nodded, slowly, hardly daring to believe that so many weeks of work had come to fruition in a piece so beautiful.

"It's almost exactly how I saw it in my head," he said on a long breath that mixed relief with quiet satisfaction. "I might add the iridescence to the interior on the next batch." He handed the bowl to Eric. "What do you think?"

But Eric shook his head. "I think it would be too much. You don't see the light in the deep pools in the creek where people swim, do you? Just along the edges, where the water is moving faster."

Henry gazed at him with the respect of one artist for the opinion of another. "I didn't think of it that way. But you're right—if I'm going to work with natural forms, they should behave the way they do in nature, shouldn't they? Otherwise, I'm serving myself and my own tastes, not what the piece is meant to be."

Eric grinned back at him, his narrow shoulders relaxing under his clay-stained *Star Wars* T-shirt. "I thought you'd be mad at me for criticizing."

"Honest critique with positive value is a different animal from criticizing. Now, let's move these over to the bench, and we'll unload the next layer and get to your lantern."

Henry removed the spacers and revealed the next layer, then bent in and took out the top and bottom pieces of Eric's lantern.

"Here you go. Put them together and we'll have a look."

The finished dome gleamed with a coppery glaze on the bottom that continued into the flat tray of the base. But above, like the sky seen through autumn leaves, the copper color gave way to a speckled blue and finally, at the knob handle, to a blue so pale it almost looked white. On the sides, the cut-out geese shapes flew from right to left, their edges smooth and uncracked.

"It's beautiful, Eric," Henry told him. "Good work. I like the color choice, even though I wasn't sure how it would turn out. Good for you for sticking by your decision when I was all hung up on the yellow instead of the blue."

The boy cupped a hand around the top and rocked it in its groove. "The bottom's still uneven. See how it doesn't sit quite right?"

"Your first major piece and you're worried about that? It'll come in time. Give yourself a chance."

"But the admissions people will see it."

"They'll be so taken up with the goose shapes and the way you graduated the color that a little unevenness in the body won't even register. This is a good piece of work, Eric. Be proud of it."

"Caleb says pride is bad."

Of course he did. "All right, then, be glad you created something that's not only useful, but it can also give pleasure to others. How's that?"

Eric touched the lantern, tracing the cutouts as if checking for any roughness he'd missed. "Do you think Mom would like it? Her birthday's in September."

"If you're going to submit it to the school, she'll see it. It won't be a surprise."

"That's okay. I want her to know it's hers, especially if it gets me admitted. Then it'll mean something, you know?"

Henry couldn't help himself. He ruffled the boy's hair, then slipped a companionable arm around his shoulders. "It already means something, kiddo. It means talent and hard work and guts. And if it comes to mean acceptance, too, then good on it, but it doesn't need the approval of other people to be a very cool piece of art."

"Is that how you feel about your batter bowls?"

And with a strange feeling of recognition, he realized he did. "Yes. Yes, I do. I mean, it's great that D.W. Frith wants them, and I'll be able to pay the taxes and fill the fridge for the rest of the year. But mostly, I'm pretty happy with what we've got here, and if I never show a single thing or get written up in another paper for the rest of my life, I still know the work is good. And for us artists, maybe that's all we need to know."

That sense of satisfaction stayed with him as he showed Eric how to pack the pieces in the crates he'd ordered from the Amish pallet shop in Whinburg. Eric's lantern got its own small crate, but before they packed it, Eric took a picture with his phone.

"To show Mom and Dad," he said, his thumbs busy typing out an e-mail.

In less than a minute, the phone pinged and Eric dug it out of his pocket again. "It's Dad." Then he handed the phone to Henry.

> To: ericnotpeter@email.com
> From: Trent_Parker@SeaboardOil.com
> Very nice. I hope it's been worth two weeks in Amish land. Pack up—I'll be there tomorrow night to get you. Mom & Justin coming in Sunday so we can pick them up at the airport on our way home.
> Dad

"Tomorrow?" Henry repeated, handing back the phone. "That soon? It feels like you just got here."

"It feels like I've been here for, like, a century," Eric said. "In a good way. At first I hated it, especially getting up so early. But Sarah's nice and Caleb is cool, too—you know, for an Amish kid."

"You're pretty cool for an *Englisch* kid," Henry informed him, reaching out to ruffle his skater-boy hair again.

Eric grinned, dodged under his hand, and scooped up a last handful of packing popcorn. "I don't want this getting busted on the way home. Can you drive me over to Sarah's? It's too heavy to carry over the hill."

"All right. And then do you know what? I think we should have a farewell party for you. If your dad is coming tomorrow, you won't have a chance to get around and say good-bye to everyone you know here."

"Oh…no, do I have to?"

"Eric, it's not a matter of have to. It's different here. You get involved with people—like Priscilla and Benny, for instance, who helped you in the first place. And Sarah, and Caleb, and Jacob and Corinne. Even Ginny. She asks about you every time I see her."

"Can you do that? Make a party like that?"

"Well, not as well as Sarah or Ginny could. Why don't we ask Sarah first? Then if she says yes, we can invite the others."

Sarah wasn't in the garden when they got to her place, but when Eric carried the crate into the house, Henry saw movement in the compiling room.

"Sarah? It's me, Henry. I brought Eric back with his lantern. It's all done." He paused in the doorway, watching the slender figure in the sage-green dress and black kitchen apron moving confidently from shelf to table.

"I'll just be a minute." Carefully, she measured a dropper full of liquid into a small brown bottle, then put a funnel in the mouth of the bottle and filled it to the top with—he squinted at the label—grape seed oil.

"What's that?"

"I'm making oregano oil. It cures toenail fungus."

That would teach him to ask questions he didn't really want to know the answers to.

"I have a customer who's *Englisch* and as stubborn as an old mule. It's taken me two months to convince him to eat his vegetables. Now he tells me he's had toenail fungus for months and did I have something to cure it. Sure I do. He has to soak his toes in white vinegar for ten minutes every other day, and then put a drop of this oil on each toenail afterward. But if he follows my instructions even once, I'll be surprised." She stuck a handwritten label on the bottle. "Why do people resist being made well?"

"Maybe they don't really believe that something so simple will help them. We *Englisch* are used to just going to the doctor and taking a pill."

She gave him a sharp glance at "we *Englisch*," but said nothing. Just in case she had ideas along that line, he changed the subject. "Eric heard from his dad this morning. He'll be here tomorrow night to pick him up. It would be nice for Eric to be able to say good-bye to the friends he's made here, but I don't think there's time for him to get around to everyone. I was wondering...could we have a farewell dinner for him here?"

"What a good idea. When?"

"Tonight?"

She glanced at her watch. "It's already nearly noon. That's not much time—we go over to Jacob's, you know, on Friday nights, so I don't have anything prepared for a company dinner. But I thought you said his father was coming tomorrow. Can you wait until then, so he can join us?"

It hadn't even entered his head. "I suppose we could, if you thought that would be better." He wasn't sure Trent Parker would fit in so well in an Amish kitchen, but what did he know? Maybe the man would surprise them all.

"It would. And since it's Saturday night, we should keep it small and quiet—and early. Many of us will want to prepare for Sunday. Church is at Lev Esh's, you know. Caleb has been helping at the work frolic over there today."

"I wondered where he was. I was thinking Jacob and Corinne, and Priscilla, and Benny Peachey, and Ginny. Those are the people Eric knows."

Sarah turned away. "Benny will be thrilled at any excuse to give Priscilla a ride over here. I'm not so sure how thrilled she'll be. Can Ginny pick her up?"

"I was going to collect Ginny." And take her home again. Which was the first time he'd thought of it, but now that he had, he didn't want it any other way.

"Oh." Sarah's voice was muffled as she squirted the strong-smelling oregano extract into another bottle, then diluted it with grape seed oil. "Of course. Well. I'll invite Jacob and Corinne, and Priscilla. You'll have to drive over to the Peacheys' to tell Benny—they don't have a phone, and there's no shanty on that spur of the road. It's a dead end."

Henry nodded, though she wasn't looking at him. "I can see you're busy, so I'll head out. I'll check in tomorrow and you can tell me what you need from town in the way of groceries."

"*Denki*, Henry."

But she spoke absently, measuring and eyeballing levels in the brown bottles, and he slipped out the door without disturbing her further, wondering what he'd said to bring on the chill.

Since he had the car out, he'd swing by the Peachey farm now and issue his invitation to Benny Peachey, and drop by Ginny's afterward instead of calling. Then again, Henry thought as he bumped and crunched his way down the Peacheys' weedy lane in low gear, it might have been smart to leave the car out on the road and do this on foot. An *Englisch* vehicle had probably not come down this drive in years, if the tall weeds swaying between the dual set of buggy tracks were any indication.

He was wrong.

When his car emerged from the trees into the yard, he found that not only was there a big Chevy diesel truck parked there already with some telecom company's logo on the side and a toy-hauler hitched to it, but the whole family was out there, hugging each other and hooting and generally whooping up such a ruckus that he wondered if he'd come to an *Englisch* farm by mistake.

But no, there were Benny and Leon, red-faced and breathless, hanging on to each other as if they'd fall down otherwise. Benny pounded on his thigh with his free hand and hollered, "I knew it! I just knew it would happen someday!" He caught sight of Henry as he got out of the car, and galloped over, Leon on his heels. "Henry! Did you hear the news?"

"Did you win the lottery?" Henry asked before he realized what he'd said.

But Benny didn't miss a beat. "Naw, even better. This ain't the wages of sin, so the bishop won't make us give it up. Dat and Onkel Crist, they finally hit it big, and that man there with the truck is the one who made it all happen."

"Who is he? What happened? Is your mother all right?"

For Ella and Linda were hugging each other on the front porch, both of them in tears—but from here, Henry couldn't tell if they were tears of joy or of despair.

"It's a shock, but she'll get over it. She and Linda, they had a hard time believing, even though they never said a word to us boys. But they'll believe now. See, Dat and Onkel Crist, they didn't plant a second crop of corn—or a third, either—this year at all. They sank the money they had left into solar panels and batteries."

"Uh-oh."

Leon chimed in. "We got talked to by Bishop Troyer, which is kinda funny because he does mechanical conversions himself, and you'd have thought he'd see where this was going."

"Where what was going?"

"It's for them cell towers, Henry," Benny said eagerly. "They run on county power, but when the power goes out, they got these big old battery packs for backup. What Dat and Crist did was invent a battery pack powered by solar panels. So not only does it use less power, but the solar chips in and helps out, so it costs less to run."

"Wow," Henry said. "Your dad and uncle must be smart men."

"They been tinkering long enough to invent the washing machine all over again," Leon said. "Batteries ain't nothing to them."

By this time, Crist Peachey had detached himself from their first *Englisch* guest and come over to see what the second one was there for. The boys quickly introduced him and brought him up to speed on what they'd told Henry, and when Henry reached out to shake hands, the other man did so with a smile. "You didn't tell him the second part of the story, boys."

"To try it out, we get our very own cell tower!" Benny burst out. "Mamm's not so sure she wants to grow metal poles instead of corn—"

"But for the money they're offering, it won't take long before she's convinced." Crist laughed. "We won't be the first— I was talking with our brother Silas Lapp, who's staying with Joshua Yoder, and he's got one in his field. We never did much with these fields anyhow," he said, turning to look past the barn to the closest one, where a crop of corn was about half the size of everyone else's. "The cell tower will be the most profitable crop they ever seen."

"Congratulations," Henry said. "Say, Benny, I just remembered what I came over for. Can you come to Sarah's for supper tomorrow night? Eric is leaving the next morning with his dad, and he wants to say good-bye to all his friends here. I figure that includes you, since you pretty much picked him up off the street and saved him from sleeping under someone's porch."

"That'd be real nice. But you know, Pris helped. Is she coming?"

Henry took the plunge. "Maybe you might collect her on the way over."

Benny's grin was even wider than it had been over the astonishing family news. "I'll do that. That sounds just fine."

Leon gave him a punch in the shoulder and their father called them over. Henry figured he'd been forgotten in the general merriment, and nodded at Crist in farewell. The man nodded back, unable to keep the grin off his face, and went to see how his wife was surviving the good news.

At least, that was what it looked like to Henry. The willowy woman with the brown hair under the organdy *Kapp* turned to Crist as he loped up the porch steps, and her hand went to her belly in a gesture as old as time. Henry had seen that protective bend of the wrist a couple of times in his youth, before his mother had told the family but after she'd told his dad.

Well. A baby might grow up in a ramshackle environment, but at least there was love enough to go around—and it seemed there would be no shortage of food on the table, either.

# CHAPTER 30

Eric and Caleb were running races up and down the lane, but Sarah had a feeling it was a thinly disguised way to keep an eye on the road for Trent Parker's SUV. She'd seen the boy take out his phone twice now and look anxiously at the screen, as though he almost expected his father to cancel at the last minute, or change the plan. They'd let Trent know that he was invited to supper and to stay the night—Eric had already put fresh sheets on Simon's bed and made it up to perfection, so that his father could sleep there and he could camp on the air mattress in Caleb's room.

But whether Trent Parker would go along with this was another question. He hadn't replied to the last message.

The windows were open and the scent of baking macaroni and cheese filled the kitchen. The boys had requested Eric's favorite dish, and since Jacob was going to barbecue outside when they got here, and Priscilla was bringing two kinds of vegetable dishes, all Sarah had left to do other than slice a loaf of bread and put out some pickles was to make a salad.

She collected her basket from the compiling room and took it out to the garden. Her crazy-quilt mix of vegetables, flowers, and herbs was at its best now, and as she brushed by the dill and mint, the sweet and spicy scents mingled in the air as if to greet her.

Up on the hillside, the "keys of heaven" was blooming, its tiny red flowers forming a mist of beauty and concealing all the hard work the roots were doing among the rocks. Where the soil was deep enough, banks of golden and orange daylilies nodded in the breeze, and the hum of bees was like a bass note under the shouts of the boys and the whisper of the leaves above her head.

Lettuce first, both butter and romaine. She knelt beside the plants and got to work. Some spinach and carrots, of course. She would grate the latter and slice in pickled beets, too, for color. Green onions, *ja*, and how about some fresh calendula petals, now that the nasturtiums were finished?

It was a good thing that *Englisch* John Casey, her vegetable-hating patient, wasn't going to be at her table tonight!

She heard a whoop of greeting, and the crunch of wheels in the lane. Buggy wheels, not rubber, which meant it was probably Jacob, Corinne, and Amanda. Sure enough, Corinne waved through the open buggy door, a big square tub of marinating meat on her lap.

"I'll start the barbecue," Sarah called, and picked up her basket. Her barbecue was fairly small, but it was propane and not the kind that used charcoal. Michael, who had learned how to cook outdoors on many a hunting trip with his father, had loved to use it in the summer.

While Jacob got the meat going, Benny and Priscilla arrived—and the latter wasted no time in getting down and hustling her two dishes into the kitchen, where the other women were washing the vegetables.

"Hi, Corinne, Sarah, Amanda...I trimmed all these beans earlier and all they need is to go in a pot. I've never seen such a crop as we've got—Mamm was so glad some of them were coming over here. And this one is fresh pea salad. I know you'll have some mint to put in it. That always makes it so nice, doesn't it? Did you hear the Peacheys' news?"

"No," Sarah said with a laugh when Priscilla paused for breath. "The way you hightailed it out of Benny's buggy, there couldn't have been that much time for conversation."

"Oh, believe me, there was time for this. Arlon and Crist have sold some kind of invention to the phone company, and they're going to get a cell phone tower in their field."

"Are they now?" Corinne's busy hands fell still—which didn't happen very often. "Have they talked it over with Bishop Dan?"

"They must have, if the tower is going in." Amanda fetched two serving bowls from Sarah's good set on display in *der Eckschank*, the china cabinet built into the corner of the sitting room next to the kitchen. "Here, Pris, put the pea salad in one of these."

"I'm glad they live on the other side of the settlement and we don't have to look at the ugly thing," Sarah said. "But think of the money. Didn't Silas say that with the rent the phone company pays, he doesn't have to farm?"

"He did," Corinne answered when it was clear that Amanda wasn't going to. "That will suit Arlon and Crist just fine. I'm glad their money worries will be over."

Would Linda and Crist move off that place now? Sarah wondered. Having some money coming in would make a huge difference to the family—but would it improve their lot, or make them more eccentric and the boys even less inclined to take up a sensible trade?

She hoped not. Surely *der Herr* had sent them this blessing for good reasons of His own. It was their place to be good stewards of it, and she could only hope that they would be.

By now, Eric and Caleb had joined Jacob at the barbecue, and Sarah could hear their voices just outside the back door. Corinne smiled at the sound, too.

"I'm glad to see that Eric is no longer quite so terrified of Jacob," she said to Sarah. "He's been a real good little helper in the barn, even though he had never even seen a cow up close before he came."

"He was a good helper because he wasn't sure what Dat would do to him if he wasn't," Amanda said with a laugh. "I'm glad he realized that his help was appreciated. Listen to them now."

It was a *gut* sound, the two boys' chatter, punctuated by Jacob's belly laugh and the thump of the barbecue lid going down. And then a car approached down the lane. Trent Parker? Or Henry?

Drying her hands on a dish towel, Sarah checked out the big front window. "Eric!" she called. "Your father is here."

Hurrying outside to meet the SUV, she saw Eric catapult around the corner of the house.

Trent slammed the car door just in time to catch him in a hug. "*Oof!* Dude, you've grown!" He looked him over, then pulled him in for another hug. "I'm glad to see you safe and sound."

Here was the unhappy man who would leave his child with strangers in order to go and work. Well, at least he didn't seem shy about showing affection after a long absence. He wore suit pants and a button-down shirt with the sleeves rolled up, but he'd clearly been driving with the windows down, because his hair was mussed. He looked like the driven executive she'd seen two weeks ago...and yet something had changed.

Absence made the heart grow fonder, and there was a lot about Eric to love. Maybe he'd been doing some serious thinking after Eric had run away.

"Dad, you remember Caleb, right? My friend? And his mom, Sarah?"

Sarah extended a hand. "Welcome back."

"I hope my kid wasn't too much trouble."

"Not at all. We were just saying in the kitchen what a good helper he's been."

"I got up at four o'clock every day and milked cows, Dad. And weeded the garden and made the beds and one day we went fishing and I caught two brookies and Caleb got skunked and we cooked them for supper!"

Trent's mouth dropped open. Then he turned to Sarah. "Is that so?"

"*Ja*," she said. "Like I told you. A real good helper and provider. We were happy to have him."

"Wow." It took the man a moment to gather words together. "*Wow.* So where's Henry, the potter? And how about this lantern? When do I get to see that?"

"It's in your room, in a crate. Henry's not here yet, but I can show you." And Eric dragged him into the house just seconds before Sarah heard another car arrive.

Henry and Ginny.

They were clearly a couple now. He came around the hood of the car to open the door for her, and when she got out, she took his hand.

Sarah's stomach plunged and righted itself, settling into a kind of hollowness that she had no business feeling. She was concerned for his soul, that was all—if he and Ginny kept on this path and decided to get married, he would be lost to fellowship. Even if he didn't go through with it, a man who loved a dead woman for ten years would love a living one for a lot longer, so how could he tie a whole sacrifice to the altar when his heart would be torn in two?

But she had said her say and it was not her place to say it again.

Sarah arranged a smile on her face and shook hands. "I'm glad to see you both. What have you got there, Henry? Is that a computer?"

"It's Ginny's tablet." He indicated the shiny sliver of metal under his arm. "We've brought something to show you, since you're in it."

Sarah didn't know the difference between a computer and a tablet, but this wasn't making sense in any case. "In it? In the com—the tablet?"

Ginny laughed. "In a manner of speaking. The video that the crew took of Henry the other week is up on the D.W. Frith website. We brought it along so we could all see it. And I can't tell you how hard it's been not to watch it before everybody else— Henry tells me he's going to make us all wait until after dinner. Why would he do that unless fame has gone to his head?"

Oh, my. The teenagers would have no problem watching this video. But Jacob and Corinne were here, too—what would they have to say about such a thing coming into the house?

"You don't want to watch me on an empty stomach, is why," Henry joked. "Say, Sarah, did I see Trent Parker as we drove in? This is his vehicle, right?"

"It is," she replied. "Eric took him inside to see the lantern he made. I think you might be needed in Eric's room."

They all trooped into the house, and while Henry and Ginny went upstairs, Sarah got herself into the kitchen to find that Amanda had finished making the salad. Jacob carried the meat in on a big platter, and in the general commotion of collecting everyone from house and yard and making introductions and getting the food onto the table, Sarah pushed away all the thoughts that were disturbing and simply concentrated on making sure her strange collection of guests was comfortable.

Trent hitched his chair closer to the table and reached for the macaroni. "Say, this looks good. I haven't had macaroni and cheese that wasn't out of a box since I was a kid."

"Dad—" Eric clutched his arm. "Not yet."

"What?" Trent looked down at the boy next to him.

"Grace, Dad."

Jacob came to his rescue as Trent slowly lowered his arm. "We say a silent grace before and after our meal, to thank God for the blessings he has given us."

"Oh. Sorry."

In the ensuing silence, Sarah did her best to focus on *der Herr* and her gratitude for His blessings, chief among them being that Jacob was here to preside at the table in Michael's place. His humility was his greatest strength. No one could be offended—not even Trent Parker—when Jacob explained their customs in such a gentle but firm way.

*Thank You for that gentle strength, Lord, because it and not anything I could do is probably the reason that Eric has been so teachable in our homes.*

Henry had a little of that humble strength, which probably helped when Eric was in his studio, learning. All in all, the menfolk around her were good examples to young boys.

When some of them weren't dating worldly women.

Jacob lifted his head and cleared his throat, and Sarah snatched her wandering thoughts from where they'd gone and stuffed them back in the corner of her mind where they belonged.

She passed the macaroni and cheese to Trent herself. "So, what did you think of young Eric's lantern? He showed it to me last night, when I went in to say good night. I thought it was beautiful—and practical, too. We're quite fond of candles around here, aren't we, Caleb?"

Caleb grinned back as Trent dished up his plate and one for his son. "It is a nice piece of work," Trent conceded. "I'm not sure it was worth putting his mother through what he did, or of inconveniencing you folks for two weeks, though."

"He did not inconvenience us." Jacob passed the platter loaded with pork chops, and followed it with applesauce. "I admit I was disturbed that he had disobeyed his parents in such a dangerous and foolish manner, but in my mind he has paid for his sin." His lips twitched as though he had thought of something that amused him. "Haven't you, Eric?"

"*Ja*, have I ever," Eric muttered. "A week of shoveling manure paid for that and every bad thing I ever did in my life."

Sarah smiled at his unconscious use of *Deitsch*. "You must still make it up with your parents," she said gently. "Remember what we spoke of."

"Yeah? I like the sound of this," Trent said.

"Eric?" she prompted.

"Help when it's not asked for, look for a way to make someone happy when I'm bored, and make the beds," he said.

"You'll make the beds?" his father asked. "For real?"

"And very well, too," Priscilla said. "I taught him how at the Inn."

"And he can make a pie as well," Sarah told Trent. "He

is better at filling than crust, but he has lots of time to practice."

"I'd buy a ticket to see that," Trent said. "I don't think anyone has ever made a pie in our kitchen at home. I don't even think we own a pie pan."

"Then I'll be the first," Eric told him. "What's your favorite?"

"Blackberry."

"As soon as we get home, we can buy the ingredients. And a pie pan. You'll see."

"Done."

Henry reached for a helping of salad. "You can be pr—glad that Eric is learning these kinds of skills, Trent. He has a natural talent with his hands, and a creative mind. I know it's none of my business, but I hope you'll reconsider your decision about the arts high school. Eric has worked hard and I believe that work ethic will carry over into his education."

Trent cut his chop and chewed for a moment. After he swallowed, he said, "If everything was as great as you say, that work ethic should carry over to his education no matter where it is."

"That's true." Henry leaned over to catch Eric's eye two places away. "But his passion is art, and harnessing that passion this young will go a long way to making him successful in the field he chooses."

"He's only thirteen."

"Our boys often know what they are going to do with the skills God has given them by the time they are thirteen," Jacob said. He took the pea salad from Priscilla with a nod. "Caleb here has turned his hand to construction, and lately I have seen him drawing barns in the dirt." Jacob lifted an eyebrow at his grandson. Even Sarah gazed at him in surprise. "You have been to a barn raising or two, haven't you?" Jacob said to her boy with affection. "You know that there is always a foreman who directs the others—a man with the design and shape of the building in his mind. Without that man, the crews are only able to do their individual parts of the work. But the foreman brings them all together to create the structure. Someday, Caleb might just be that man."

Oh, he was a clever one, was her father-in-law. Without saying a word about it, a person could get his meaning if they were so inclined—that God directed every part of a young man's life and the people in it so that His plan could be realized. None of them knew what God's plan was for young Eric. But she had done her individual part for him, and so had Henry, and so had Priscilla and Benny. Maybe his time here would set him on a different path. Maybe it wouldn't. But her job now was to leave him in God's hands as he left her own, and pray for him.

"So what you're saying is that I should support this art school plan, even though his mother and I both feel it would be rewarding bad behavior?"

"The cows have done that already," Eric mumbled.

When Jacob and Corinne remained silent, Sarah realized that they were prompting her to speak. "Eric has made a good point," she said with a smile at him. "I don't think his stay with us was quite the holiday he might have expected, but he rose to the challenge. He has learned a little of the value of obedience and hard work, and he reaped the reward of learning from someone who has done well in his craft. Wouldn't you say so, Henry?"

"I would, compliments aside," Henry said. "And Eric, even if your dad says that art school isn't in the plan, you'd be very welcome to come back here next summer and study with me again."

"You could stay with us!" Caleb said. "And Simon will be home then and you can meet him."

Sarah didn't expect Trent to say yes to this school plan, and he didn't. But as he cleaned the last of the food from his plate, she could see that he was thinking hard.

She rose and began to clear away the dishes, and Priscilla got up, too. Then, to her surprise, Eric did as well—and of course if he did, then Caleb couldn't very well sit while his guest put himself in the place of the servant. So she had more helpers than a woman could ask for and the table was cleared, the food put away, and the dishes done in record time.

Trent didn't miss this behavior, either, and rubbed Eric's shoulder affectionately when they all seated themselves again to watch the video on Ginny's tablet. Even Corinne and Jacob hovered behind Sarah's chair, their curiosity combining with courtesy toward her *Englisch* guests. They would never criticize or comment on the device in her home, she saw now. It would go away with Ginny and that would be that.

The website came up and there was a picture of one of Henry's batter bowls, one whose handle ended in a spray of— were those peony leaves?—on the side of the bowl. Ginny tapped a little arrow and music came out of the tablet.

The picture changed to the long view from the top of Sarah's hill, out over the farms and fields of her neighbors, the camera moving from left to right as though someone were taking it in. And there in the distance was her own house, and her bent figure in the garden.

"That's you, Mamm!" Caleb said.

Sarah blushed scarlet, though anyone outside her family would never be able to tell who it was. She couldn't help it—

she glanced in appeal at Jacob. "They asked my permission, but I told them they must not show my face."

"They have not," Jacob said. "Many of our friends have been in these films in the past. It means nothing to us, daughter, and if it helps our neighbor Henry in making his living, then it has done no harm."

Sarah relaxed in relief. After this, she could almost enjoy the little film. The light in it was beautiful—they had caught the sun at her favorite time of day, when it lay soft and golden on the garden.

"In the fields and lanes of Amish country, you're likely to see horse-drawn buggies and a simple people dressed in clothes like those their grandparents and great-grandparents wore," said a friendly woman's voice. The scene changed and a horse clopped past pulling a buggy. The viewer got a glimpse of a beard and a hint of an organdy *Kapp* through the open windows. The buggy passed the camera and Caleb stifled a giggle.

"That was Paul Byler's buggy!" he said, his voice choked with laughter. "Oh, won't he be surprised he's on a video!"

Thank goodness they had not been able to see full faces. Paul would be a lot more than surprised—if he ever found out about it. As Jacob had said, it meant nothing to them.

"Nestled among the flowers and trees is the studio of Henry Byler, whose artistry was recently discovered on a trip to Amish country," the woman said warmly.

The picture changed to Henry's lane, then focused on the barn. The viewer passed through the door to see Henry at the potter's wheel, working on a batter bowl. The camera narrowed in on his hands, and Sarah was struck once again by the strength in them, and the gentle but sensuous way he manipulated the clay to encourage it to take the shape he wanted.

"Henry's natural talent with clay and glazes has blossomed in his Amish home," the lady said. "He observes the shapes and curves found in nature and transforms humble clay into beauty for the home, bringing Amish simplicity and that same closeness to nature into pieces for your kitchen."

Henry sat back, as if he had been pushed away from the screen.

The camera focused closely on a batter bowl, following the curve of the handle, the light hitting it just right so that the leaf shape where it met the body of the bowl glistened. And behind it, in the near distance, hung an Amish man's straw hat, as if to make the connection between it and Henry's art.

"Oh, no," Henry whispered.

But the lady wasn't finished yet. "Let D.W. Frith share Amish beauty and simplicity with you this autumn, and bring nature and all its goodness into your own home."

On the road that ran in front of Henry's and Sarah's places, another buggy clopped past and receded into the dip where the creek ran, then came up the hill on the other side. The viewer's last sight was of the buggy cresting the rise, as if to say, "Buy a bowl and be uplifted."

Henry pressed a depression in the front of the tablet, and the music shut off and the screen went dark.

"What's the matter, hon?" Ginny said. "I thought it was beautiful."

"I did, too," Priscilla said. "Even your cousin Paul's buggy."

"Oh, it was beautiful, all right," Henry said. "Too bad it was all a story. Every word in it was true—and at the same time, a complete lie."

# CHAPTER 31

Why?" Eric asked, puzzled. "Aren't you selling your bowls at D.W. Frith after all?"

Henry did his best to get a grip on himself, but he wasn't sure he succeeded. "I am—but only because it's too late to pull out. Don't you see? I told them specifically I wasn't Amish. I told them over and over again." He pushed his chair back and got up from the table. "Not once does it say in that video that I'm Amish, and yet the whole thing implies it. It's a lie. How am I going to explain this?"

"Who do you have to explain it to?" Ginny's amber eyes searched his face. "We all know it's an advertisement, and only little kids believe everything in an ad is true."

"What if someone comes down here on a holiday and visits the studio?" Henry turned to her in agitation. "They'll see in a minute that I'm not Amish. They'll think I'm a liar, riding the Amish coattails to make a buck."

"They'll be coming to see your pottery, hon, and buy quilts and eat good food." Ginny's gaze was sympathetic, her tone as soothing as though she were calming a spooked horse. Which was exactly how he felt. "Besides, if anyone makes comments about false representation, you can tell them you didn't make the video. D.W. Frith did."

Not so helpful. She wasn't seeing the point. But maybe only someone who had once been Amish and had chosen to leave would know what it was like to be strapped into that harness, to be thrust back under the same standard, even if it were only in the mind of the viewer.

Which was not something he could articulate in a roomful of his Amish neighbors, all of whom he liked and respected.

"Ginny's right, Henry," Priscilla put in, her young face bright with encouragement. "People will be coming for your pottery, really, not to see if you're Amish. And besides, now that you and Ginny are engaged, it will be so obvious you're not Amish that folks will realize it has to be the store's fault, not yours."

"Engaged?" Sarah and Ginny said together.

"Why, sure." Priscilla's smile filled her whole face. "I totally forgot until this minute to say how happy I am—and congratulations!"

If Henry had been having a hard time getting his feelings out before, it was nothing to what he felt now. He stared at the girl, his mouth working around words that wouldn't come, and watching as both light and smile faded from her face.

"Oh dear," she said. "Was it supposed to be a secret? Did I do wrong by speaking up?"

*Ginny.* What was Ginny thinking? Henry turned to see the same flummoxed look on her face as must be on his own.

"I—we—who—" His mouth flapped but no sense came out.

"So it's true, then," Sarah said, visibly pulling herself together.

"I can't think where you might have—"

But Benny cut him off in a rush. "If that's true, then is the rest of it true? You're going to go and live at the Inn with Ginny? Because I'll tell you this, no matter what Sarah says to my aunt, she ain't coming to live on his farm and leaving us. Not now that we finally got something going with the phone company. She needs us, and the baby needs us, and we need her!"

"Live on the—"

"Who says they're—"

"Baby!" Sarah's voice cut through the babble and commotion like a scalded knife. "What baby? Is Linda expecting?"

"*Ja*," Benny said. "She told us at supper last night and you should just see how happy Onkel Crist is. But that don't mean they're going to do like you said and move onto Henry's place. Why should they?"

"Now, wait just a minute here!" Henry roared. He wasn't the type to holler. In fact, he didn't think he'd raised his voice in at least a decade. But the sudden silence that fell in Sarah's kitchen because of it felt good, and he leaped into the breach without a second's hesitation.

"First of all, Ginny and I are *not* engaged, and even if we were, it's nobody's business but ours. And second of all, no one is moving onto my farm! I don't know where you got such a crazy idea, Benny, but my studio is there, my home is there, and Paul and the boys farm it. I have no intention of opening a boardinghouse for Amish couples."

"But Sarah said—"

Sarah—whose gray eyes were huge and whose face was nearly as white as her prayer covering.

"What did Sarah say?" Henry pinned her with a gaze that demanded the truth.

"I—I—" She swallowed, and glanced at Jacob as if he might offer her some help.

But Jacob was as surprised and confused as anyone in the room. Eric had sidled over next to his dad and was pressed up against him. Priscilla was nearly in tears at having ruined the dinner party. And Benny's face had so reddened with agitation that his freckles had nearly disappeared.

"*Dochder*," Jacob said to Sarah in quiet *Dietsch*, "if you have caused a misunderstanding, you had best clear it up before you cause offense and real damage."

To Henry's surprise and dismay, he understood every word.

"I never meant to cause offense." Tears filled Sarah's eyes, and the color flooded back into her face with a vengeance when she realized everyone around the table was looking at her. "I just—I was treating Linda, and was thinking out loud to her one day that if—if Henry and Ginny decided to marry, that maybe he would go and live at the Inn and the farm would come open and Linda and Crist might be able to farm it and—and have their own home."

"They have a home now," Benny said. "It's a good home. *Ja*, sure, some people think maybe Dat and Crist should pay more attention to the fields than their inventions in the barn, but it ain't the fields that made that solar pack and they sure ain't bringing in the money now like having that cell tower standing in 'em will."

"You were thinking out loud one day?" Corinne's forehead was furrowed with concern. "You were talking with Linda and advising her to leave her home with Ella and Arlon? Oh, Sarah."

Sarah wilted under the pain in her mother-in-law's face. "She couldn't conceive. I thought it would be for the best— that if she had calm and quiet and her own home, she might be able to."

"Who says we ain't calm and quiet?" Benny burst out. "We have prayer time same as anybody else."

"I'm sorry, Benny. I judged your family," Sarah whispered. "It was prideful of me and presumptuous and I beg you to forgive me."

"It ain't me who needs to forgive," he said, the indignation leaking out of him at Sarah's miserable humility. "It's Aendi Linda and Onkel Crist."

"You're right," she said. "I'll see them tomorrow after church and ask their forgiveness, too." Her shoulders slumped and she patted her pockets. Amanda pulled a hankie out of hers and handed it to her with such a look of sympathy that Henry got irritated all over again.

"Don't Ginny and I get an apology?" he asked.

"Henry." Surprise laced Ginny's tone. "She didn't mean to spread gossip. Looks like a little bitty speculation got out and started growing into a fact before anybody noticed."

"She had no business speculating about us."

But Ginny seemed a lot less bothered about it than he would have expected a woman to be after hearing her name and private business bandied about all over the district.

"There's a lot worse things could be said about me than that I was getting married to you," she pointed out with a glimmer of her usual good humor.

"It's offensive." When her gaze fixed itself on him, he realized how that must have sounded. "I mean, being talked about is offensive."

"Please forgive me, Henry," Sarah said from behind the handkerchief. "And Ginny."

"Of course I forgive you, sweetie," Ginny said. "If that gossip ever turns into reality, believe me, you'll be one of the first to know."

But for some reason, this didn't seem to make Sarah feel better, and Henry had had about enough. He took Ginny's yellow sweater from the back of her chair and helped her into it, shook Trent's hand, wished Eric well, thanked the room in general for a great dinner, and in five minutes was walking out into the summer evening, where darkness had nearly fallen. Fireflies winked on and off all over the lawn and in the fields beyond it, males trying to impress the females with their brilliance and all but a lucky few not finding any success.

"Poor Sarah," Ginny said once they were in the car and accelerating in the direction of town. "I feel sorry for her."

"I don't," Henry said. "You can't talk about people like that and not have it come back to bite you."

"But it wasn't malicious. She was trying to do the right thing."

"Who knows what the right thing is when it comes to people? I don't even know the Peacheys except for Benny, and even I can see that encouraging a woman to leave her family is overstepping the line."

"She wouldn't have gone alone." Ginny settled back in the passenger seat. "But be that as it may, it was kind of fun being engaged for thirty seconds. I'd forgotten what it was like."

"It's nothing to make jokes about, if you ask me. Here I'd just seen myself in an ad campaign that was a total lie, and the next thing I know I'm being congratulated on another lie, and there's my neighbor, in the middle of both things. I don't know how she does it."

"It's not fair to blame her for being in the video. So were you."

"I'm just saying."

"So was she. Talk is cheap. Like telling people it was offensive, the thought of being engaged to me."

*Wait. Whoa.*

He pulled off the road in a spot where the wagons gained access to someone's field and there was a shoulder wide enough for a car.

"That's not at all what I meant. The gossip offended me. Not the thought of being engaged to you."

He couldn't see her face very well in the dark interior of the car—only the splash of her curls and the straight outline of her nose, but her posture seemed to soften. "It's kind of a nice thought, though, isn't it?"

Shifting in his seat, he touched her hair. "I admit it's flickered through my mind once or twice. But we haven't actually known each other that long."

"I think I know you better after a couple of months than I ever knew my husband in fourteen years of marriage. But then...I suppose getting to know myself was a big part of that. If a person doesn't know herself when she's young and takes a big step like marriage, how can she expect to know anyone else?"

"You're a wise lady, Ginny Hochstetler," he said softly.

He would go a long way before he found a woman like this again. True, there were some obstacles to their being together—living and working arrangements, for one. How could an innkeeper live on a farm and keep an inn? How could a potter live in an inn when his studio was two miles away on a farm? But those were just logistics.

The important thing was the softness in his heart when he looked at her. The joy he sometimes allowed himself to feel in her company. That sparkle in her eyes that told him she felt the same way.

*Don't let her get away. If this is the moment, don't lose it.*

Because heaven knew he was done with being connected to

the Amish. With Ginny, he could cut that tie for good, and begin his life over again for the second time. It would be twice as good as the first time, because he wouldn't be alone.

"Ginny?"

Her hand slipped into his. "Hmm?"

"This is probably the most unromantic location ever for a moment like this...but...would you ever consider giving some truth to that rumor—for real?"

With a low chuckle, she said, "You might have to take back what you said to poor Sarah."

"Sarah has nothing to do with this. Ginny, do you ever think about sharing your life with me?"

"I'm doing that right now, and I think that I like it."

"I mean in a more formal way. I guess—what I mean is—would you marry me? Someday? When we both feel the moment is right?"

Now she took his other hand. His own were cold, which made hers seem all the warmer. "Protecting my reputation from the ravages of gossip, are you?"

"No. Mine."

She laughed, and he raised her hands to kiss the backs of her knuckles. "Will you?"

"Unromantic location or not, you are a very romantic man and I'm very close to kissing the breath out of you right now. But Henry, you haven't said one very important thing. Do you love me?"

Mentally, he kicked himself. Of course he should have said that first. "If love is wanting to hear your laugh first thing in the morning...looking for you in a crowd to see what crazy earrings you've got on today...wanting to hear your voice just to assure myself that I'm not all alone on the planet...then yes, I love you."

"I love you, too…minus the earrings. Yes, my very dear man, I will marry you. Remind me to thank Sarah Yoder for spreading rumors the next time I see her."

This time, it was he who kissed the words right off her lips, right there on the side of the road.

And even the *clip-clop* of the buggy passing on the other side didn't make either of them come up for air.

# CHAPTER 32

As married women, Linda and Ella Peachey sat fairly close to Sarah in church in Lev Esh's huge basement room, but there was of course no opportunity to speak until the service was over. She did her best to let her soul calm itself during the slow singing of the hymns, and to remember that during each hour of a Sunday morning across the time zones of the country, somewhere an Amish congregation was singing the "Lob Lied" at exactly the same point in the service and lifting up God's name in praise.

During the fellowship meal afterward, Sarah didn't have the nerve to bring up such a sensitive topic in case others heard. But when she saw Ella and Linda strolling near the rockery that was Saloma Esh's joy, admiring the variety of plants, Sarah saw her opportunity.

She joined them and, for the span of a single second, thought it might be all right—that Benny might have cleared the way before her.

But no. The delight in the garden that had been in Linda's eyes faded into politeness, and Ella's face closed the way certain flowers did at night, to protect themselves from things that stung and nibbled. Sarah could not go back and leave this damage unrepaired. She must go forward in the humblest way she knew.

"Ella—Linda—please, may I speak with you?"

They exchanged a glance in which Sarah clearly saw Ella say without a word, *It's up to you, Schweschder.* Linda nodded.

At which point the careful speech she had prepared early this morning while she was making breakfast completely fled her mind.

"I have done a very hurtful thing," she began. "I have been so caught up in my pride and in my little skill as a healer that I completely forgot that God is the healer and His will must be done."

The two sisters-in-law stood waiting, and Sarah despaired that she would ever find the words to make right her error.

"In my foolishness, Linda, I thought that if you had a home of your own, and quiet and security, that you would be better able to conceive." Linda's hand moved over her flat belly in a way Sarah instantly recognized. "But Benny told us last night that God has done what I in my blindness could not."

"I believe your herbal drinks helped," Linda said at last.

"But my putting ideas in your head about leaving your home could not have." Oh, she must not cry before she got these words out. "When Benny was telling us last night, I could see that I had caused offense in him. And if I did that, then Ella, what must you feel?"

"Our home is not perfect," Ella said stiffly. "But it is our home, and God is there."

"I know that now," Sarah whispered. How could she explain this?

Her gaze, blurry with unshed tears, fell on Saloma's rockery, and the jaunty "keys of heaven" plants that waved and bloomed on the edges.

And then the words came, as though the *gut Gott* Himself had put them there.

"You see those plants there, the ones with red flowers?"

"The Jupiter's beard?" Ella asked.

"*Ja.* They are also called keys of heaven, and while they don't have a use so much to an herbalist, they've taught me a lesson. You see, they grow where the soil is thin and rocky and it doesn't seem as though there should be enough to sustain them. But God has made them so they find what they need, and they like it best right where He puts them. What I never saw until now is that the plant doesn't think *thin and rocky* at all. The plant thinks, *Here is where I belong, where I can get what I need to grow best.*"

"And you think that is how I am?" Linda's face had softened, and the light had begun to return to it. "Because I do. I belong on the farm with my family, and the boys, and that barn full of inventions." She gave Ella a fond smile. "There is where I have what I need to grow best. Both of us do. And that is why you couldn't really convince me to leave."

"We had quite a job calming Benny down last night," Ella said. "To hear him, you would think Crist and Linda had a wagon loaded, ready to pick up and move into Henry's place."

*Henry.*

Sarah heaved a sigh that seemed to come right from her shoes. "I have that seam to mend, too. But I could not go another day without making it right with my sisters in the church. Will you forgive me for letting my pride and wrongheadedness get the best of me?"

"Of course I forgive you," Linda said, and leaned in to hug her. "I am so happy right now that I cannot bear to let anything get in the way of it. I am sure your herbs have helped

God's hand along. Taking the herbs is the only thing that has changed for me, so it must be so."

"And you, Ella?" Sarah asked. "Will you forgive me?"

"No wrong has been done except in your own mind, and God has taken care of that." Ella extended a hand. "I would not want us to not be in fellowship together. I forgive you, if you will forgive yourself."

Sarah pulled her into a hug, and to her great relief, Ella came. They stood close together, admiring the rockery and the keys of heaven with its jaunty red flowers.

"I wonder I didn't see this lesson before," she mused aloud. "Look at Eric, the *Englisch* boy that Priscilla and Benny found purely by chance, and brought back here. He was not content to grow in his place, which he found very rocky, and so he ran away. I know how I felt when Simon and Joe went to that dude ranch without telling me exactly where they were going. I can't even imagine what Eric's parents went through before they knew he was safe—so young, and so reckless."

"I have been afraid for Benny and Leon many a time, but they always seem to land on their feet," Ella said. "Even still, they don't seem inclined to run away."

"Benny loves his home," Sarah said. "I could see that. I only hope this Eric learns to be content where he is. I certainly don't want to find him on my doorstep again and face his father's anger. Once was enough."

Linda looked past Sarah's shoulder and waved. "My *gut Mann* has brought the buggy around, so we must go. And here is your Caleb, too."

"I hitched up Dulcie, Mamm," Caleb said, hanging back respectfully in case he was interrupting them.

"I'm ready, and leaving with a lighter heart than when I came." She smiled at Linda and Ella, and her heart softened even further at the sincere smiles of forgiveness and friendship they gave her in return.

God really did answer prayers, she thought as she let Caleb take the reins and drive the four miles home. Later, when he had gone over to his Daadi to talk cows and barns and what Jacob jokingly referred to as "the meaning of life," she sat on the back steps next to the lemon balm, whose gentle scent filled the air and whose vigorous branches were now crowding the porch. She could almost lean on it as she would the shoulder of a friend.

Scripture said, *It shall be given you in that same hour what ye shall speak*, and God had been faithful in showing her that humble little plant in the very moment of her need.

Which told her something. Eyes closed, she lifted her face to the summer sky and let the sun fall on it in blessing as she approached the Lord.

*Lord, help me to look to Your creation to find my help, and not to my own thinking. In that way lies pride, and offense, and the breaking of relationship with my sisters and brothers. Help me to be as humble as that little red plant, the keys of heaven, growing in my place and learning to love it there. To want no other place but the one You have given me. Thank You for teaching me, and for softening my heart and those of my sisters in the church. I hope this will bring us closer together, so that we can share the joy of the new life You are creating.*

From far away, she heard a voice hailing her, and opened her eyes to see a lean figure coming over the top of the hill.

Henry.

And not with his usual amble, either, that told the onlooker he was more concerned with looking at plant forms than where he was going. He was walking with a purpose, as if he had news to tell her.

Well, she had news for him, too. She'd learned a lesson, and she hoped he'd be happy to hear it so that they could clear up every misunderstanding and truly be friends again.

Her step was light as she made her way to meet him through the flowers blooming in the field.

# READING GROUP GUIDE

1. The "keys of heaven" plant grows in rocky places where the soil is thin and other plants don't find survival easy. Yet it thrives in its place. Who would you say is thriving in his or her place in this novel?

2. Who is trying to move out of his or her place? Do you think it's a wise move? If you were in that place, would you do the same?

3. Sarah and the other Amish people in Willow Creek are friendly with the *Englisch* among whom they live, but they are aware that they cannot "have fellowship" with them. What do you think about this?

4. Do you like the character of Ginny Hochstetler? Do you think she and Henry are right for one another?

5. Sarah tells Silas Lapp that she's dedicated to her new calling as a healer and declines his courtship. Was this the right thing to do? Do you think she'll regret it?

6. Sarah felt she was doing the right thing to encourage Linda Peachey to push for a home of her own. Do you think this blinded her to what was best? Do you think she was following God's will?

7. Eric ran away to pursue his passion. Would you have taken steps this extreme if you felt strongly about something?

8. What do you think of Sarah and Henry encouraging Eric to stay in Willow Creek instead of returning him to his parents right away?

9. If you had been Eric, would you have chosen two weeks in an Amish home over two weeks in New York City?

10. What do you think Henry is coming to tell Sarah at the end of the book?

# GLOSSARY

*Aendi:* Auntie
*Ausbund:* The Amish hymnbook
*Bidde:* please
*Bobblin:* Babies
*Bohnesupp:* bean soup, often served at lunch after church
*Bruder, mei:* my brothers
*Daadi, Daed:* Grandpa
*Daadi Haus:* "Grandfather house"—a separate home for the older folks
*Dat:* Dad, Father
*Deitsch:* Pennsylvania Dutch language
*Denki:* thank you
*Dokterfraa:* female healer
*Druwwel:* trouble
*Eckschank, der:* the corner cupboard
*Englisch:* non-Amish people
*freind:* friend
*Gelassenheit:* humility, submission
*Gmee:* church community in a district
*Gott:* God
*Grossmammi:* Great-grandmother
*Guder Mariye:* good morning
*Gut:* good
*Gut, denki:* Good, thank you.
*Ja:* yes

*Kapp:*  prayer covering worn by Amish and Mennonite women

*Kinner:*  children

*Kumme mit:*  Come with me.

*Lauscht du:*  Listen.

*Liewi:*  dear, darling

*Maedel(in):*  young girl(s)

*Mamm:*  Mother, Mom

*Mammi:*  Grandma

*Mann:*  husband, man

*Maud:*  maid, household helper

*Meinding, die:*  the shunning

*Neh:*  no

*Nichts?:*  Is it not so?

*Onkel:*  Uncle

*Ordnung:*  discipline, or standard of behavior and dress unique to each community

*Rumspringe:*  "running around"—the season of freedom for Amish youth between sixteen and the time they marry

*Schweschder:*  sister

*Uffgeva:*  giving up of one's will, submission

*Verhuddelt:*  confused, mixed up

*Warum has du gelacht?:*  Why did you laugh? (Colloq. What's so funny?)

*Was duschde hier?:*  What are you doing here?

*Was ischt?:*  What is it?

*Wie geht's:*  How goes it?

*Wunderbaar:*  wonderful

*Youngie:*  Young people who are running around

Coming in summer 2015

If you enjoyed the first two books in Adina Senft's Healing Grace series, look for the next installment,

# BALM *of* GILEAD

## A Healing Grace novel

Turn the page for an excerpt.

*In the ancient world, a tree known as Balm of Gilead, or the Mecca balsam, provided healing balsamic oils. In the new world, a species of poplar tree possesses similar properties and is also known as Balm of Gilead. Its fragrant, sticky buds are harvested and infused with oil to make a salve for the treatment of skin conditions.*

*In plant lore, poplars are considered to be protective trees, which may be why the Amish and Englisch alike plant them as windbreaks in fields and along roads. There is also a belief among ancient peoples that in the whisper of the poplar tree's leaves, you can hear the still, small voice of God.*

An Amish woman's year, Sarah Yoder had always thought, was governed not so much by the twelve-month paper calendar on the kitchen wall than it was by the hand of God. Instead of crossing off squares, a woman lived according to the cycle of the preaching on every other Sunday, and the blossoming and fruiting of the trees and plants in garden and orchard.

Because of the wet spring and hot summer they'd had this year in Whinburg Township, the gardens had gone crazy—and still were, here at the tail end of September with its chilly nights and crisp blue days. A branch on one of the old Spartans in Jacob and Corinne Yoder's apple orchard had actually broken from the weight of its apples, so the word had gone out and sisters' day had been moved up to deal with the emergency.

Autumn was Sarah's favorite season. Every one held its blessings, it was true—spring for the tender greens and shy flowers and the seeds going into the soil, summer for the long days of growing and canning and putting by, winter for the rest the plants took under their blanket of snow and for the lamplit evenings spent with family and friends. But there was something about autumn that Sarah loved more than any of these. Maybe it was the sense of the earth giving back all that the work of her hands had put into it. Maybe it was the full pantry with its rows and rows of jewel-toned jars of canned fruit, pickles, and vegetables. Or maybe it was just the quiet in the air now that the work was coming to a close—air that was still enough that she could smell burning leaves and hear the shouts of the little scholars going into the one-room schoolhouse on the other side of the county road.

Her younger son Caleb had had a brief—very brief—moment of nostalgia for those innocent days he'd left behind, earlier at breakfast. As he tucked away ham and eggs and biscuits and strawberry jam, he'd said, "It's hard to believe my school days are gone for good, Mamm. I don't even have to keep my work journal anymore. Can I have another piece of ham?"

She'd forked a piece onto his plate and tried not to smile. An eighty-year-old man couldn't have reminisced any better about the days of yore. "Are you looking forward to your first day of work with Jon Hostetler?"

His mouth full, Caleb nodded vigorously. With a mighty swallow, he said, "Daadi Jacob says I'm to keep humble and do as I'm told, and before I know it, I'll be running a work crew and maybe even my own outfit."

Sarah stifled a pang at the thought of how quickly those words came out of a man's mouth. The years would run by just as quickly and her boy, fourteen now, would be working and marrying and going to his own home that he would probably build with his own hands.

Which is just as it should be, if God willed it.

But for now, she would value every moment with him, even the ones where she swore she would wad up the dishcloth and stuff it in his mouth to keep him from talking her ear off. There would come a day, she knew, when she would give anything to hear him talking, even if it was about something mystifying, like helping Henry Byler on the next place fire his pieces of pottery in the kiln.

But then, the whole subject of Henry Byler was mystifying, and one best avoided if a woman were to keep peace in her heart.

Her walk across the fields on the path that she, Caleb, and her older son Simon had worn into the soil brought her to her in-laws' place. Already she could hear the voices of women raised in encouragement, exclamation, and laughter. She picked up her pace, cut through the backyard, and walked around the laurel hedge into the orchard.

Half a dozen women and a few young men stood on ladders, their dresses and shirts making them look like brightly colored birds in the trees.

"Sarah!" Corinne, her late husband's mother, was filling a basket next to the poor abused Spartan, which thankfully was old enough and low enough that she didn't need to climb up on a ladder. In her late sixties, Corinne still had the sunny smile of a girl as she waved, the breeze catching at her purple dress. "Choose any tree you like. We're determined to lighten the load on the branches by at least half, and make as much applesauce as we possibly can by dinnertime."

"And pie," called Corinne's youngest daughter Amanda, who at twenty-one was the only child still at home. "Not to mention tarts, strudel, and Schnitz."

She was still at home … but not for lack of Sarah's attempts at matchmaking. She and Corinne were going to have to put their heads together and see if they couldn't improve their results in that department. They thought they'd found a likely candidate earlier in the summer, but he'd had the bad judgment to prefer Sarah instead, so that plan had been a failure.

Yes, it was true that God had His plan for Amanda, and He would reveal the special someone He had in mind for her in His own good time. But plans could be helped along, couldn't they? Didn't the Scripture say that all things worked together for good to them that loved God, and were called according to His purpose?

If the Bible said it, then it was so.

# THE HEALING GRACE SERIES

### *Herb of Grace*
## Book One

To help make ends meet, Amish widow Sarah Yoder becomes an herbal healer using the plants she grows in her garden. As Sarah compiles her herbs, she awaits God's healing in the life of a man who rues a decision he made years ago, and in Henry Byler, a lonely prodigal with whom she shares a budding—and forbidden—attraction.

**And coming in summer 2015**

### *Balm of Gilead*
## Book Three

Sarah Yoder buries herself in her work after Henry Byler announces his engagement to a worldly woman. But when she is called upon to treat him, will her heart be able to withstand the test—and will he be able to resist the call of God?

**Available now from FaithWords wherever books are sold.**

*Visit the neighboring community of Whinburg, Pennsylvania*
*in the Amish Quilt Series*

### The Wounded Heart

Widowed with two young children, Amelia Beiler struggles to run her late husband's business until Eli Fischer buys it. Eli has a personal interest in her, but when she's diagnosed with multiple sclerosis, Amelia feels she must keep her distance from him in order to protect him.

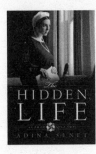

### The Hidden Life

Thirty-year-old Emma Stolzfus cares for her elderly mother by day and secretly writes stories by night, her hidden life shared only among close friends. But when a New York literary agent approaches her about her work, it will change her life in unexpected ways.

### The Tempted Soul

After years of marriage, Carrie and Melvin Miller fear they'll never be blessed with children. Carrie is intrigued by the medical options available to the *Englisch* in the same situation, but her husband objects. Is God revealing a different path to motherhood, or is Carrie's longing for a child tempting her to stray from her Amish beliefs?

**Available now from FaithWords wherever books are sold.**